Books by Mark Cheverton

The Gameknight999 Series
Invasion of the Overworld
Battle for the Nether
Confronting the Dragon

The Mystery of Herobrine Series: A Gameknight999 Adventure
Trouble in Zombie-town
The Jungle Temple Oracle
Last Stand on the Ocean Shore

Herobrine Reborn Series: A Gameknight999 Adventure
Saving Crafter
The Destruction of the Overworld
Gameknight999 vs. Herobrine

Herobrine's Revenge Series: A Gameknight999 Adventure
The Phantom Virus
Overworld in Flames
System Overload

The Birth of Herobrine: A Gameknight999 Adventure
The Great Zombie Invasion
Attack of the Shadow-Crafters
Herobrine's War

The Mystery of Entity303: A Gameknight999 Adventure
Terrors of the Forest
Monsters in the Mist
Mission to the Moon

The Gameknight999 Box Set
The Gameknight999 vs. Herobrine Box Set
The Gameknight999 Adventures Through Time Box Set

The Rise of the Warlords: A Far Lands Adventure
Zombies Attack!
The Bones of Doom
Into the Spiders' Lair

Wither War: A Far Lands Adventure
The Wither King (Coming Soon!)
The Withers Awaken (Coming Soon!)
The Wither Invasion (Coming Soon!)

THE RISE OF THE WARLORDS BOOK THREE

AN UNOFFICIAL MINECRAFTER'S ADVENTURE

SKY PONY PRESS
NEW YORK

Copyright © 2018 by Mark Cheverton

Minecraft® is a registered trademark of Notch Development AB

The Minecraft game is copyright © Mojang AB

This book is not authorized or sponsored by Microsoft Corp., Mojang AB, Notch Development AB, or Scholastic Inc., or any other person or entity owning or controlling rights in the Minecraft name, trademark, or copyrights.

All rights reserved. No part of this book may be reproduced in any manner without the express written consent of the publisher, except in the case of brief excerpts in critical reviews or articles. All inquiries should be addressed to Sky Pony Press, 307 West 36th Street, 11th Floor, New York, NY 10018.

Sky Pony Press books may be purchased in bulk at special discounts for sales promotion, corporate gifts, fund-raising, or educational purposes. Special editions can also be created to specifications. For details, contact the Special Sales Department, Sky Pony Press, 307 West 36th Street, 11th Floor, New York, NY 10018 or info@ skyhorsepublishing.com.

Sky Pony® is a registered trademark of Skyhorse Publishing, Inc.®, a Delaware corporation.

Visit our website at www.skyponypress.com.

10 9 8 7 6 5 4 3 2 1

Library of Congress Cataloging-in-Publication Data is available on file.

Cover design by Brian Peterson
Cover artwork by Vilandas Sukutis (www.veloscraft.com)
Technical consultant: Gameknight999

Print Paperback ISBN: 978-1-5107-2739-7
Print Hardcover ISBN: 978-1-5107-2833-2
Ebook ISBN: 978-1-5107-2743-4

Printed in the United States of America

ACKNOWLEDGMENTS

As always, I must acknowledge the support I receive from my family. Their tireless acceptance of my writing obsession, which often goes until late at night and sometimes even into the wee hours of the morning, makes it possible for me to put quill to parchment and craft these stories. I also want to thank the great people at Skyhorse Publishing. Their faith in my first novel made all the subsequent ones possible. Their editors, especially Cory Allyn, and marketing and sales people are the best! Lastly, I want to thank my agent, Holly Root, from Root Literary. Her faith and encouragement toward me and my stories is always appreciated and never taken for granted.

NOTE FROM THE AUTHOR

I've really enjoyed the feedback I've received from the readers of the Rise of the Warlords series. Everyone seems to love these books, and I'm thankful to all of you who are telling their friends about them. I know some of you have even told your teachers, and entire classes are now reading them. Thank you for spreading the word. You've all embraced Watcher, Blaster, Planter, Cutter, and, of course, Er-lan, and I appreciate you taking them into your lives.

Your emails (you can send them to me through my website, www.markcheverton.com) are the highlights of my days. I love reading what you all think about the stories, and I have especially enjoyed seeing your fan fiction with these new characters. Your creativity at crafting new tales not just with my characters, but with your own, is inspiring. I love the comments many of you leave on my website, complimenting others on their stories or artwork—the community warms my heart. I'll be looking forward to more stories from you all . . . please keep them coming!

With respect to the online game, based on the first book of this series, the results are in: it's a hit. Thousands of you have played the game and I've had numerous videos sent to me, showing you slaying the Wither King in the game. I'm so glad all of you are enjoying the game . . . it's been fun playing it with many readers.

If you don't know about the online game from *Zombies Attack!* you can find information about it here: http://markcheverton.com/zombies-attack-rpg-game/.   You can get to the game by going to the Gameknight999 Minecraft server—the IP address is mc.gameknight999.com—or you can find information about the server at www.gameknight999.com. Come check it out; there is free stuff there, as well as images of things built on the server. Look for me, Monkeypants_271, and my son, Gameknight999, there, and maybe we can play a game of paintball, but I'll warn you . . . I'm not very good.

Look for me on Twitter, too, @MarkC_Author, or on Facebook @InvasionOfTheOverworld, and say hello.

Keep reading, and watch out for creepers.

Mark

Failures have a way of uncovering the deepest parts of our character and revealing the true self that many of us keep hidden. Only through confronting obstacles and learning how to vanquish them do we learn who we really are, and what we are capable of. Embrace the challenges in your life, for each is an opportunity to grow and become more than you were yesterday . . . and who knows who you'll be tomorrow?

CHAPTER 1

I t was a strange sight: so many villagers living their lives in a huge savannah community without a single weapon in sight. At times, Watcher almost felt naked without his bow or enchanted sword, Needle. They were tucked away in his inventory, kept hidden away out of respect for the nonviolent beliefs of the NPCs (non-playable characters).

Watcher gazed out at the village and surrounding terrain from atop the cobblestone watchtower. The view was fantastic. He could see over the tall barricade that ringed the community and out into the savannah desert surrounding the village. Pale grass grew across the undulating plains, the delicate blades swaying back and forth under the caress of the constant east-to-west breeze. Acacia trees dotted the landscape. Their dark trunks were twisted and bent in unique ways, as if a child had been sculpting them out of clay, distorting them into different and imaginative forms. Watcher loved the shapes; it was like they were frozen mid-dance, a snapshot of their joyous celebration now captured for all to see.

He had come to the tower to see the sunrise; it was his favorite time of the day. But now, the blushing red sky had already faded to a deep blue, the rectangular clouds fleeing the rising sun. The Far Lands seemed peaceful and content. Being millions of blocks from the center of the Overworld, this land was isolated from the turmoil of Minecraft and its constant struggle between users and monsters. In the Far Lands, there were no users and never had been, just villagers and creatures, and at the moment, all seemed in balance.

Animals moved about through the savannah, as well as the occasional zombie or skeleton. None of the monsters approached the village; the imposing wall made it clear any attacks would be futile. That was a good impression to give; if the mob had attacked and gotten inside the walls, the inhabitants would have done nothing. The NPCs in this community were pacifists and refused to partake in any violence. They'd let the zombies scratch and pound at the stone and brick walls that surrounded their village before they raised a weapon to stop them.

Watcher, his friends, neighbors, and companions had only been in this village for a couple of months. They'd come here after destroying the skeleton warlord and his horde of monsters in the Hall of Pillars. During that conflict, the skeletons had demolished Watcher's village, burning it to the ground and leaving them all homeless, but fortunately, these villagers had taken Watcher and his friends and neighbors in with open arms; it was a kind gesture they all appreciated and respected.

With the clucks of chickens and moos of cows greeting the new day, the villagers were slowly beginning to awaken. Glancing at the landscape one more time, Watcher turned and mounted the ladder that descended to the ground floor. Once at the bottom, he left the cobblestone structure and walked to the village well, the center of the community. He leaned on the edge of the cobblestone wall ringing the water source and stared out at the buildings that made up the village.

The blacksmith was stoking one of the furnaces, likely smelting iron ore into ingots. Yeasty aromas drifted from the bakery as freshly baked loaves of bread were placed on windowsills to cool. Farmers and planters were heading for the fields, ready to tend their crops as others brought hay and seed to animals in pens; the village was slowly coming back to life after a long night's sleep.

"Hi, Watcher." The voice startled him.

Glancing over his shoulder, he found Planter leaning on an adjacent side of the well, a warm smile lighting up her beautiful face.

"Don't you just love it here? The massive wall they built around their community keeps all the creatures out, making it so they don't have to fight them off." Planter walked around the well and stood in front of him. "It makes this place seem so peaceful."

The morning light from the square sun shone down on the courtyard, making Planter's long blond hair appear to almost glow; the sight took Watcher's breath away. She said something to him, but he didn't hear; his mind was enraptured by the image before him.

He thought about their history together. Growing up in the same village, Watcher and Planter had played together since they learned to walk, but now, she no longer seemed like the childhood friend from the past . . . she was more. At the end of their last adventure, Watcher had wanted to tell her how he felt: that he liked her, not just as a friend, but more. Unfortunately, that opportunity had slipped away, along with his courage. Now, it no longer felt like the right time anymore, and he was afraid to say something to her.

I want to tell her how I feel, but what if she doesn't feel the same? he thought. *I might end up looking like a fool, and at the same time destroy the friendship I treasure so much.*

When it came to Planter, uncertainty and fear ruled his mind. He kinda missed the old days when they were just friends, but he knew things were different now. . . . He wanted more.

She said something, but Watcher was lost in his thoughts.

"Ahh . . . what?" he said.

"Were you even paying attention?" Planter shook her rectangular finger playfully at him, then smiled. "You were daydreaming again, weren't you?"

"Yeah . . . sure, that's it."

"Well, pay attention." She sat beside him. "I was saying . . . I think I like the non-violent attitude of these villagers. They refuse to fight with the monsters and they reject all weapons. No swords means peace."

"That's fine, if the monsters agree with you," Watcher said. "As soon as they step outside these walls, their non-violent attitude might get them killed."

"Oh Watcher . . . you always see the dark side of things."

"That's not true, I just—"

"Someone . . . help!" a voice suddenly shouted, interrupting them.

Watcher immediately took off towards the sound, Planter just a few steps behind him. As he ran, he pulled on pieces of his enchanted iron armor. The iridescent glow from the metallic plates painted the ground with a subtle purple light. At the same time, Planter donned her enchanted chainmail, the links jingling together like delicate wind chimes. Reaching into his inventory, Watcher found the handle to his magical sword, Needle, but refrained from drawing the weapon, remembering the villagers in this community didn't even like seeing swords or bows.

He dashed around the corner of a large house, heading for what sounded like someone crying. Before him was the entrance to the village mine. A woman sat on the steps weeping, her tan smock with a wide brown stripe down the center stained with dust and dirt.

"She's down there . . . someone must help her!" The

woman saw Watcher approaching and stood. "Please, you have to help me."

"Of course we'll help," Watcher said reassuringly. "Tell us who you are and what's wrong."

"It's my daughter, Fencer . . . she's down there and she's hurt." The woman stood and faced Watcher. Her long black hair, braided into a ponytail, lay dangling across her shoulder. Brightly colored pieces of cloth were tied to it, though the decorations were now stained with dirt. "She fell into a cave and she's hurt. I think there are monsters down there."

"Don't worry, we'll take care of her." Planter reached out and wrapped her arms around the woman. She burst into tears, weeping into Planter's shoulder. "Show us where your daughter fell."

The woman released the hug and wiped at her cheeks, then faced Watcher. "Saddler."

"What?" Watcher asked, confused.

"My name is Saddler and that's my daughter, Fencer, down there in the cave." She turned and ran down the steps. "Come . . . she's this way."

The woman ran with surprising agility down the steps leading into the mines, with Watcher and Planter following close behind.

"What's going on?" a voice asked from behind them.

Watcher glanced over his shoulder and found Blaster following them, his black leather armor blending in with the shadows in the passage.

"Blaster, I'm glad you're here," Watcher said. "Someone needs help."

"Then let's get moving faster," Blaster replied.

"She's down here," Saddler said, her voice echoing off the walls. The mother was beginning to sound frantic.

They reached the bottom of the stairway, then turned to the left and followed the main tunnel. Multiple passages split off to the left and right, each showing huge sections of dirt and stone having been dug up where the miners were looking for coal, iron, diamond, redstone . . .

"This is like a maze down here." Planter's voice bounced off the stone walls of the passage and came back to Watcher from all sides; it made him smile.

"Notice the torches?" Watcher pointed to the torches on the walls. "They're all on the right side of each passage. That tells you whether you're heading deeper into the mine or back toward the entrance. Torches on the right, you're going in deeper. Torches on the left, you're heading out."

Planter nodded in understanding.

"Here it is." Saddler stopped at an intersection of two passages. A redstone torch was planted on the ground, the crimson glow pushing back on the darkness. "I put this torch here so it would be easy to find."

"Saddler, what happened to your daughter?" Planter asked.

"She was down here, taking her turn in the mines like everyone else in the village, when she fell into a cavern."

"What happened? How did she fall in? Did she . . ."

"She's right over here." Saddler ran through a narrow passage, then stopped at another redstone torch. "I don't know what happened. Maybe she was digging straight down?"

Next to the torch, a hole opened to a large cavern under the tunnel. Lava bubbled somewhere nearby, filling the air with ash, but also lighting the chamber with an orange glow.

Watcher knelt and stuck his head into the hole. Far below, he saw the girl laying on her side, motionless. Suddenly, the clattering of bones filled the air.

"There are skeletons down there, and who knows what else." Watcher stood up. "We need to get to her . . . fast."

Blaster pulled out an iron pickaxe. "Step back."

The boy dug into the wall of the tunnel, creating a larger hole. Then, he carved into the stone, forming steps as he descended along the edge of the chamber.

Watcher pulled out his enchanted bow and notched an arrow to the string. Saddler saw the weapon and scowled in disapproval, moving in front of the boy.

"No weapons . . . no violence," she said.

"There are monsters down there. If we don't stop them before they find your daughter, it'll be over for her." Watcher stared into the woman's square face. "If you want us to save your daughter, this is how it's done."

The woman looked at the pointed tip of the arrow, then back to Watcher, finally nodding reluctantly as she stepped out of the way.

Watcher followed Blaster down the newly hewn steps, Planter drawing her enchanted golden axe and was a step behind. The iridescent glow from the magical enchantments in the axe and the bow lit the stairs with a shimmering light, helping Blaster to see.

The moans of a zombie added to the clattering of skeleton bones.

"We need to hurry," Watcher said.

Blaster dug as fast as he could. When they were almost to the floor, Watcher jumped off the stairs, landing hard on the stone. Pain burst through his body as he flashed red, taking damage, but he didn't care; he had to get to Fencer before the monsters did.

Sprinting through the darkness, Watcher ran toward the girl. She lay on the ground ahead, bathed in the orange light from a nearby pool of lava. The sounds of monsters were getting louder. A zombie moaned off to the right. Watcher stopped and listened. The decaying creature growled again. Drawing back an arrow, he released the barbed shaft toward the grumbling voice. The fire-arrow burst into flame and struck the zombie, lighting it on fire. The flickering glow illuminated another monster nearby. Watcher launched another burning arrow, this one at the creature's neighbor. As the flames licked their green, decaying bodies, Watcher put away the fire arrows and used just normal ones. He fired again and again, striking the zombies until they disappeared, pained and sad moans on the creatures' lips.

"Hey . . . save some for us," Blaster shouted.

By now, his two friends had caught up to him. They sprinted toward the prone figure, the three friends in lockstep. Suddenly, the clattering of bones filled the darkness to the left.

"I'll take care of them." Blaster drew two long, curved knives from his inventory, then disappeared, his black armor making him practically invisible in the shadows.

Watcher ran toward Fencer. She was lying on the ground, unconscious. It seemed that she was fading in and out, as if about to disappear; her HP (Health Points) was dangerously low. Watcher offered her an apple, but the girl seemed barely aware of what was going on.

"Fencer, are you okay?" Watcher asked.

She moaned, but didn't respond.

"We have to get her out of here." He glanced at Planter, who had a worried expression on her face. Even when scared, she was beautiful, he thought. "I'm going to . . ."

An angry growl echoed throughout the chamber.

"Look out!" Planter charged past him, her enchanted axe streaking through the air.

She slashed at an attacking zombie, blocking the monster's razor-sharp claws with the handle of her weapon, then kicked the creature hard in the stomach. With a grunt, the zombie took a step back, but Planter did not relent. She charged, her axe smashing into the fiend with merciless accuracy.

Two more monsters charged out of the darkness. Watcher stood with his blade drawn right next to Planter. The two friends fought in a synchronized rhythm as if they were performing a choreographed dance. It was almost as if they knew each other's thoughts: When Planter attacked, Watcher blocked. When Watcher thrust Needle at a monster, Planter was there with her golden axe to guard his back. The attacking creatures were destroyed in minutes, leaving the cavern deserted.

The sound of bones clattering to the ground came from the shadows off to the right. Blaster emerged from the darkness with a smile on his face, his curved knives reflecting the orange light from the lava pool. "I solved our problem with the skeletons." He smiled, nonchalant.

Watcher shook his head, amazed.

"We need to get Fencer up to the village," Planter said.

Watcher put away his sword, bent over and picked the girl up in his arms, then ran for the stairs they used to get into the cavern, the glow from his enchanted iron armor still giving him enough light to see.

Fencer moaned and opened her eyes for a moment, a confused look on her face.

"Don't worry, Fencer, we're taking you out of here," Watcher said. "We'll get you to the village healer, and then you'll be okay."

She moaned again, then drifted back into unconsciousness.

Watcher could tell Fencer was badly injured, her health almost gone.

"I hope we weren't too late to help you, Fencer," he whispered to the girl, then sprinted up the stairs and back to the village.

CHAPTER 2

Shakaar, the spider warlord, paced back and forth in the Gathering Chamber. The claws at the end of each leg clicked a syncopated rhythm on the stone floor as she strode from one end of the cavern to the other.

"He sssaid he would be here." Shakaar glanced around the chamber, her eight red eyes burning with anger.

Lava spilled down one wall, casting an orange glow on the surroundings. Other pools of lava sat on the ground, adding more light to the Gathering Chamber. Smoke and ash drifted through the air, creating a gray haze that might have choked a villager, but was a welcome aroma to a spider. Shakaar stared at the entrance, wishing her anger gave the spider some kind of magical power to somehow force the wither to appear. She clicked her sharp mandibles together in annoyance.

Suddenly, a chill seemed to spread through the room. The short black hairs that covered her dark body all stood up straight as she tensed, ready for battle.

"You seem impatient, Shakaar," a deep voice said.

"Maybe she wasn't going to wait for us," a scratchy voice said. "I told you she couldn't be trusted."

"Calm down, Left," a soft, lyrical voice added. "She wasn't going anywhere, were you, Shakaar?"

The spider turned and found herself staring up at Krael, the self-proclaimed King of the Withers. The dark creature had three heads atop its broad shoulders. The center head wore a golden crown with tiny black skulls embedded along its rim. It was the Crown of Skulls, a powerful enchanted relic from the Great War between the NPC wizards and monster warlocks. The crown sparkled with magical energy, the glow pulsing like a heartbeat as if it were alive.

Shakaar knew there were rumors that two more crowns existed, both of them like this one. Stories passed down from the spider elders suggested that the three crowns, if worn by a single monster, would give unstoppable powers to that creature. But many spiders thought they were just tales to scare the hatchlings into doing their chores.

"You are late," Shakaar said. She wanted to make sure the wither understood who was in charge in the spiders' lair.

"My apologies," Center's voice boomed, filling the chamber. "We were retrieving an ancient and powerful tool for the spider warlord."

"A tool?"

All three heads nodded. "There is a wizard in the Far Lands, and he plots the destruction of all spiders." The center head paused, letting that information sink in. "This wizard destroyed the zombie warlord as well as the skeleton warlord. And now, this wizard has focused his attention upon the spider warlord."

"How do I know you ssspeak the truth?" the spider warlord said.

The left head glared down at Shakaar, but the spider warlord ignored his gaze. She kept her eight red eyes focused on the center skull, the one wearing the Crown of Skulls. That was the one clearly in charge of the other two.

"Withersss have a way of usssing othersss to the benefit of the withersss and to the detriment of othersss." She clicked her mandibles together, then tapped one of her claws on the ground. This was a signal to the other spiders in the chamber to approach.

The right head glanced around, watching the other monsters approach, then glanced at the other wither skulls. Center nodded but kept his gaze fixed upon the spider warlord.

"I see you doubt our word," Center said. "That can be understood. I will show you we speak the truth." The wither flicked his body forward, causing an object to come out of his inventory and land on the ground before the spider. "This is an ancient artifact from the Great War. It was made by one of the monster warlocks and is a powerful tool."

The spider reached out with a claw and picked up the item. It was a glass lens attached to a long black strap. The eyepiece gave off a soft, iridescent glow.

"It is called the Eye of Searching, and it is now yours." Krael leaned forward. "Put it on."

Shakaar wasn't sure if it was a request or a command, but she knew any magical relic from the Great War could be a powerful weapon for the spiders. Reaching up with two legs, she positioned the lens over one of her eyes, then wrapped the straps around her fuzzy head, tying them at the back.

Instantly, the relic stabbed at her HP, drawing power from her health as she flashed red and moaned.

"That is natural," Center explained. "The magical weapons and tools from the ancient warlocks use the health of the wearer to provide power to the enchantment. But the Eye of Searching will let you see anyone you can think of." He paused, letting the spider process the information.

A blue cave spider cautiously approached, a clump of green moss held between his mandibles. Carefully, he passed the moss to his warlord. Shakaar held the moss for a moment, then stuffed it into her mouth, rejuvenating her health.

"Now, think of a wizard . . . a young wizard with blue eyes and reddish-brown hair." Center's voice was deep, like the rumbling of distant thunder. "Focus on that thought, and then look through the Eye."

Shakaar gasped. An image formed in her mind of a young boy wearing enchanted armor and wielding a magical sword. He was in an underground chamber, fighting a group of zombies alongside a girl wielding an enchanted axe, her long blond hair swaying from side to side with each stroke. The boy fought like a seasoned warrior, the enchanted blade streaking through the air at incredible speed.

"I sssee him."

"He is our enemy." The lyrical voice of Right was soothing, almost like a song. "We will help the spider warlord destroy him."

"Destroy him . . . yes," the scratchy voice of Left added.

Right cast Left an angry glare.

Pain blasted through Shakaar's body again as the Eye of Searching recharged its power. She stuffed more green moss in her mouth, then removed the relic from her head and put it into her inventory. "What isss it you need from me in exchange for your help? All monssstersss know withersss do nothing out of kindnesss; you alwaysss want sssomething."

Left growled, ready to reply out of anger, but Center intervened first. "We know you've been capturing some of the NPCs and bringing them here as captive slaves. We only wish to use some of them for our own purposes."

"I need every one that we've captured," Shakaar replied.

"Then capture more," Left said, his voice filled with anger, as always.

"My impatient skull is correct." Center's voice was deep and calm, silencing Left. "You need only capture more NPCs to meet your needs, and we can both profit by mutually helping each other." Krael floated higher into the air, as if getting ready to leave, though it was still speaking. "If this wizard can roam about, unchallenged, he will attack you with a huge army of villagers. They will enslave your hatchlings, putting them to work in mines, digging for diamonds. Your spiders will be made to suffer, working to death just to satisfy the wizard's greed. They will have nothing but a life of misery and despair."

"That I cannot allow," Shakaar said, her rage building.

"Do you wish our help against this wizard?" Krael asked. "Or do you want to suffer the same fate as the zombie and skeleton warlords?"

Shakaar was furious as she considered the monster's words. The rumors about the demise of the skeleton and zombie warlords had moved through the Far Lands as fast as lightning. Perhaps the wither was right; she needed help. Things were going well in the Hatching Chamber. The initial experiments with the witches' potions looked promising, but they needed more time to perfect everything. If the wizard attacked the spiders' lair now, before they were ready, it could ruin everything. She had no choice.

Shakaar nodded. "Very well, Krael, we will work together in thisss endeavor."

"Excellent. We will show you where to find this wizard."

Shakaar clicked her claw on the stone ground again, this time in a different rhythm. A group of spiders came into the Gathering Chamber and stopped near the entrance, waiting for instructions.

"Show my sssissstersss where to find thisss wizard, and they will dessstroy him, jussst like during the Great War." The spider warlord turned toward the group of spiders. "Sssissstersss, follow Krael's directions. Go out and find the boy-wizard and dessstroy him. If he isss not there, then punisssh the NPCsss who aid him. We will turn the livesss of thossse around him to misssery."

Right and Left turned to Center and nodded, then all three wither skulls smiled evilly. With malice in his three sets of eyes, the king of the withers floated to the entrance of the chamber, ready to show the monsters where to find his enemy.

CHAPTER 3

Watcher paced back and forth outside the baker's house with fists clenched, impatiently waiting for news of Fencer's condition. "What's taking so long?"

"Your dad and Mapper are in there with Baker." Planter's voice was soft and calming. "Just be patient."

She put a hand on his arm, stopping his repetitive march.

Watcher glanced at her deep green eyes and started to smile, but then a sound came from inside the wooden building. Watcher turned his gaze to the door, slowly clenching and unclenching his hands. He heard Planter sigh but didn't understand why.

"Patience is not a skill Watcher has mastered yet." Blaster gave his friend a grin.

"This village doesn't really have a healer," Er-Lan explained. The zombie stood with his friends, concerned for the young girl. "There are few injuries because they never leave their community. Some healing potions exist, but apparently, they are old and weak. Er-Lan is not sure how well they will work on Fencer."

"They aren't making healing potions . . . that's insane." Watcher felt himself growing frustrated.

"They should always have new potions ready, just in case."

Some of the village inhabitants glared at Watcher, staring disapprovingly at his enchanted armor; it was something made for war, and all the NPCs in the village disapproved of violence.

Planter moved closer to Watcher and lowered her voice. "These people haven't experienced what we have, Watcher. They're pacifists, and don't believe in violence."

"A zombie doesn't care if you believe in violence or not," Watcher said. "Their claws are just as sharp, regardless of what you believe."

"Not all zombies use claws for violence," Er-Lan said in a low, moaning voice.

"I know, Er-Lan, sorry." Watcher looked away from the door and glanced at his zombie friend. "It was a metaphor."

"Er-Lan understands." The zombie moved to the door of Baker's house and peeked through the window, the voices of those inside audible to the zombie's sensitive ears. He stepped away from the door and stood next to Watcher. "Fencer fights for her life. Food has not helped, nor have the old healing potions." He glanced at Saddler, the zombie's eyes filled with compassion. "Mapper and Cleric have done everything possible." Shuffling to Saddler, he put his green hand on her shoulder to console the mother. "Fencer needs a Notch apple to save her life. Nothing less will do."

"A Notch apple," Saddler moaned, her posture slumping in defeat as she thought of her daughter. "We don't have any here in the village. In fact, I don't think we've ever had one."

"I know where to get one," Watcher said. He turned and faced Saddler. "A witch can make one for us."

"Witches are uncooperative," Er-Lan said, his green, scarred face creased with worry. "How will Watcher gain their assistance?"

"I'm gonna ask really nice, and then if that doesn't

work, I'm gonna ask not very nice." Watcher's voice rang with confidence.

"I can help with that." Cutter's voice boomed through the village. "I'm good at being not very nice." The big villager pushed through the crowd of NPCs clustering around the baker's home. They glared at his armor, the ornate decorations on the shining metal as offensive to them as the magical enchantments that protected the metallic plates. "We'll just go find us a witch and explain the situation." He drew his diamond sword. Many of the villagers gasped in surprise, some of them muttering insults under their breath. "I'm thinking this will help with the explanation."

The big NPC held the weapon in front of him for all to see, his accusatory glare moving from villager to villager. "Sometimes, being non-violent doesn't work. Sometimes, the fight comes to you, and it'll be necessary to make a choice." He moved between Planter and Watcher. "*We* are making a choice to help this girl, even though we're just visitors here, and nothing is going to stop us."

"That's right, and—" Watcher didn't even have a chance to finish.

"You accepted us after we defeated the skeleton warlord," Cutter continued. "And we appreciate that. So, a few of us are going to find a witch and bring back a Notch apple for that girl, whatever her name is."

"Fencer," Watcher muttered under his breath.

"Yeah . . . Fencer." Cutter sheathed his sword. "We're going out there to help Fencer."

Planter stared up at Cutter as if he were the bravest person in the world.

He didn't even go down there in the cave to save her, Watcher thought. *I did that, not him.*

He glanced at the ornate ribbons of metal on Cutter's armor, shaped into curves and spirals, making the chest plate appear as if it were meant for a king. Running his hand over his own armor, Watcher looked down and the mundane metal. All it had was a few rivets to hold the plates together; it was as unremarkable as he was.

Just then, the door to the baker's house opened. Mapper and Cleric stepped out and faced the crowd from the raised porch.

"I heard what Cutter was saying," Cleric said.

"It was really me that started it," Watcher whispered, but no one heard.

"A small party of NPCs could find a witch in the swamp to the south." Cleric glanced down at Watcher. "Son, will you lead this group into the swamp and get us a Notch apple?"

"Sure," Watcher replied with pride. "I'll need—"

"I'm going!" Cutter blurted out. "Blaster should be with us, as well as Planter and her awesome axe." He flashed her a smile. "Oh . . . and Watcher, too. That should be enough."

"I'm going as well," Mapper said. The old man was obviously excited about the adventure. "There will be an ice spikes biome on the way. I've always wanted to visit one of them."

"Er-Lan will go as well." The zombie stepped forward, many of the villagers stepping back. They still weren't accustomed to a zombie that was nonviolent. Er-Lan moved to Watcher's side and spoke in a low voice. "There was a vision."

"A vision?" Watcher pulled the zombie aside and spoke in a low voice. "You saw a vision of the future?"

The zombie nodded.

Watcher knew about Er-Lan's ability to see glimpses of the future. The visions had foretold events on their past adventure, and Watcher had learned to trust them. "What did you see?"

"Watcher and his friends were in a huge forest, with trees taller than anything Er-Lan had ever seen." The zombie glanced about. All of the villagers were staring at them, straining their ears to hear. "There was a black rain in the forest, with huge, dark raindrops falling all around."

"A black rain?" Watcher sounded confused. "Are you sure this was a vision of the future?"

Er-Lan nodded. "But the strangest part was that the huge drops of rain glowed with red embers, as if burning from within."

"That makes no sense."

"Er-Lan agrees, which is why this zombie must accompany the others . . . to make sure all are safe." The zombie stared into Watcher's blue eyes, his gaze unwavering.

Watcher knew his friend would not take no for an answer and would likely follow them anyway, even if they tried to refuse.

"Very well." The boy raised his voice. "Er-Lan goes with us."

"There you go, a party of six." Cutter sounded proud.

"Seven . . . it will be a party of seven," a voice said from the back. Saddler stepped forward.

Many of the villagers murmured to each other; clearly, they were shocked that Fencer's mother would leave the village and join the new group on their mission. Saddler pushed through the crowd until she was standing at Watcher's side. She stared up at Cleric defiantly.

"I'm going as well," she said.

"You can't go out there," one of the villagers said. "There will be monsters out there. You might need to fight for—"

"My daughter is fighting, right now, for her life. I'm not gonna hide behind our walls while these visitors go out to help her." Saddler turned and glared at the other NPCs. "I don't like violence any more than the next villager." She lowered her voice to a whisper and cast her gaze to the ground as if she were ashamed. "But this is my daughter we're talking about, my little Fencer." Slowly, Saddler raised her head and cast her gaze across her neighbors' faces. She stood tall, her chin held high as she spoke in a loud, clear voice. "I don't care what any of you think about me. If it's necessary, I'll take up the sword and face a thousand monsters if that's what it takes to save my little girl."

Many of the villagers shook their heads in shock at the declaration, but Saddler held firm, refusing to be shamed into backing down.

"We'll need supplies," Watcher said, speaking to Saddler.

"Don't worry; I'll get you whatever you need," she replied.

"There's something I need that I don't think you can get." Blaster ran his fingers through his dark, curly hair, trying to wrangle the disobedient locks into line. It didn't work.

Saddler glanced at his crazy hair and smiled. "What is it?"

Blaster glanced at Watcher. "You remember that wand you used to duplicate all those Frost Walker boots before we battled the skeleton warlord?"

Watcher nodded. He reached into his inventory and pulled out the magical relic and held it in front of him. It looked like a stick, crooked and bent, but near the end, it split into two identical pieces, each capped with gold, forming the shape of a "Y."

"What's that?" Saddler asked.

"It's a relic from the Great War," Watcher explained. "I don't know what it's called, but it—"

"It's the Wand of Cloning," Mapper said as he approached. "I read about it in one of the ancient books of magic for the old days."

"The Wand of Cloning?" Saddler seemed confused. "What does it do?"

"I think we should do this out of sight from the other villagers." Blaster walked toward the wall that ringed the community. It was far from any of the other NPCs. Reaching into his inventory, he pulled out his last block of TNT and placed it onto the ground. "My dad always told me, 'When you start something, begin it prepared, as if you plan on being successful.' TNT has a way of being the key that opens many locks. I wouldn't want to go hunting witches without any explosives with us."

"We aren't hunting," Watcher said warily. "We're searching for them, and then *asking* them to help us."

"And if they don't agree to help us, then we force them . . . right?" Blaster smiled.

"Well . . . I guess—" Watcher began.

"Exactly," Cutter interrupted.

"Who knows what we're going to bump into out there." Blaster pulled out a piece of melon and some cooked chicken. "We need the TNT."

Watcher sighed. "Very well. Get ready with the food."

"What's going on?" Saddler asked, confused.

"Just step back and trust us." Planter pulled her back, away from the block of TNT that sat on the ground.

Watcher gripped the Wand of Cloning tight in his hand. He was hesitant to use it, as he knew what it would cost: pain, a lot of pain. But it also cost something else: part of his identity. *Am I really a wizard, like the zombie warlord and skeleton warlord both accused me of being? Even the King of the Withers thinks I'm a wizard, but I don't feel like one. I'm just Watcher. I don't want to be a wizard—I just want to be me.*

All the attention and looks of surprise when he used these magical artifacts made him feel disconnected, as if he were no longer *one of them.* If he was a wizard, then he was something different, forever removed from his peers.

Watcher knew what it felt like to be singled out and separated from the main group. In his old village, he was never part of the crowd, but always an outsider; the NPC who was too small, too skinny, too weak . . . He'd always felt that barrier between him and everyone else. Slowly, that barrier had worn away, but now, it felt as if it was growing again.

He sighed, but knew he had no choice; they had to have this TNT.

With the Wand of Cloning over his head, he swung it around in a circle. The purple glow around the relic was faint at first, but then grew bright. At the same time, Watcher grunted as the wand stabbed at his health, drawing upon his life force to power its magical enchantment. He flicked the wand at the TNT. A sparkling mist appeared on the ground. When it cleared, there were two blocks of TNT instead of just one.

"How did that happen?" Now Saddler was *really* confused.

Watcher did it again and again, his body flashing red over and over as the enchanted wand tore into his HP, converting his health into magical energy. Finally, with his skin as pale as the bones of a skeleton, he stopped, his body completely exhausted.

Blaster caught him just as he was about to fall. He quickly stuffed the melon into his mouth. Watcher dropped the wand and gobbled down the fruit, then took the cooked chicken and devoured it as well. Slowly, color returned to his face as his HP regenerated.

Bending over, Watcher retrieved the wand and put it back into his inventory.

"That was incredible. You have any other surprises I need to know about?" Saddler's eyes were wide with surprise.

"Show her the bow," Planter said.

Watcher reached into his inventory and pulled out a large white bow made from bone. "This was the bow of the skeleton warlord."

"We took it from him," Cutter added.

Watcher wanted to correct him—*I took it from him, you mean*—but he kept his comment to himself. "It's called the Fossil Bow of Destruction, and it's another ancient artifact from the Great War."

"What does it do?" she asked.

"Well . . . it will shoot an arrow that can kill anything

with one hit. The arrow tracks the target, and will pass through just about anything to reach it." Watcher could still remember the pain the weapon had inflicted on him the last time he'd experimented with it. He was hesitant ever to use it again. "It extracts a price, though, just as the Wand does. It's one of the reasons why I don't like using these things unless we have to." He put the bow away. "For now, I have my own bow." He drew an enchanted bow from his inventory. "It has served me through many adventures."

"Maybe you could use that enchanted chainmail we took from the zombie warlord," Blaster asked. "You remember, it was called . . ."

"The Mantle of Command." Mapper gave them a satisfied grin.

"Right . . . I knew that . . . the Mantle of Command." Blaster smiled back at the old man. "Maybe you could use that armor to find a witch. It would make this little trip a lot shorter."

Watcher pulled the magical chainmail from his inventory and held it far from his body, as if it were poisonous. It sparkled with an iridescent light, pulsing with power as if it were alive. He could feel the enchantment reaching out to him, seeking to use his HP as a source of power. The last time he'd put on this armor, he'd been able to see the hiding place of the skeleton warlord as well as some spiders and the wither king, but it had come at a terrible price. The Mantle had almost killed him. . . . He had no desire to try that again.

"It's too dangerous." Planter put her hand on Watcher's, then pushed it down toward the ground, forcing him to put away the Mantle. "We all know what it did to him before . . . we aren't trying that unless it's absolutely necessary." The finality in the tone of her voice made everyone wary of challenging her decision.

"I'm not a fan of weapons, as you all know." Saddler moved to Watcher and Cutter. "But if we must have weapons with us," she glanced at the young boy, "I'd rather have the best ones."

"Now you're talking our language." Blaster nodded and smiled.

"I'll get the supplies we need, then we'll leave." Saddler turned to Mapper. "How about you come and help?"

Mapper nodded and the two rushed off to the supply shed.

"Watcher, you think it'll be hard to find a witch?" his father asked.

The boy shook his head. "All we need to do is find the witch's hut, and the witch should be inside, brewing potions. My understanding is they only leave their huts when it's absolutely necessary. We should find one soon enough."

"You be careful," Cleric said. "Your sister and I will keep everyone in the village out of trouble while you're gone."

His sister, Winger, smiled, then stood next to their father.

"I see Saddler and Mapper by the front gates." Planter pulled out her golden axe and red shield. Both items glowed with magical enchantments. "Let's go."

They all ran to the gates, leaving Watcher to stand there, staring at his father and sister. For some reason, he felt as if everything was about to change. A feeling of dread seemed to wash through his soul, as if it were some kind of warning sent to him from the distant past. Full of trepidation, he turned and followed his friends out of the village and into the savannah.

CHAPTER 4

"Do you think they've found the witch yet?" Winger's voice sounded concerned. "I'm worried about my little brother."

"I'm sure Watcher's okay." Cleric glanced down at his daughter. "Winger, you don't need to worry about Watcher. He's a smart boy and I'm sure he'll be careful." He put his arm around her and hugged her tight. "By the way, don't think I forgot . . . Happy birthday!"

She smiled. "What did you get me?"

"Well, with our village crushed and burned to the ground, and having just survived a huge battle with the skeleton warlord and his forces, I didn't really get you anything, other than a cake. Baker will be pulling it out of the furnace soon."

Winger sighed, then smiled at her father. "A cake will be good. Besides, I'm just glad we survived those terrible battles and that adventure."

Cleric smiled and gave his daughter a hug.

Just then, more NPCs emerged from their homes. The shadow from the looming wall around the community slowly shrank as the morning sun drifted higher into the eastern sky. The village was waking from its long evening slumber, its activity slowly building. "How long do you think the members of this savannah village will let us stay here?"

Cleric shrugged. "I don't know. We told them our village was burned to the ground by the skeleton warlord and his minions. There's really no place else for us to go, but they also know we've been battling with zombies and skeletons. They don't approve of our fighting."

"Do they approve of the skeletons destroying our village?" Winger asked.

"Well . . . I'm sure they—"

"Do they approve of the zombies attacking us and taking everyone prisoner?" Her voice was growing louder

"I doubt they—"

"Do they approve of the zombies killing all the old and sick NPCs from countless villages?" Winger's anger was still building.

Cleric put a calming hand on her shoulder. "Listen, daughter, these NPCs have their own beliefs, and we need to respect them. There are only fifty members of our village still alive, but there are about a hundred of the savannah villagers. We need to respect their wishes and be good community members. In this village, we are the minority."

She sighed. "I know . . . I just get frustrated."

"We are guests here in their village, and we need to be respectful."

"Yes, father." She rolled her eyes.

The constant east-to-west breeze grew warmer as the morning progressed. It carried with it the smell of dry grass and the tangy smell of the acacia trees. Winger took in a huge breath and let the aromas flow into her body. It was fantastic.

But just then, a strange noise floated in on the wind. The sound reminded Winger of the cobbler at their old villager, carefully hammering nails into the soles of a shoe. But instead of one cobbler, it was as if there were a thousand of them, all tapping on their nails as fast as they could. Winger glanced at her father, confused, and the expression on Cleric's face made her worry. The old man wasn't just curious about the sound; he was scared by it.

"What is it?" she asked.

"Spiders," he whispered. "Go around and wake up all of *our* villagers. Make sure they're all armed and wearing their armor."

She nodded and sprinted through the village, pounding on doors to wake up the members of their villager army. After she woke a few, Winger sent out others to wake the rest as she sprinted back to Cleric.

She found her father surrounded by a group of concerned villagers. The clicking was louder, as if it was just outside of the walls.

"Dad, I think *they* are on the other side of the wall." Winger reached into her inventory for her bow, but Cleric put a restraining hand on her arm and shook his head.

"We know spiders are out there." The village leader, an old NPC named Miner, stood atop a slab of cobblestone and stared down at Cleric and the other visitors. "But we won't use weapons. If we just leave them alone, they'll leave us alone. That's why we built this wall."

"But you don't understand about spiders," Winger said. "They can just—"

"If you are to live here, you must accept our rules." Miner glared at Winger as if she were a petulant child, then turned his back on her.

"This is bad," she whispered to her father. "Spiders right outside the wall . . . this is very bad."

"I know you're frustrated, daughter. Just be patient."

She sighed and said nothing.

Suddenly, a spider crested the top of the wall. It was a large, black, fuzzy thing, with eight bright red eyes and wicked-looking curved claws at the end of each leg. Like a black fog, more of the dark nightmares crested the top of the barricade; their eyes were glowing embers of hate. The villagers moved away from the wall as more of the monsters scaled the barricade and stared down at them from the top. One by one, the spiders lowered themselves down on thin strands of spider's silk, settling noiselessly into the courtyard.

Miner stepped forward and confronted the terrifying beasts.

"The ssspider warlord hasss given commandsss for thisss village," the largest of the spiders said.

"We want no part in anyone's war. We will offer aid to all creatures who need it, but we will not be pulled into someone else's war." Miner stood tall, seemingly unafraid.

"You dare challenge the ssspider warlord, Ssshakaar?" The monster took a step closer, the other spiders spreading out, keeping their hateful eyes on the villagers. Miner stood his ground, standing calmly before the horde, his arms held behind his back.

"We mean no harm to spiders nor any other creatures of the Far Lands," the village leader said.

"Then you will tell usss where the boy-wizard isss hiding?" The spider's eyes grew bright, its mandibles clicking together impatiently. Some of the other spiders clicked their mandibles together, the sound echoing off the tall stone walls.

Winger glanced at her father, her hand moving to her inventory. He shook his head ever so slightly.

"We don't know anything about a wizard." Miner held his hands out, showing they were empty and he was not a threat. "They are a thing of the past. We're just a peaceful community, living in harmony with the land."

"Ssshakaar told usss you would lie," the spider hissed as it swung a sharp claw at the villager.

Winger noticed there was some kind of dark green ooze coating the point.

The razor-sharp edge tore through Miner's smock and dug into his flesh. Instantly he flashed red, taking damage. He groaned and clutched at the wound, then fell to the ground.

"What's happening?" Miner groaned. "What did you do?"

He flashed red again.

"I'm jussst making an example of you." The spider glared down at the wounded NPC. "You have been infected with a new poissson. Your HP will be gone sssoon. Hopefully, the next villager will be more cooperative."

The other monsters stepped forward, ready for battle.

Miner glanced up at his wife. She knelt at his side and offered him food to help rejuvenate his health, but nothing slowed the terrible poison. Cleric reached into his inventory for his sword, but the injured villager saw the move and shook his head. *No,* the old man mouthed, his dedication to non-violence unwavering even as the poison ravaged his body. His HP dropped lower and lower until, with a tear in his eye, he disappeared, leaving his inventory to float on the ground, no longer needed.

Cleric turned his head and spoke something softly to one of his villagers. "Go get as many pails of milk you can carry."

The NPC nodded and ran from the congregation, heading toward the animal pens, a couple of companions with him to help.

Scanning the crowd with its eight blazing eyes, the spider pointed to a small boy trying to hide behind his mother. "You . . . boy . . . come here."

The young villager hid behind his mother's leg.

"Come here now, or my ssspidersss will attack." The other monsters clicked their mandibles together; it had a hungry sort of sound to it.

The mother sighed, then stepped forward, her son still hidden behind her.

"You will tell me about the boy-wizard, or you will tassste my poissson." The spider's eyes were like red-hot embers.

"We don't know what you're talking about," the mother pleaded. "Just leave us alone."

"Thisss isss your lassst chance." The monster held out a dark-green claw, an acidic stench coming from its poisonous coating.

"I know this wizard," Cleric suddenly said in a loud, clear voice.

The spider pushed the mother and boy out of the way and turned toward the voice.

Pushing through the crowd, Cleric approached the fuzzy creature, his hands held calmly behind his back.

"Tell me what you know . . . now!"

Cleric glanced over his shoulder at Winger and nodded, then faced the monster. He murmured something softly.

"What did you sssay?" the spider hissed impatiently.

Cleric said it again, mumbling unintelligibly.

The spider moved closer. "Ssspeak louder!"

"I said . . . NOW!"

His iron sword flashed out from behind his back and fell upon the monster. At the same time, Winger pulled out her enchanted bow and shot at the creature. Her arrows instantly caught fire, the *Flame* enchantment giving each shaft fiery life. The burning projectiles hit the spider, pushing it back a step. Advancing, Cleric struck the monster again and again, causing it to flash red as it took damage. It swung its claw at Cleric, but was blocked by the villager's iron sword. More arrows from Winger's enchanted bow struck the spider until it disappeared, the creature's HP finally exhausted.

The NPCs from Cleric's village all charged with weapons drawn, but to his surprise, those from the savannah community also charged forward. Some had shovels, others with axes, while some just wielded sticks. They fell upon the spiders, their rage at seeing their leader murdered driving them to fight.

Expecting the pacifists to just cower and yield, the spiders were not ready for the ferocity of their attack. They tried to fight back, but were badly outnumbered. They slashed at the NPCs with their wicked, curved claws, some of the sharp points finding flesh. Fortunately, only a few spiders had poisonous claws, and infected villagers were quickly given the only antidote to spider venom: milk.

Winger's bow hummed the song of battle as her bowstring buzzed with every shot. She drew and fired her flaming shafts of death as fast as she could, striking out at the creatures before they could fall upon the villagers of this savannah community. The NPCs' courage was admirable, but they had no idea how to fight, and many of them were getting hurt.

A spider slashed at a farmer, its sharp claw tearing through their brown smock. Winger kicked the monster back, the buried three arrows into the creature before it could stand. The farmer said something to Winger, but she didn't stay around to listen; she was already firing on other targets. The creatures screeched in pain, echoing the villagers who were wounded.

"Don't let any of them get away!" Winger shouted. "KEEP FIGHTING!"

She turned her bow upon the spiders trying to climb the wall. Two of the hideous creatures burst into flames as her fire arrows struck them, but one of them still made it to the top. The creature glared down at the villagers, looking pleased and thinking it had escaped, but suddenly, Cleric and a group of warriors appeared atop the barricade, their iron swords tearing into the monster. The creature tried to flee, but the villagers would not relent. They attacked it from both sides, blocking the spider's attacks, eventually silencing the creature forever.

The villagers cheered, the taste of victory sweet.

Cleric climbed off the wall and ran to the center of the courtyard. One villager was lying on the ground, grievously wounded. Winger gave the NPC food to help them rejuvenate their HP. Many of the villagers patted Cleric and his armed companions on the back while others glared at the weapons in their hands.

"Just because you are nonviolent, it doesn't mean the monsters are as well." Cleric glared at the villagers, a stern expression chiseled into his square face. "There's something going on with the spider warlord, something that threatens us all. They knew we were here and came hunting my son."

"Didn't the spider call him a wizard?" one of the villager asked, confused.

"That's what the other warlords called him as well, for some reason," Winger explained. "We don't know why."

Cleric nodded. "If the spiders sent this small group here to find my son, they will send more. In time, the spider warlord will send all her forces here. They'll wipe this village off the surface of the Far Lands, leaving no survivors." He turned and glared at the villagers, letting his words set in. "The safety of this community depends upon us, the NPCs from my village, not your wall."

Many of the inhabitants nodded their square heads as they listened, some standing proud with an axe or shovel in hand.

"We can send an emissary to the spider warlord," someone shouted. "Explain we aren't involved in their war."

"Anyone sent to the spiders' lair will be destroyed." Winger moved to his father's side.

"Maybe we can defend our village," another said hopefully.

"Look around you." Winger glared at the speaker. "You know nothing of warfare. You have no weapons, no armor. There are barely a hundred of you. The spider warlord probably has hundreds and hundreds of monsters under her command. You wouldn't stand a chance."

"My daughter is right," Cleric said. "You can no longer stay here. When these spiders fail to report back, more will be sent to investigate."

"So what do you suggest we do?" Miner's wife asked, still on the ground, her eyes bloodshot from grief.

"We must abandon the village so when the spiders return, they find nothing." Cleric's voice was calm and wise. "Hide Fencer and a few people in the mines to take care of her, and the rest go with us."

"If we abandon our village, where will we go?" someone asked, worried.

"We go after Watcher and help him to find the witch. He'll never be able to fight an entire army of spiders on his own." He reached out to Miner's widow and helped her to her feet. "If we are to save Fencer, we must also go help my son, or all of us will end up like Miner."

The NPCs glanced down at Miner's belongings, still floating on the ground, then turned their gazes towards the weapons held by the warriors. Many looked disgusted by the swords and bows, their will to fight already fragile and close to shattering.

"I'll go with you," an NPC said bravely.

"What is your name, friend?" Cleric asked.

"I'm Farmer, and I won't let a bunch of spiders terrorize our village." He glanced at his friends and neighbors. "This is our home, and if we must fight to keep it, then so be it."

Everyone was silent in the courtyard, with no other NPC willing to come forward, until . . .

"I'll help," a young voice said. It was the boy who had been threatened by the spider commander. "This is my village, and my friends live here. Spiders are mean!"

The NPCs smiled at the young boy's bravery.

"My son's right," his mother said. "I'll help."

"Me too . . ."

"And me . . ."

"And me . . ."

One by one, all of the villagers came forward, the flame of their bravery rekindled by a young spark. They looked at the weapons, now with hope in their eyes instead of disdain.

"Okay, here's what we need." Cleric pointed to a group of men. "We need every horse, plus food, and iron for weapons and armor, and . . ." He doled out the responsibilities, transforming the village into a fighting force. As the NPCs moved throughout the village, gathering supplies, Cleric turned to his daughter.

"I know you're worried about Watcher, but we're going after him. We'll make sure he's safe."

Winger nodded and smiled. "You know, I'm not sure this is what I really wanted for my birthday . . . another dangerous adventure with a host of monsters trying to destroy us."

"I know, little one, but this is all I have for you."

"Well, since we're at least helping out Watcher and our friends, then I guess I'll take it."

Cleric smiled and gave his daughter a hug. "Let's go help the others prepare. I think we're in for a long day."

CHAPTER 5

Shakaar paced back and forth across the Hatching Chamber, looking at the hundreds of eggs spread out across the cavern, each shell as black as night with a smattering of bright red dots across its smooth surface. Blocks of spiderweb cushioned each egg on the stone floor of the chamber or held the precious cargo tightly to the walls and ceiling.

Streams of lava oozed from the walls of the cavern, collecting in pools across the uneven ground. The molten stone cast a sulfurous orange glow through the cavern, making it easy for the dark-blue cave spiders to scurry about and tend to the eggs; that was their only purpose in Minecraft. Many of the poisonous spiders held clumps of green moss in their mandibles; the nutritious plant was a favorite food to newborn spiders. The smaller spiders moved through the tunnels and caves of Minecraft, searching for the hidden dungeons where the moss grew. After the plants were stripped from the mossy cobblestone on which it grew, they were brought back to the Hatching Chamber. Placing the verdant clumps of moss around the eggs, the cave spiders prepared first meals for the hungry new mouths that were soon to emerge.

The spider warlord smiled as she watched the tenacious little spiders, the "brothers," as they were known. They weren't very strong, but their poisonous claws tended to dissuade other creatures from bothering them while they performed their task. Shakaar envied them this poison; it made the cave spiders extremely dangerous.

A group of fuzzy black spiders, the "sisters," passed by the opening to the Hatching Chamber, with newly-imprisoned witches alongside the monsters as they entered the tunnel. They'd just been captured from the great southern swamp and were now being taken to their new quarters in the spiders' lair. It was likely the last home they'd ever know; prisoners never escaped from the spider warlord . . . at least, not alive.

"Sssoon, you will be brewing poisssonsss for me," Shakaar said to the defeated prisoners who shuffled past. "Enjoy your new home. Resssissstance is futile."

One of the witches glanced up at the spider warlord, a look of uncertainty on her square face. She glanced at the spiders around her, then a flicker of hope blossomed into life within her eyes. Suddenly, the witch turned and made a break for freedom, hoping the others would not notice . . . but Shakaar did.

"Sssissstersss, a witch isss trying to get away." Shakaar pointed with a dark claw. "Dessstroy her!"

A pair of spiders scuttled after the escaping witch. The monsters ran along the walls of the passage, zipping passed the doomed witch, then leapt to the ground, blocking her escape route. The witch skidded to a stop, then reached into her inventory and pulled out a sparkling potion. She held it high, ready to throw it at the two spiders barring her passage.

Shakaar moved with lightning speed, dashing out of the Hatching Chamber and across the uneven ground. She snuck up behind the witch and brought her razor-sharp claws down upon the woman. The witch screamed in pain, dropping her potion. It splashed to the ground, coating the witch and Shakaar, but causing no harm. It was just an Awkward potion, the precursor to many other concoctions, but harmless on its own. It had been a bluff. The spider warlord slashed at the witch, tearing into her HP with a vengeance. Finally, the prisoner collapsed to the ground, her black, conical hat tumbling off her head.

The witch stared up at Shakaar, her eyes bright with defiance. "We will stop you somehow," she said. "People will notice our absence."

"You fool. The villagersss hate you. Witchesss have been ssshunned from the NPC comunitiesss since long ago." Shakaar moved closer, knowing that the witch was too weak to stand. "They no longer care about you, jussst like you care nothing about them." She raised a claw high in the air, ready for the final strike. "No one will come for you. Witchesss will sssoon be extinct."

Before the witch could answer, Shakaar brought her claw down upon the helpless NPC, taking the last of her HP. She disappeared with a look of terror on her square face, a few useless potions and items falling from her inventory to the ground. Only one of those items seemed interesting: a golden apple. It was something Shakaar had seen before, but this one glowed with an iridescent purple luster, as if enchanted. She stepped forward and collected the items, then gave them to another spider.

"Sssisssster, put thessse itemsss into the chessstsss in the Gathering Chamber." She clicked her mandibles together impatiently. "They might be of ussse. Perhaps we will have the witchesss make more."

The spider nodded, took the items and scurried through the tunnel toward the Gathering Chamber. Shakaar turned back to the other spiders and their prisoners.

"No one essscapes from the sssspidersss' lair." She moved closer to the captives, her eyes burning with anger. "You will be desssstroyed before being allowed to leave thisss place. Obey usss, give up all hope, and you might sssurvive." She glanced at the sisters. "Take them to the brewing chamber. Make sssure they work on improving the poissson. The ssspider eggsss will be hatching sssoon and will need a new coating, but we need sssomething ssstronger. The poissson mussst make thessse new hatchlingsss vicioussss, with an inborn hatred for all living creaturesss, except for ssspidersss, of courssse."

"Yes, warlord."

One of the spiders turned to the witches and struck the nearest one with her claw. The woman screamed in pain, but it forced her forward, and the other prisoners followed close behind.

Shakaar smiled, then returned to the Hatching Chamber. She cast her gaze across the cavern, trying to count the hundreds of eggs.

"You will hatch sssoon, my children," Shakaar said to the unborn spiders. "With the poissson the witchesss are brewing, you will all have the venomousss clawsss the brothers have." She smiled. "After we treat your egg ssshellsss, the poissson will become infusssed within your bodiesss and your mindsss, filling you with hate. You will then be the perfect fighting machinesss."

She climbed the wall of the chamber, then scurried across the ceiling. Attaching a piece of spiderweb from her spinnerets, then lowered herself down, hanging in mid over her unborn children.

"Sssome of the sssisssstersss have complained thisss poissson will make my children violent and angry. They sssay that isss no way for a child to grow up." She glared down at the eggs below here. "What do I care about your childhood? All that isss important isss the ssspidersss ruling all of the Far Lands. Sssoon, it will all belong to usss, and a new age will begin; the Age of the Ssspidersss." Shakaar laughed, her eyes like bright red lasers. "And there isss no one to ssstop usss, just asss the wither king predicted."

Closing her eight eyes, Shakaar imagined what the war would be like, when all the eggs hatched, and the spiders were free to move across the Far Lands like a deadly black wave, destroying everything they touched. It made her smile.

"Sssoon . . . very sssoon." Shakaar smiled toothy, frightening grin.

CHAPTER 6

Watcher's feet crunched through the frozen layer of snow covering the ground. His breath billowed in front of his face like soft clouds, the cold chilling the tip of his nose. They'd entered this frozen biome just as the moon set behind the western horizon. Now, the sun was peeking its radiant face over the mountains to the east, splashing warm reds and rich oranges across the world. The light cast brushstrokes of crimson and gold upon the snow, making it glow as if the frosty layer were covering molten stone. Rays of light from the rising sun pierced the frozen spikes of ice jutting up from the landscape, and as the light shone through the translucent blocks, the clear ice split the sunbeams into rainbow colors, decorating the snow.

"Er-Lan sees rainbows." The zombie sounded stunned as he shuffled through the hard-packed snow.

Planter gasped at the beautiful sight. "Watcher . . . you seeing this?"

Watcher nodded.

"Come walk next to me." Planter's voice was soft and melodic, like beautiful music. She glanced at him and gave a welcoming smile that was more than just that of a friend.

What's that supposed to mean? Watcher's thoughts bounced around his head as he tried to understand the meaning of her invitation . . . and that smile.

Moving to her side, Watcher felt as if fireworks were going off inside his chest. He and Planter walked side-by-side, their footsteps crunching through the snow in a synchronized beat, *crunch . . . crunch . . . crunch . . . crunch.* Occasionally, their hands brushed against each other.

Was that on purpose? Watcher contemplated the meaning of the passing touch as if it were an enemy's battle strategy, but he couldn't tell if it was intentional or not.

She pointed with her enchanted golden axe at the vibrant display. "Look at the color." Her voice was high-pitched with excitement.

Watcher nodded and glanced at her. Some of the multicolored light was shining down upon Planter's wonderful long blond hair; it made him smile. "Yeah . . . I see, it's spectacular."

A gentle snow started to fall, the crystalline flakes gracefully dancing on the breeze as they fluttered to the ground. The snowfall seemed to still the biome into a peaceful quietude, the sound of their feet breaking through the snow the only noise to be heard.

Maybe I should say something to her now. Watcher glanced around at his companions; everyone seemed preoccupied with the colorful display. Waves of fear crashed through him, tearing away at his courage. *I must do it . . . now.*

But before he could act, Cutter spoke up.

"When we're done finding a witch and saving Fencer, maybe we can build some ice sculptures." Cutter's voice boomed through the silence like a hammer through glass. His iron armor clanked as he walked faster, pushing his way between Planter and Watcher. "I bet if we built a tall ice spike of our own; it would really break up the sunlight."

"That would be fun." Planter gave the big warrior a smile.

Watcher's heart sank. He scowled at the big NPC, but Cutter didn't notice.

Did Cutter just move between us so he could be closer to Planter? Jealous thoughts spread through the dark parts of his soul as Watcher tried to understand why his friend would do something like that. *It was probably nothing.*

"First, we have to save Fencer," she added.

"Of course," Cutter said. The big warrior smiled at her.

For the first time, Watcher noticed Planter staring back at the hulking NPC. It was as if she were noticing him for the first time, much like how Watcher had recently noticed Planter as something more than just a childhood friend.

"I doubt we'd have time to play around with ice, Cutter." Watcher scowled. "After we save Fencer, we still need to rebuild our own village, then we'll likely need to construct some defenses for the village. I don't want another monster army to flatten our homes to the ground again. We'll be *way* too busy to play with ice." He glared at Cutter, but the big NPC was oblivious to his stare.

"Hey, we're just talking here," Cutter glanced down at the boy. "Lighten up a bit."

"Wow, Mr. Serious is telling the daydreamer to lighten up." Blaster laughed as he chimed in. "This is quite the role reversal."

Planter laughed along with Blaster, and even Cutter smiled. But not Watcher.

"I don't need to *lighten up a bit*." Watcher was now getting angry. "We have a lot of work ahead of us, and we need to stay—"

"It's not a big deal. Don't worry about it." Cutter's voice had a tone of finality, signifying the conversation was over.

Why am I having this argument? Watcher searched his thoughts. *Was I wrong?* Cutter and Planter and the whole situation dominated his thoughts. *Why does it all seem so confusing?*

An uneasy silence spread across the group; they could all feel Watcher's tension. As an attempt to change the topic, Watcher moved next to Fencer's mother.

"Saddler, have you ever been in this biome?" Watcher asked.

The woman shook her head, her long, black ponytail dancing about on her back. "I was born in that savannah village and had never left before today."

"You mean, you've never gone out and seen the different biomes in the Far Lands?" Mapper sounded shocked.

They curved around a steep pile of ice, the translucent cubes almost taking on a diamond-like appearance in the morning light. Watcher and Saddler walked in lock-step.

"When I was born, the wall was already there." Saddler sighed. "This is the first time I've ever been out of the village."

"Well then, to see your first ice spikes biome must be a treat," Mapper said.

She nodded. "It is. I never imagined anything so spectacular."

"Saddler, can you tell us why your village has sworn off violence?" Mapper asked.

"Yeah . . . it doesn't seem like a very good idea." Blaster shook his head, confused. The boy had removed his favorite black armor and was now wearing white, blending in with the background again.

"Blaster . . . be nice." Planter cast him a scowl. He just smiled in response.

"Something happened a long, long time ago, causing the village to take a pledge of non-violence. Some think it happened during the Great War, but no one is really sure."

"Don't you have anything written down in books?" Mapper asked.

She shook her head. "No, there's nothing written down anywhere. All of the buildings have been searched and there's no mention of what happened. All we know is the wall was there before anyone in the village was born."

"Your parents and grandparents and great grand-parents . . . all of them were born with the wall being there?" Mapper glanced at Watcher, a surprised expression on his wrinkled face.

Saddler nodded.

"So, leaving the village with these companions . . . that was difficult?" Er-Lan's voice was filled with compassion. "This zombie understands the difficulty of such a choice."

Saddler glanced at the zombie and nodded. "I'm sure the other villagers feel as if I betrayed them." Her voice was solemn and sad. "We all swore to never take up arms against another creature and to stay within the confines of our village, but I couldn't just give up on my little girl, Fencer." She turned to Watcher. "I will always be indebted to you for saving her. None of my neighbors or friends would have gone into that cave knowing there were monsters down there."

"So they're afraid. . . . They're cowards?" Blaster asked.

"Avoiding violence does not make one a coward." Er-Lan's voice was barely a whisper, but loud enough for all to hear.

"That's right, Er-Lan. Sticking to your principles doesn't make someone a coward," Mapper corrected. "It makes them brave."

"But to leave that little girl down there in a cave with monsters closing in on her . . . that's terrible." Blaster shook his head in disgust.

"I agree with Blaster. . . . They're cowards." Cutter's deep voice boomed across the landscape.

Watcher glanced at Planter and rolled his eyes. "They aren't cowards." His voice was terse. "They're just trying to follow their beliefs."

"Well, Cutter and Blaster do have a point," Planter said as she curved around a huge column of ice that stretched up high into the sky. "They would have just abandoned Fencer if we hadn't been there."

Watcher sighed. "Knowing who you really are and following your path can be difficult. Though we don't understand the NPCs in that savannah village, it's important to respect their dedication to their principles. Sometimes it can be hard to follow your beliefs."

Cutter laughed and glanced at Planter, waiting for a response. She remained silent.

"Come see what's up ahead." Blaster ran over a snow-covered hill and disappeared behind its peak.

Watcher drew his enchanted sword, Needle, from his inventory and chased after his young friend, the rest of the party two steps behind him. When he reached the top of the snowy mound, he found Blaster standing in front of a round dwelling, constructed from blocks of packed snow.

"Look . . . it's an igloo." Planter's lyrical voice fluttered with excitement.

"What is it?" Er-Lan sounded confused. "It just seems like a mound of snow."

"I've never seen one of those!" Mapper exclaimed as he sprinted down the hill, slipping on a block of ice and tumbling the rest of the way.

"Mapper, are you okay?" Er-Lan knelt at the old man's side.

As he struggled to stand on wobbly legs, Mapper smiled bashfully. "I've heard about these appearing in the Far Lands only recently, but have never seen one."

"Well . . . come on." Watcher put a hand on Mapper's left arm, Er-Lan on his right. "Just don't take another dive."

Mapper laughed, then sprinted toward the entrance, the two friends on either side.

Watcher followed Mapper and Er-Lan into the domed structure. Inside, white carpet covered the floor, and there was a bed on one side of the igloo, with a crafting bench and furnace on the other. A lone redstone torch burned, providing enough light to see without melting any of the snow.

"Is this all?" Cutter stomped around, shattering the bed with an axe to see what was underneath.

Blaster turned his pickaxe upon the furnace, then shattered the crafting bench too, putting both into his inventory. "This is pretty anti-climactic. I thought we might find something useful."

"Yeah. This is a waste of time . . . let's go." Cutter stormed out, followed by Blaster and Saddler.

Er-Lan growled as if sensing something.

"It's not a *waste of time*. Hold on." Watcher moved to the edge of the white carpet, then knelt and stared at the fuzzy floor covering. "There's something underneath the rug."

"What are you talking about? How can you tell that?" Cutter's question was more like an accusation, as if he were showing off to someone.

"See how it rises up just a bit?" Watcher pointed with an iron axe at the far edge. "I think there's something here."

Swinging his axe, he tore into the carpet, destroying each square. The pieces floated off the ground, then flowed into Watcher's inventory as he continued to cut into the floor. When he destroyed the last piece, right at the slight bump, he found a trap door hidden under the white carpet.

"You see?" Watcher smiled.

"He was right." Blaster patted him on the back.

"Let's see what's down there." Cutter sounded impatient.

Watcher glanced at Planter, expecting some sort of recognition for his discovery, but she was already following the big NPC down the ladder.

"Wait!" Watcher shouted, but it was too late.

With Needle in his hand, Watcher followed his friends into the dark passage, Mapper and Saddler right behind him. The ladder descended about twenty blocks, then ended in a torch-lit room. The walls were made of stone brick and covered with dust; it was clear no one had been here in a long time.

One wall consisted of two cells, iron bars across the front. Clearly, they were prison cells, with a cauldron of water and a stone bench in each. Er-Lan stood before the cells and stiffened, then snarled.

"What is it?" Watcher moved to the zombie's side.

"Monsters have been kept here." His dark claws unconsciously extended from his decaying fingers. "Creatures were tortured here and left to perish. Great suffering happened here . . . Er-Lan can sense it."

"You can sense it?" Mapper asked.

The zombie nodded.

"Maybe it's best if you went to the surface to guard the entrance," Watcher said.

Er-Lan nodded his head, then slowly stepped away from the cells and climbed the ladder back to the surface.

Watcher surveyed the rest of the chamber. A brewing stand stood atop a wooden desk, a bottle still mounted on it, its potion dark and foreboding. Mapper reached out and took the bottle from the stand, then smelled its contents.

"Ahh . . . a splash potion of slowness." The old man smiled. "This might be useful." He stuffed the bottle into his inventory.

Watcher scanned the rest of the space. On the other side of the room was a large chest and a cauldron of water. He carefully opened the box, the hinges squeaking as if they hadn't moved in a century.

"All of you should look in here," Watcher said slowly, shocked by its contents.

Inside were a couple dozen swords, scores of bows, and stacks and stacks of arrows. Leather and chainmail armor filled many of the slots, followed by a stack of shields, but one shield sat in its own slot, which was curious. Watcher reached in and withdrew the shield. It was painted a bright red, the rim decorated with gold. Across the center were painted three wither skulls, each face with a different expression. The shield shimmered with magical energy as enchantments pulsed through the wood and metal.

Planter gasped when she saw it, her eyes wide with surprise.

"That looks just like the one we found while we were chasing the skeleton general and his forces a few weeks ago." Planter pulled out her shield; it was an identical copy.

"Apparently someone made many of these shields." Mapper lifted the shield and inspected its surface. "Clearly it's enchanted. I suspect this was made during the Great War. Maybe at one time, there were hundreds of these shields being used to protect villagers."

"Give it to Saddler." Watcher took it from Mapper and handed it to Fencer's mother. "You should use this. Maybe it will keep you safe."

"Why me?"

"Why not?" Watcher answered. "Someone should use it. I think it should be you. Does anyone disagree?"

Everyone remained silent.

"There you go . . . it's unanimous," Watcher said.

She smiled.

"Look, Saddler, we're shield sisters now." Planter held her shield up and smiled, then glanced at Watcher and gave him a smile.

Watcher's soul exploded with fireworks.

"Take all the weapons and armor," Cutter said. "You never know when we'll need more."

Watcher filled his inventory with armor and swords while Blaster, Cutter, and Mapper took the rest. They all filled their inventories to the brim.

"Let's get out of here." Cutter slammed the lid closed.

"I agree." Watcher climbed to his feet. "I'd like to find a witch before nightfall."

"That would be good," Planter added. "I'm worried about Fencer."

"We all are, of course," Cutter flashed her a confident smile, then climbed the ladder to the surface.

Before Watcher could say anything, Planter climbed up after him, disappearing into the dark passage. Waiting for the others to go to the surface, Watcher glanced around the room.

"Why was someone stocking weapons here, under an igloo?" His soft voice bounced off the stone walls and came back to him.

With a sigh, he climbed the ladder and stepped into the igloo. Moving to Saddler's side, he handed her an iron sword. "You'll likely need this."

She stared down at the weapon, a look of disgust on her face. Reluctantly, she grasped the hilt and held the sword away from her as if were about to bite.

"Here's some armor as well." Watcher gave her some chainmail. "You should put it on before we leave, just to be safe."

The woman nodded and put on the clinking armor, then held the blade out as before, trying to get as far from the weapon as possible.

"Let's go." Cutter stepped out of the igloo, then stopped just outside the frozen structure as a growl floated through the air.

"What was that?" Saddler asked, sounding worried.

"Was that Er-Lan?" Planter asked.

"It was not Er-Lan." The zombie stood at the back of the igloo.

Watcher stuck his head out of the igloo and scanned the terrain. Snow still fell from the sky in silent little clumps, each delicate geometric shape different from the next. The frozen shower made the biome seem still and peaceful.

But then the growl sounded again, driving the

peaceful stillness away. Watcher turned toward the sound. Standing nearby was a polar bear with two cubs, the animals' white fur blending in with their surroundings.

Cutter drew his diamond sword, then glanced at Watcher. "We need to move in that direction, but the bear is right in our path. It needs to go." He held his sword out as if showing it to Watcher. "You ready for a fight?"

"No, don't!" Saddler cried out as she emerged from the igloo. She reached up and grabbed Cutter's arm, forcing the big NPC to lower his sword. "We don't need to kill them."

"That bear is right in our path," Cutter pointed with his other hand. "If we go around, it might charge at us. There's no choice."

"You always have a choice when you decide who you want to be." Saddler sounded as if she were lecturing a misbehaving child. "You don't have to use violence. Make another choice."

Decide who you want to be. Saddler's words bounced around in Watcher's head as if they were some kind of universal truth, though he didn't understand their significance. *I don't want to be the person that destroys a bear just because she's protecting her cubs.*

"No, we won't attack." Watcher sheathed his sword. "There must be another way."

"You say it might . . . charge?" Mapper's voice cracked with fear, but then the old man smiled. "I know how to get past the polar bear without hurting it." He reached into his inventory and pulled out the slowness potion. "I'll use this. Is everyone ready to run?"

"What is it?" Cutter asked.

But Mapper didn't reply. Instead, he charged straight at the beast, the splash potion held high in the air. When he was within range, he threw the bottle at the animal. It crashed on its furry, muscular chest, coating the animal with the dark liquid as it reared up on its hind legs, brandishing dark claws. Instantly, colored spirals floated around the animal.

Mapper veered to the right and ran around the bear as it tried to pursue him, but the furry beast moved sluggishly now. "Come on, the bear is too slow to catch anyone now."

Watcher nodded, then took off running, the rest of the party following. Half went around to the left of the bear and the rest went to the right. They passed by the creature without having to fight it, leaving the furry mother to tend to her cubs.

"Good thinking, Mapper," Planter said, patting him on the back.

The old man beamed.

"Let's get moving." Watcher glanced to the sky. "It'll be dark soon."

They took off across the frozen landscape, heading for the distant swamp. Watcher hoped they could find the witch and get back to the savannah village soon. But a nagging thought tickled the back of his mind: *If we don't find a witch soon, Fencer will be doomed.*

Watcher shuddered as he ran, the icy fingers of dread slowly kneading at his soul.

CHAPTER 7

As the party neared the edge of the ice plains biome, the smell of rot and decay filled the air. Watcher glanced at Er-Lan, wondering if the smell was coming from his friend, but he knew the zombie had been taking regular baths since he'd abandoned the tyrannical rule of the zombie warlord and joined their community.

Planter scrunched her face at the offensive odor. "What is that?"

"Zombies, maybe?" Cutter pulled out his diamond sword.

Er-Lan shook his head. "The smell is wrong. It is not zombies."

"It must be the swamp." Mapper pulled out a stained and dog-eared map and held it up to the noon sky, making the features on the ancient document easier to read. "Yep, we should almost be to the end of this frigid biome. The swamp should be very close."

"There it is." A voice shouted from up ahead. Blaster was standing atop a small hill, his white armor making the boy difficult to discern from the snowy background. "We're at the swamp, and I can see a witch's hut."

"Do you see a witch?" Watcher ran up the hill.

"Nope, but maybe she's inside." Blaster removed his white armor and replaced it with a dark-green set. "They never venture very far from their huts unless they're searching for supplies."

"If the witch isn't there, we'll have to find another hut." Planter glanced at Saddler. The mother had a worried expression on her square face. "I'm sure she's there . . . I hope."

A tiny square tear tumbled from Saddler's eye. It fell to the ground and instantly froze into a miniature cube of ice. She wiped at her cheek, then scowled, a look of grim determination on her face. "If this witch isn't there, then we'll find another." She gritted her teeth and stomped up the snow-covered hill. "Come on, everyone."

Saddler reached the top of the hill, then sprinted down the other side, her iron sword in her hand.

They followed Saddler down the frozen slope, then stepped into the shallow waters of the swamp. Instantly, the temperature went from freezing cold to uncomfortably humid; the change felt like a kick to the chest. Jumping from lily pad to lily pad, they made their way closer to the structure, everyone in the company trying to keep their feet out of the stagnant waters. But eventually, their only choice was to slog through the knee-deep mire, trudging their way toward the witch's hut.

Watcher placed a block of dirt on the ground and stood on it, surveying their surroundings. It was difficult to see very far, but it was the best he could do. Watcher knew slimes liked to spawn in the swamps, and he'd rather see those green gelatinous creatures before they bounced toward them to attack. Fortunately, there were none nearby. He pushed his way through the still waters toward a small island, a lone oak tree standing at the center. Long green vines hung down from the branches and along the trunk, making it look sad for some reason.

With an axe in hand, Watcher climbed the vines on the trunk, then chopped away at the leaves when he reached the branches overhead. He made a set of leafy steps and climbed to the top of the tree, gaining a much better view of the swamp. A blue sky stretched from horizon to horizon, the overhead azure background dotted with white, rectangular clouds drifting in their persistent westward trek. Holding a hand over his eyes to block out the sun, Watcher peered across the swamp. The assorted colors of clay, dirt, sand, and gravel under the shallow water created a colorful patchwork of shapes and hues. Green lily pads punctuated dark spots in the quilt-like pattern with circles of color against the muted tans of the swamp floor. Across an open section of water, the witch's hut was clearly visible. A side window flickered with light, as if a torch was burning within.

"What do you see?" Planter asked.

"There's a light inside the hut." Watcher glanced down at Saddler. "Maybe we're in luck and she's there." He sprinted to the edge of the tree and jumped, landing lightly in the shallow water. "We need to be careful when we approach. If we scare the witch, she'll throw some potions at us. I don't think a potion of harming would be very helpful right now."

"Don't be afraid." Cutter moved closer to Planter. "I can take care of the witch. Come on, let's get her."

"I didn't say I was afraid; it's just . . ." Watcher started to say, but no one was listening. His companions were trudging on through the swamp, their splashing footsteps covering his voice.

He glared at Cutter's back, frustration building up inside him. Drawing his bow, he nocked an arrow to the bowstring, and moved through the water as fast as possible, keeping his eyes swiveling to the left and right, searching for the witch; he had no intentions of being poisoned today.

When they were at the edge of the hut, Planter built a set of steps out of blocks of dirt, allowing Cutter to climb onto the small porch jutting out from the doorway. Still no witch.

"Wait for us." Watcher's voice was just loud enough for Cutter to hear, but, of course, the big NPC ignored him.

Screaming his battle cry, Cutter charged into the hut. Blaster glanced at Watcher, a confused expression on his square face. Watcher just shrugged, then climbed the steps.

"There's no one here," Cutter said from inside.

Watcher stepped into the small home and glanced around; it was indeed empty. A cauldron sat in the corner, filled with water, next to a crafting table. A furnace was on the other side of the crafting chamber, flames slipping from the opening and casting a flickering glow throughout the room. On the opposite wall, a small wooden desk sat, a brewing stand on top with three bottles ready for brewing. Grabbing one, he smelled the contents. They were just filled with water . . . clearly, the witch was getting ready to brew something.

A chest sat in one corner, the lid open. Items lay on the ground as if pulled from the chest and tossed aside. Watcher looked in the box, but found it empty.

"Strange . . . why would the chest be empty, but items strewn all over the floor?" Mapper asked.

"What's this?" Saddler picked up a small red object. It was round and had something hanging from the end.

"That's a spider eye," Planter said.

"What?!" Saddler dropped the eye. "How did it get here?"

"Witches use them to make different potions." Mapper picked up the eye and tossed it into the chest.

"Spiders also drop them when they're killed," Cutter added. "Maybe there was a fight here and the witch took a spider out."

"If that's true, where are the balls of XP?" Watcher picked up the other items and put them back into the chest. "And where's the witch? If she destroyed the spider, she'd still be here."

"There are a couple of blocks of spiderweb over here," Er-Lan said, pointing to a shadowy corner. "Maybe some spiders trapped the witch there."

"Or maybe the witch was just messy and those are cobwebs." Cutter sheathed his sword. "There's no one here—let's move on."

"I agree." Planter gave Cutter a smile, then stepped out of the hut and jumped to the wet ground below.

Watcher saw that look and seethed in anger. *What's going on with those two?*

He moved toward the door, but Cutter pushed past him and leapt off the porch. Watcher heard Planter giggle when the warrior said something after landing in the water. He couldn't hear what they were saying, but he knew whatever it was, he didn't like it.

With his bow out, he sprinted down the stairs and scanned their surroundings. The sun was descending from its apex, toward the western horizon, allowing the landscape to slowly cool.

We must find the witch before dark, Watcher thought. *It'll be dangerous to try to catch one at night.* None of them wanted to be the recipient of a splash potion. He glanced at Mapper. "Which way to the next hut?"

"My map said there should be a hut to the southwest." Mapper pulled out the map and stared at the tiny letters and symbols, then nodded and put the item back in his inventory. "If it gets dark before we find a witch, we'll need to use torches."

"No, we shouldn't use any torches," Watcher said. "The monsters would see them. We need to try and stay invisible, at least for now."

Cutter rolled his eyes, then cast Planter a smile. She giggled again.

Watcher scowled, then started walking south-west. They moved in silence, sprinting across islands and jumping from lily pad to lily pad when possible, going as fast as they could, even though the stagnant water and mud of the biome made it difficult going.

"I see something up ahead." Watcher's keen eye-sight was the best in their village, if not in all of the Far Lands. "Something out there is flickering . . . it must be the next hut."

They trudged through the muck, moving closer to the structure. It seemed just like the last hut: a square building with a sloped roof standing atop four posts. A tall oak tree on a small circle of land stood next to the wooden structure. A small porch stuck out in front of the door with a window on one side. As they approached, a witch could be seen moving past the window, her purple smock and conical black hat unmistakable to anyone knowing what to look for.

But then, a dark shape Watcher had first thought was the shadow of the nearby oak moved on the roof of the hut. Eight bright red eyes blinked as they scanned the swamp.

"Spiders." Watcher notched a sparkling red-tipped arrow to his bowstring and pointed it toward the monster. The distance was too great, but he still held the weapon at the ready.

The witch dashed out onto her porch. She turned and threw a potion at another spider fast on her heels. The potion shattered on the head of the spider, caus-ing the creature to stumble and fall. Turning, the witch jumped off the porch and landed in the water. A stream of spiders charged out of the hut and followed, splash-ing down next to her. They coated the witch with blocks of spiderweb, immobilizing her arms and quickly mak-ing the NPC their prisoner. The witch glanced toward the villagers, making brief eye contact with Watcher. He could see fear in the NPC's eyes.

They ran through the swampy waters, closing the distance to the witch and spiders.

"Come on, we need to help her!" Watcher shot the magical arrow at the spider on top of the hut. Instantly, bright flames burst into life as the shaft leapt off the bow. The fire arrow streaked through the air, making a graceful arc towards its target, but the monster leapt off the hut at the last moment.

The spiders gathered their prey and bobbed about in the water, their feet too short to reach the soggy ground. But then, somehow, they started moving with incredible speed. Watcher pushed through the murky water as fast as he could, trying to get closer, but the spiders were now somehow running off as if they were on land, not in water. By the time Watcher and the others reached the hut, the monsters were long gone.

"What just happened?" Blaster asked, bewildered.

"It seems the spiders took the witch," Er-Lan explained.

"I know they did that!" Blaster put away his knives. "I mean . . . *why* did they do that?"

"I don't know." Watcher's voice was filled with anger. The look on the witch's face was that of someone accepting the arrival of their death. It was sad and terrible, and Watcher wasn't about to let that happen, not even to a witch. "But we're gonna find out."

Quickly, they searched the hut, hoping to find some clue that would tell them what was going on; they found nothing. The chest, as with the previous hut, was empty. No potions, no golden apples . . . nothing useful was left behind, just a few unimportant items scattered across the floor.

"Something is going on with the spiders and witches," Watcher said in a low voice.

"You think?" Blaster said sarcastically, smiling.

"We need the witches so we can help my little girl." Saddler's voice was filled with sadness, but also with rage as well. "I'm not gonna let a bunch of spiders get in the way of saving my daughter."

"None of us will let that happen." Watcher drew Needle from his inventory and nodded reassuringly to the mother.

Saddler drew her own iron sword and nodded to the

boy, a scowl on her face. "What are we waiting for?" She turned and jumped out of the hut. "Let's go!"

Blaster glanced at Watcher. "She's got spirit." He turned and followed her, as did Cutter and Planter.

"Looks like this might take a bit longer than we thought," Mapper said. "I hope you're ready for another adventure." He smiled, then headed out of the hut, leaving Watcher with Er-Lan.

"Er-Lan, why do you think the spiders would want to capture a witch?"

"It is uncertain. Spiders are not liked by any of the other monsters, and witches are shunned by the NPCs."

"That's not true," Watcher said defensively. "We don't shun them."

"Witches are not welcome in the villages so they must live in swamps, alone." Er-Lan glanced at the solitary structure. "Witches and spiders are both alone in their respective worlds. Perhaps there is a bond there."

"It didn't seem as if they were bonding." Watcher stepped out onto the porch, his companions waiting below. "I saw the expression on her face; that witch was terrified."

"Er-Lan is not sure what is happening, but if it involves the spiders, then it is not good." The zombie moved to the porch with his friends. "Spiders only cause harm and destruction. Nothing good will come from this."

Watcher pondered the zombie's words, then jumped off the porch and landed in the swamp. He found his comrades trudging through the water, trying to follow the spider. When he caught up with his friends, Watcher saw how the spiders had been able to move so quickly through the murky water.

"Look, there's a trail of spiderweb blocks in the water." Blaster pointed at the fuzzy blocks with a curved knife.

The trail of white, sticky cubes extended through the swamp. Blaster tried to stand on one of the cubes, but slowly sank into it, becoming entangled in the many tacky strands.

"We can't use their path, but we can make one of our own." Watcher pulled out a cobblestone block and placed it on the ground. "Come on, everyone, follow me."

Watcher jumped onto the block of stone, then placed another one three blocks away. He jumped to that gray cube, then placed another and jumped. They leapt from block to block, now moving quickly through the foul biome.

Watcher glanced over his shoulder at Mapper behind him. "I'm tired of adventures, but I'm not gonna fail Saddler's little girl."

And with a grim look of determination on his face, he sped through the swamp.

CHAPTER 8

Winger held her arms tightly around her father's waist as he kicked their horse into a gallop. Behind her, the rest of the NPCs from the savannah village charged across the landscape, most riding double on horses, but some on foot, sprinting as fast as possible. Occasionally, a rider would stop and dismount, giving those on the ground a chance to ride and rest their weary legs; there weren't enough horses for everyone.

"You know, Dad, so far, this isn't a very good birthday present." Winger chuckled.

"Think of it as a sightseeing trip, with me as your guide."

"Yeah . . . and a horde of spiders out there somewhere, ready to destroy us."

Cleric nodded.

"I'm so glad the villagers agreed to help us," she said. "This isn't really what I had in mind for a birthday present, Dad. But if it helps Watcher, then I'm happy."

"Me, too." Cleric pulled to the left on the reins, causing the horse to veer around a large oak tree. "I just hope we can reach them before the spiders do."

"We will," Winger reassured him.

They passed a man and wife who were walking hand-in-hand, their tired feet dragging on the ground as if they were exhausted. Cleric brought his animal to a halt. Both father and daughter jumped off their mount and gave the reins to the couple. Quickly mounting, the man and wife thanked Winger and Cleric, then rode off.

"Everyone, keep your HP up by eating!" Cleric shouted. "We need to move as fast as possible."

He winked at his daughter, then took off running, her footsteps close behind.

The group of villagers soon entered an ice spikes biome, the cold air causing the horses and villagers to puff clouds of white mist as they ran, breathing heavily. In the snow, footsteps were visible, showing the path of Watcher and the others. The villagers followed the frozen trail until they stopped at the sound of a voice.

"An igloo is up ahead," the forward scout shouted.

Cleric reached a small hill and gazed down at the rounded structure, the rest of the army standing on the frosty mound, uncertain what to do.

"Watcher would have already searched it. . . . Keep going!" Cleric called as he ran down the hill and past the igloo. He glanced up at the sun—its shining yellow face was on its way to the western horizon, but they still had a few hours of daylight left.

A villager clothed in a chocolate-brown smock with a tan stripe running down its center pulled his horse to a halt and leapt off, then handed the reins off to another NPC, who jumped on and galloped away.

"Wish we had more horses," the first villager said wistfully.

Cleric nodded. "What's your name?"

"I'm Farmer." He pointed to the tracks in the snow. "That's your boy out there . . . right?"

Cleric nodded again.

"What's that stuff about him being a wizard?" Farmer asked.

"The spiders seem to think he has magical powers," Winger said. "Oh . . . hi, I'm Winger, and that boy is my brother, Watcher."

"Ahh . . . he's also the one that saved Fencer in the caves?"

Both Cleric and Winger nodded, then smiled with pride.

"He must be a brave boy."

"The bravest," Winger replied.

"Why do the spiders think he's a wizard?" Farmer had a confused expression on his face.

"It's not just the spiders. It's the zombies and skeletons too." Winger suddenly grew quiet as her father cast an angry glare at her.

"Perhaps you said too much?" Farmer winked at her. "No worries. I know these villagers are just nervous about anything that might bring violence to their homes. They don't want to be embroiled in any war."

"When monsters declare war on *all* villagers, it makes everyone part of it, whether they like it or not," Cleric said. "The war just hadn't reached them yet. Now, it seems it has."

"That's for sure," Farmer replied.

"Enough rest, it's time to run," Winger said, then sprinted down the hill, Cleric and Farmer following close behind.

Watcher's tracks led away from the igloo and across the ice plains biome. Cleric, Winger, and Farmer ran across the ice plains, alternating between running and walking. At times, they traded with some of the mounted villagers, riding double on a horse to rest, although the weary horses received little to no respite. The villagers reached the edge of the frozen landscape with an hour of daylight left, but the tracks they'd been following now disappeared into the swamp.

"We can't take the horses into the swamp," Cleric said. "Let's follow the edge of the swamp for now."

"Everyone change riders." Winger dismounted from

the brown and white mare. "Anyone who's tired should be riding for a while."

Villagers changed positions, then ran or trotted as the group moved around the border of the swamp. Winger kept her eyes toward the distant edge of the biome, hoping to spot a figure moving through the mire, but all she saw were lily pads and vine-covered oak trees.

"I see something," a villager shouted.

Winger ran over to see where they were pointing. Out in the swamp, a square house constructed atop stilts was visible, light spilling from the doorway.

"Is there anyone moving in it?" Winger sounded a bit frantic, her concern for her brother evident in her strained voice. "Does anyone see anything?"

The villagers grew silent, their sympathetic eyes directed toward the worried older sister.

"I don't think there's anything there, Winger." Cleric put a reassuring hand on her arm. "Everyone . . . keep going."

"You think we went in the wrong direction?" Winger spoke in a low voice, meant only for her father's ears.

"I'm not sure." Cleric put an arm around his daughter. "If we don't spot them before it gets dark, we may be in trouble."

"You mean *they'll* be in trouble."

Her father nodded, frowning.

"I think maybe we should—"

"I see some cobblestone out there in the swamp!" someone shouted.

Winger stopped and stared in the direction the NPC pointed. Sure enough, there were cobblestone blocks placed in the water, just barely poking up out of the stagnant waters. "They were probably jumping from block to block so they could move faster."

"But why would they need to move faster?" a villager asked.

"Maybe they were being chased by something," another suggested.

This possibility brought an uneasy silence to the group of villagers. No one spoke, but many cast concerned gazes toward Cleric and Winger.

"I can see some spiderwebs in the water as well." The voice came from the top of an oak tree. One of the villagers had climbed to the top of an oak tree and was searching the landscape for their friends. "The line of cobblestone blocks seems to be heading in the same direction as the spiderwebs."

"The spiders must somehow be involved with the disappearance of the witches," Winger said.

She glanced at the villagers behind him. Those from the savannah village were nervous about being outside their walls. Many tried to show a determined expression, but fear lingered behind their eyes.

"It's normal to be afraid," Cleric said in a kindly voice. "What you do with your fear is the real question. Do you panic and let the fear control you, or do you use the fear to keep you on your toes and safe? Fear can be a good thing if you respect its warnings. Right now, we're safe, so everyone can relax. But when we aren't safe, I'll be the first to let you know."

Some of the NPCs relaxed at his assurances.

"We're going to continue along the banks of the swamp, following the trail left by my son, but we need to move fast so we can catch our friends and warn them about the spiders." He drew an enchanted iron sword and held it high over his head. "Come on, everyone! We have a spider horde to catch."

He kicked his horse into a gallop, then reached down and pulled his daughter into the saddle behind him.

"Those are seven words I never thought I'd hear you say in a single sentence." Winger tried to smile, to push back on her fears, but her face couldn't do it. Instead, as the NPC army sped around trees and shrubs along the edge of the putrid swamp, she thought about her brother and their friends, hoping they were safe.

CHAPTER 9

Shakaar clicked her claw on the stone floor. The spider warlord was about to explode with impatience.

"Why haven't the sssisssstersss returned with more witchesss?" Her eyes glowed dangerously bright.

"We have ssspidersss out looking for them, warlord," one of her generals, a spider named Sharum, said cautiously. "They will be found sssoon."

Shakaar clicked her mandibles together in agitation.

Sharum took a step back. "I will persssonally go out and watch for them. The sssisssstersss and their new captivesss will be found."

"Very well . . . go."

The spider general bowed her head, then scurried from the Hatching Chamber and into the twisting passages leading to the surface.

Shakaar turned from the cavern opening and stared at her domain. The floor and walls were covered with sticky cubes of spiderweb, red-spotted eggs cradled within their silky embrace. The smaller, dark-blue cave spiders—the brothers—scuttled about, moving from egg to egg, adding clumps of green moss here and there, the nutritious fibers ready to be consumed by the newborn hatchlings.

"Warlord, this hatchling is ready." One of the brothers waved a leg in the air, his claw colored a dark, dark green.

Shakaar knew the dark green was from the poison pulsing through the brother's veins. Cave spiders were notoriously poisonous; their venom made up for the diminutive size. And that poison was something the spider warlord wanted for her sisters.

Sprinting across the chamber floor, Shakaar wove her way around delicate eggs until she reached the one gently rocking in its silken cradle. A tapping sound was audible from inside the egg; the hatchling was trying to break through its calcified cocoon and enter the world.

A narrow crack formed along the surface of the spotted shell; it was jagged and crooked, like a bolt of lightning. Just then, a tiny, dark-green claw pushed through the narrow gap, causing the crack to widen. The nearby brother reached out with his own poisonous claws to help the hatchling break through the shell.

Shakaar hissed and struck the cave spider, causing him to flash red with damage. The brother looked up at his warlord, an expression of confused terror filling his eight red eyes.

"The hatchlingsss mussst get out of their ssshell on their own." Shakaar glared down at the male. "If they are not ssstrong enough to emerge fully on their own, then they are no ussse to our ssspider nessst. Ssspidersss too weak to fight or contribute to the collective mussst be driven from the nessst or dessstroyed. You know the rulesss."

"I am sssorry, warlord. Forgive me." The cave spider lowered his head and bowed.

"You are forgiven thisss time, brother." Shakaar put the tip of her claw on the creature's head and let it dig into his dark-blue scalp. "But next time, the punisssshment will be sssevere."

"Yesss, Shakaar." The brother backed away from the cracking egg.

The spider warlord turned her attention to the struggling hatchling. The young spider had split open its shell and was pushing itself through the jagged crack. The gooey green gel coating the surface of the egg made the young spider's escape more difficult, but Shakaar didn't care; it would only make the spider stronger. She knew the sticky coating was one of the witch potions being tested on this young sister, and if it worked, the balance of power would be forever shifted toward the spiders.

Finally, a huge section of the shell fell away, revealing a small spider, her fuzzy black hair matted to her dark skin. The newly hatched sister stared up at the warlord, tiny red eyes glowing bright with an expression of crazed violence. Shakaar smiled.

"Sssomething to be happy about?" a spider asked.

Shakaar turned and found Shatil next to her. This sister was one of her commanders and a stout fighter. "Yesss, another sssissster has hatched." She pointed at the hatchling. "Look at her eyesss. The poissson not only ssspread to her clawsss, but hasss alssso infected our newborn sssissster'sss brain. I have made her into a killing machine with the witchesss' potionsss." Shakaar smiled, unconcerned about the damage done to the young creature's mind.

Shatil glanced down and nodded. "Why are you ssso concerned about having more sssissssters? We already have ssso many."

"We will need many troopsss if we are to take over the Far Lands." Shakaar's eyes glowed a bright red. "The wither king tellsss usss the villagersss move againssst usss already. We will need many sssisssstersss on the battlefield when the Great War returnsss again." She turned back to the newborn spider. "Thisss time, the ssspidersss will be the victors. Thisss time, it will be the villagersss who sssuffer."

The tiny hatchling extended her legs out of the shell and climbed out, then glared angrily at her warlord.

Shakaar could see the young spider's claws were a dark green instead of black, like her own. *Good, the poison from the witches seemed to work,* she thought.

"The wither king let the zombiesss and ssskeletonsss help with preparationsss for the war, but they were ssstupid and incompetent. The boy-wizard defeated them." At the thought of the young wizard, Shakaar clicked her mandibles together. "But with thisss relic given to me by Krael, King of the Withersss, I can sssee where my enemy hidesss."

She pulled out the single, glowing lens of the Eye of Searching. With her clawed arms, she put the strap around her head and positioned the lens over one eye. It instantly glowed purple, then stabbed at her, the relic devouring part of the spider's HP to power its hungry enchantments. She groaned as she flashed red, taking damage.

Closing her eyes, she thought about her enemy, the boy-wizard, as Krael had taught her. Instantly, an image formed in her head of the small boy, his reddish-brown hair bouncing about as he jumped from block to block, moving through a swamp. He had a small handful of companions with him, but nowhere near enough to defeat her sisters.

"I sssee you," she whispered to herself, then raised her voice. "Our enemy isss with a sssmall band of NPCsss. We will let them draw nearer, then catch the foolsss in a trap." Shakaar smiled. "Sssend the sssis-sstersss to the foresst of giant treesss. We will catch them there and dessstroy the boy-wizard for Krael. Thisss will prove our worth to him. When he unleash-esss hisss army upon the Far Landsss, we will be hisss ally inssstead of hisss victim."

She flashed red again as the ancient relic drank more of her HP, then removed the Eye of Searching, put it back into her inventory, and turned to the young hatchling. The tiny spider had crawled out the shell and across the blocks of cobwebs and was now munching on the green moss supplied by the brothers. She reached out to stroke the young spider's soft, velvety head. The newborn hissed at Shakaar and swiped at her with her claw, missing, then went back to her meal.

"Eat well, my sssissster. Your ssstrength and lethal clawsss will be very important sssoon." The spider warlord smiled, then turned from Shatil and moved through the Hatching Chamber, checking the eggs. A few others were covered with the experimental dark-green slime, just as the last one had been; more tests of the enslaved witches' potions.

"Sssoon, you will all have the brotherssss' venom, but the sssissstersssss' ssstrength and my wrath. Then my army will be unsssstopable!"

The other spiders in the chamber turned toward their warlord, clicking their mandibles together as their anticipation for battle and their thirst for violence grew.

CHAPTER 10

They left the smelly swamp just after sunset. That was a good thing, because Watcher was running out of cobblestone, and none of them looked forward to slogging through the stagnant waters again. Before them stood a forest of massive spruce trees, some of them soaring twenty-five blocks into the air, if not higher. The ground was a mixture of grass and the brown-speckled podzol blocks. Short, green ferns spread their fronds, trying to catch the odd errant rays of sunlight that penetrated the leafy canopy overhead. In the shady spots, where neither grass nor fern could survive, brown mushrooms flourished, their curved domes unique in the blocky landscape.

A wolf howled in the distance, followed by the moo of a cow.

"The spiders' trail is gone." Cutter sounded agitated. "When they were putting down their blocks of web, they were easy to follow. But they don't need to use their webs anymore. How are we going to follow them now?"

"Well, we can assume they're continuing in the same direction." Mapper pulled out his map, but the faint silvery light of the moon made it difficult to read. "Though they might head somewhere else and give us the slip."

"We can still track them," Watcher said.

"How?" Cutter demanded.

"Just look." Watcher knelt and ran his hand across the brown and tan spotted ground. He felt the tiny tufts of soil that had been torn up from the sharp claws of the spiders. "Their claws leave tiny little holes in the ground. All you have to do is look."

"I see it. They're headed that way." Planter pointed with her glowing axe, then smiled.

Watcher grinned back; her smile was like fireworks. He loved it when Planter was happy; it just made his heart burst with joy.

"Well, we can't just stand around here, grinning like idiots. Let's get moving." Cutter stomped past Watcher, heading in the direction Planter indicated. "Nice job reading their trail, Planter."

She glanced around, unsure how to respond. "Thanks . . . I guess."

Watcher scowled. "Cutter, why is it you always discount what I do as accidental, but with others, you think they're being clever or smart? I was the only person that saw the tracks of the spiders, yet you just complimented Planter . . . what's that about?"

"What's the big deal?" Cutter turned and faced him. "You want compliments all of a sudden?"

"I don't want compliments. . . . I just want a little recognition now and then."

"Okay then." Cutter glanced at Planter and rolled his eyes. "Good job finding the spiders' trail, Watcher." The big NPC turned away, then spoke in a low voice. "I think this wizard-thing is going to your head."

Watcher growled softly, frustrated with Cutter. But then a thought drifted through his head. *Is this about him wanting recognition,* he thought, *or is it jealousy over Planter?*

He saw the way Cutter gazed at Planter, and how she looked back at him. He wanted her glances only for himself, but some of them seemed to be in Cutter's direction as well.

Or maybe this is about my own insecurities. Sometimes, I wish I was as confident as Cutter or Blaster. But instead, I always have this self-doubt, like I don't know who I am.

He sighed, frustrated with himself, then noticed everyone was staring at him.

"Well?" Blaster pointed to the spiders' trail. "Lead on, master tracker."

They moved through the forest, following the faint telltale signs of the spiders' passage. Watcher kept his enchanted bow out, a magical fire arrow notched to the string, and Planter did the same. Another howl floated to them on the gentle east-to-west breeze; the wolves in this area were restless. Fortunately, the animal sounded far away, so it didn't pose much of a threat.

They scanned the dark forest, watching for signs of an attack, but so far, the spiders appeared uninterested in their pursuers; haste seemed to be their priority.

"Saddler, I was surprised when your village took us in," Mapper said suddenly. "Are they always so welcoming?"

The woman nodded. "Many people have sought refuge in our village over the years. Everyone is accepted as long as they can contribute."

"That's commendable." Mapper nodded.

"In fact, my husband was one of those visitors." Saddler smiled as some memory flitted through her mind. "He was almost dead when he found our village. I personally nursed him back to health, then fell in love with him. He was the light of my life, my best friend, my confidant . . . my soul mate."

"You said *was*," Blaster said. "What happened?"

"Well . . ." she grew quiet for a moment, taking a strained breath, then spoke in a low voice. "Cobbler had strong arms, so he worked in the mines, digging for iron and coal. He loved fining a rich vein of ore that would provide for others in the village. Well, one day, he said he found a huge deposit of iron ore. Many of the diggers went down into the mines with him, to get all that ore. While they were digging, a zombie appeared in the passage. The monster attacked and . . ." She grew silent for a moment, likely reliving the terrible memory. "The other diggers told me later how ashamed they were of my Cobbler."

"What happened?" Planter's voice was filled with sympathy.

Saddler sighed. She wiped away a tear. "They told me the zombie attacked Cobbler, and he used his pickaxe . . . as a weapon." The woman paused, as if expecting there to be some reaction to this statement.

"So?" Cutter said. "He was protecting himself."

"He'd sworn an oath of non-violence . . . hadn't he?" Mapper asked, realization dawning on the old NPC's face.

Saddler nodded.

A large cluster of mossy cobblestones barred their path. They curved around the green and gray stones, then picked up the spiders' trail again.

"We all swore that oath, saying there was no excuse to use violence." Saddler sniffled. "The other diggers were ashamed when Cobbler struck back with his pickaxe."

"He was just protecting himself. No one should have to—" Watcher began.

But Saddler continued, interrupting him. "The diggers said my husband killed the zombie after taking a lot of damage, but another emerged from the shadows and finished him off. He died, alone, in that mine shaft."

"What did the other diggers do?" Planter asked.

"They just hid in the shadows and watched as my love battled for his life . . . and lost."

"And they were ashamed by Cobbler?!" Planter's anger was growing. "They stood there, doing nothing, and yet judged him as the villain . . . that's ridiculous."

"That is the law of the village." Saddler wiped her cheek with a dirty sleeve.

"Saddler, I'm so sorry." Planter moved next to her and wrapped an arm around her. She squeezed the woman tight.

"All I have left from Cobbler is his pickaxe." She pulled the iron tool from her inventory. The wooden handle was painted with delicate, child-like flowers, and curving vines spiraled up to the metallic head. "Fencer decorated this for her father; it was his favorite possession in the world, and I will never part with it while I still draw breath." She paused. "After that tragedy, Fencer became my entire world and the only reason to continue living. And now she's on the brink of death." She glanced desperately at Watcher. "You must help her."

"We will," Watcher replied. "We'll catch that witch and get a Notch apple from her . . . that will heal your little girl, I promise."

She nodded, then glanced back at the ground, the colorful pickaxe clutched tightly to her chest.

"Why aren't we gaining on the spiders?" Blaster asked, his black leather armor making him nearly invisible in the dark forest.

"Look at this." Mapper bent down and picked up a bottle from where the empty vessel had been discarded next to a tree. "It seems as if the spiders dropped this. There's still some potion in it."

He wafted the vapors to his nose, smelling the contents. Tipping the container, he put the smallest drop on his finger and put it to his lips. "Potion of swiftness . . . *that's* why we aren't getting any closer."

"Spiders are faster than NPCs on foot. They probably made the witch drink it so she could keep up," Cutter said. "They must be afraid of us."

"Or maybe their captive is more important than we are," Blaster said.

Watcher nodded in agreement. "Likely they'll only attack if they have superior numbers. I don't think they want to risk losing the witch."

Cutter took the bottle from Mapper and smelled the contents, then cast the bottle aside. "When they have more spiders, you can be sure they'll turn and attack."

"That witch must be important to them." Saddler adjusted her iron helmet, pulling some of her long black hair from her face and tucking it behind an ear. "But she's more important to me." She put Builder's pickaxe away and drew her iron sword again. Glancing at each companion, she gave them a look of grim determination, then started running again, following the spidery trail.

"Saddler, doesn't a battle with the spiders make you scared?" Planter asked the villager as she caught up to the running mother. "You seem so confident, as if fear can't touch you for some reason."

The villager glanced at Planter, then reached out and ran her fingers through the girl's long blond hair. "My daughter, Fencer, has hair much like yours. Cobbler used to say it was like liquid sunshine."

"Don't worry, we're gonna catch those spiders and save that witch." Watcher's voice was barely a whisper. "Then we'll get a golden Notch apple for Fencer."

"But how are we going to catch them?" Saddler was almost in tears as frustration bubbled up inside her, filling her voice. "They're too fast for us. We'll never save that witch."

"I don't know, but we'll think of something. You just need to trust me and trust all of us. We stand with our friends; their problems become our problems, and right now, saving Fencer is our problem."

Saddler sighed, but it sounded as if some of the frustration and worry had evaporated away.

"Er-Lan smells something." The zombie moved to Saddler's side, his short, stubby claws extended.

Watcher stopped and moved behind a tree, the others doing the same. Peering around the trunk, he scanned the forest, looking for threats. Nothing moved. Ahead, the tall forest seemed devoid of any motion. The gentle sway of the ferns and blades of grass was gone, as if an invisible hand had stopped their motion. Even the animals in the forest seemed to feel the tension and fell silent. The hairs on the back of Watcher's neck stood up, the warning driving icicles of fear into every nerve and chilling his blood.

"What do you see?" Planter stood next to him. "I thought I saw something move."

Watcher remained motionless, allowing his eyes to take in the entire scene. And then he saw it: something moving out from behind a cluster of mossy cobblestone blocks. He glanced at Planter and smiled, then laughed and moved out from behind the tree.

"It's just a bunny." Watcher walked toward the cluster of green cobblestone and smiled.

More rabbits emerged from the shrubs, the black and white bunnies mixing in with chocolate browns.

"Ahhh . . . they're so cute." Planter ran forward and picked one up.

The creature nuzzled its furry head against her cheek. An expression of joy spread across Planter's face. It made Watcher happy to see her so enraptured in delight.

"Great job finding the rabbits." Cutter smiled sarcastically at Watcher.

The boy rolled his eyes, then turned back to the others. "Come on, everyone, there's nothing dangerous here." Watcher continued running with Saddler in lockstep beside him. "Let's keep moving. We have a spider horde to catch."

CHAPTER 11

They eventually slowed to a walk, everyone, including Watcher, tired from the chase. Moving next to Planter, he looked down at the black and white bunny she held in her hands.

"Have you been carrying that all this time?" Watcher asked.

Planter glanced at him with her bright green eyes. She said something, but Watcher wasn't paying attention; he was lost in those emerald pools.

"What?" He asked, shaking his head.

"I said 'No, I just found this one and picked her up.'" She smiled as she scratched the fluffy animal's ears. "Aren't they fantastic?"

"It's just a rabbit." Cutter's voice boomed through the forest, always louder than necessary.

Planter scowled at the big warrior, but he was too distracted adjusting his armor to notice.

Watcher smiled.

"I didn't know rabbits were part of the mega taiga biome," she said.

"Yep, there are lots of animals in this forest." Mapper paused to catch his breath, then continued. "Let's see, there are chickens and sheep and wolves and—"

"Wolves?" A concerned expression came across Planter's face. "Don't wolves eat rabbits?"

"Wolves eat just about whatever they want to eat," Cutter added. The big warrior moved between Planter and Watcher, feigning interest in the tiny animal in her arms. His armor clanked as he walked, scaring the little rabbit. It squirmed in Planters arms, then jumped to the ground and scurried away. Cutter just grinned. "I love wolves. They're a ferocious animal that knows how to fight and won't just run away when attacked. Wolves are a creature to be respected."

"Standing your ground isn't always the right thing to do," Watcher pointed out.

Cutter remained silent, as if he was ignoring the comment.

"Mapper, you have any idea where these spiders are heading?" Planter asked as she stopped walking and pulled out a loaf of bread, taking a huge bite.

"I'm not quite sure," the old man replied. "I saw some ancient structures built by the wizards on the map, but the spiders don't seem to be heading toward them. It's almost as if they just want us to follow them. . . . It's strange."

Just then, a sound, like distant thunder, floated through the forest. The noise was almost imperceptible, but often even the faintest sounds were still detected by Watcher's sensitive ears.

"Did any of you hear that?" The boy scanned the forest for threats.

"Hear what?" Cutter drew his diamond sword and held it at the ready.

"I thought I heard something like thunder, but look up . . . there are almost no clouds overhead." Watcher glanced up and could easily see the sparkling stars overhead, with just the occasional cloud drifting by.

"I didn't hear anything." The big warrior surveyed their surroundings one more time, then put away his sword. "I think it was nothing, or maybe something from that famous imagination I've heard so much about."

Watcher blushed when Planter giggled, then put away his bow.

"It's okay, Watcher, sometimes I hear things too," Mapper said in a soothing voice.

"But I felt something in the ground rumble as well, like a very faint tremor." Watcher lowered his voice and whispered to the old man. "Something's coming toward us . . . I can feel it."

"Just keep it to yourself until you know what it is for sure," the old man whispered back. "We don't want to panic everyone for no reason."

"Right." Watcher nodded, but he knew his face showed what he was feeling: fear.

Er-Lan moved next to Watcher and grabbed his arm. "This is the forest."

"What?"

"From the vision," the zombie said. "The black rain . . . it draws near."

Glancing to the sky, Watcher checked again for storm clouds. "I can see the stars, Er-Lan. There aren't any clouds up there. I think you're mistaken about the black rain."

"Visions are never mistakes." Er-Lan glanced around, fear covering his scarred face. "All must be careful . . . the black rain comes."

Watcher nodded and patted his friend on the back, then refocused his attention on their surroundings. They continued through the spruce forest, the massive trees looming high overhead, their tops barely visible in the darkness. The path before them was difficult to see, as the few rays of moonlight piercing the leafy canopy were not very bright. Only Watcher's keen eyes could still discern the trail of the spiders.

Suddenly, a clicking sound seemed to filter down through the branches and leaves ahead. Watcher skidded to a stop and peered into the forest. A small opening in the dark canopy overhead, letting moonlight shine to the forest floor, pushing back on the night. It allowed

Watcher to see the forest just around him, but sections further away were completely masked in darkness; anything could be out there, including that rumbling something.

Just then, a huge cluster of clouds floated across the moon's pockmarked face, masking its lunar glow and causing a black, velvety curtain of darkness to envelop the forest. More things clicked in the treetops.

"Everyone look around." Watcher's voice was barely a whisper.

"I don't see anything," Cutter boomed dismissively.

"Shhhh." Planter took out her enchanted shield and golden axe. An iridescent glow surrounded the girl from from the weapons' purple radiance.

With his bow in his hand and a sparkling fire arrow notched to the string, Watcher closed his eyes and allowed his ears to direct his attention. He listened to the strange clicking, then finally recognized it.

"Spiders . . ." he said, his voice barely a whisper. "In the trees."

Drawing back on the bowstring, he aimed at the clicking noises, focusing his shot on the sounds overhead. Stilling his body and his mind, he released the arrow. Instantly, it burst into life as it streaked through the air, flames licking its pointed tip. A magical halo of light surrounded the shaft as it flew, shining a radiant glow on the treetops.

Planter gasped, pointing. "Spiders in the trees!"

Watcher's arrow sliced through the air and embedded itself with a *thunk* into the thick bark of a towering spruce. The flickering glow suddenly revealed countless spiders, all descending from the forest roof at the end of thin strands of spider silk.

"Fire at the spiders!" Watcher launched more of his fire arrows at the treetops, lighting the green canopy so the others could see.

His companions pulled out bows and launched arrows at the creatures descending from the treetops like a dark, deadly rain. Pointed shafts streaked through the air, striking the spiders' dark, fuzzy bodies. The monsters screeched in pain, clicking their mandibles together rapidly. One of them disappeared, its glowing balls of XP falling to the ground like a multicolored hail.

"Work in pairs," Watcher ordered as he fired at a nearby spider with his flaming arrow. "Fire at the same spiders!"

Moving next to Planter, he pointed at a spider, then fired. Their arrows flew in parallel, both hitting the creature in the side. After another volley, the fuzzy creature disappeared, adding more colorful XP to the ground. They fired as fast as they could, but there were so many spiders, it was hard to tell if it made any difference. The monsters slowly moved down their thin strands of web, their eyes glowing like hot, angry embers.

All throughout the forest, the lethal rain fell. There were scores of spiders descending on their gossamer strands, and even more clicking still coming from the treetops.

"They're all around us." Planters fired at a nearby monster, cutting through its web. The creature fell to the ground screaming, then became silent.

Watcher turned, taking in everything around him. There were just too many of them; their arrows weren't slowing the mob at all. Some were near and easier to shoot, but others were far away, their dark, fuzzy bodies merging with the darkness; they were impossible to hit.

"I don't like this." Mapper fired his bow as fast as he could, but everyone knew he was a terrible shot. "When they all reach the ground, they'll charge and overwhelm us."

"Just keep shooting." Blaster shot at the monsters nearest to the ground, his shafts hitting with deadly accuracy. When the first of the spiders touched down, he took out his dual curved knives and charged at them.

"Blaster, wait!" Watcher yelled, but the boy ignored him.

The spiders clicked their mandibles together excitedly as Blaster streaked toward the monsters, his dark armor making him nearly invisible. He slashed at the creatures as he darted by, tearing into their HP. Some, who had been wounded by the arrows, disappeared under the first knife thrusts, while others lingered a bit before the boy destroyed them.

"Blaster, get back here!" Cutter boomed. "More spiders are landing on the ground. We need to stick together."

The monsters continued to settle noiselessly on the ground, forming a thick, angry circle of claws and fangs around the villagers. Blaster dashed back to his friends and stood between Cutter and Mapper. The companions held their weapons at the ready as hundreds of angry red eyes glared at them from the darkness.

"We're surrounded," Watcher moaned, the taste of defeat heavy on his soul. "Everyone get back-to-back and form a circle."

The villagers pressed their backs together, with Mapper and Er-Lan at the center. The old man fumbled with potions, but he had nothing that would harm the spiders. Watcher fired as quickly as he could, drawing and nocking like a seasoned warrior, the other villagers doing the same, but their sharp hail of arrows had little effect. There were so many spiders approaching, the flow of pointed shafts was insignificant.

"Er-Lan saw the black rain," the zombie moaned. "The visions are always true . . . always true."

"I don't suppose you saw how this ends?" Blaster glanced at the zombie between firing arrows.

"Er-Lan only receives glimpses, no more." The monster sounded terrified, but grew silent as the last of the spiders reached the forest floor.

Suddenly, the fuzzy black creatures stopped clicking their mandibles and became eerily quiet. An uneasy silence spread through the forest as all those blazing red eyes stared at the small band of NPCs. The spiders moved forward slowly, their fuzzy black bodies bumping into each other, making it hard for them all to approach; that was the only thing delaying their charge.

Watcher slowly lowered his bow. *We're trapped . . . it's over,* he realized as he glanced at Planter and a sadness such as he'd never experienced washed over him.

"Keep firing," Cutter yelled, but Watcher was numb to everything, the feeling of despair overwhelming his mind.

The ground shook again, as it did before, but this time, the thunder boomed from the darkness, as if the storm were about to descend upon them. But it didn't matter; he'd failed, and now all his friends would be destroyed as well.

Planter, I failed you the most, he thought. *You relied on me to keep you safe, and I foolishly thought I could do it, but my courage was just a lie.* Drawing another arrow, he raised his bow again and shot at one of the closest spiders, but knew the situation was hopeless.

Maybe that storm will just wash us all away and end this nightmare, he thought as he fired as fast as he could, hitting spider after spider as their circle of claws drew tighter around the defenders, getting ready for the final charge.

This was the end.

CHAPTER 12

Watcher thought he was at the center of a titanic storm. The thunder grew so loud that the spiders stopped their advance to look up at the sky with their hateful, red eyes, uncertain and afraid. At the same time, the ground shook as if a giant was hammering the towering spruce trees into the ground like so many nails, making the forest floor quake in fear.

Then suddenly, a single battle cry pierced the air, just barely audible over the thunder, and then more joined the first, filling the forest with shouts a hundred strong . . . and in that moment, Watcher recognized one of the voices and smiled.

Cleric, riding on a large black stallion, emerged from the night leading the most beautiful cavalry Watcher had ever seen. The NPCs rode double on the backs of the horses, the front riders holding the reins while the back riders carried bows or swords or axes or shovels in hand.

"ATTACK!" Cleric shouted.

The mounted warriors charged through the spider ranks, raining arrows down upon the fuzzy monsters. One group of mounted warriors pulled away from the main body and attacked the opposite side of the spidery enclosure. Many of the double riders were wielding farming tools such as shovels or hoes, but the blunt edges of their weapons did not limit their ferocity or rage. They fell upon the spiders with a vengeance, the startled creatures stunned and surprised, unsure how to respond.

Behind the cavalry came a group of soldiers on foot, led by Winger. They crashed into the spider ranks, slashing at their fuzzy backs, catching their enemies completely unprepared. Winger's flaming arrows were burning meteors of death as they sped through the air. They hit spider after spider, igniting the creatures with magical flames. Turning to face this new threat, the spiders charged at the infantry.

"We have to help them." Watcher drew Needle and held it high into the air. "Charge!"

Watcher sprinted toward the monsters, hoping to close the distance to Winger's troops, his friends following close behind. Needle slashed through the air. It was a bolt of razor-sharp, iron lightning, slicing into the monsters' HP with lethal precision. The weapon slashed into spiders to the left and right as Watcher carved a path to his sister. To his left, Planter wielded her enchanted axe like a seasoned warrior, while to his right, Carver wreaked terrible havoc with his own diamond blade.

A claw swiped at his chest, scratching across his enchanted iron armor. Watcher kicked at the creature, sending it toward Cutter, who quickly finished it off. Suddenly, Blaster bolted past, his curved knives swiping enemies as he sped by. He darted through the battlefield, moving so fast, the spiders had little time to react. He whittled away at their HP, making the monsters easier to defeat when they finally reached Watcher and his friends.

A wicked, curved claw streaked through the air, heading straight for Watcher's face. He ducked, allowing the sharp tip to flash over his head, then drove Needle into the creature. The spider took a step back, then attacked again with two legs, each aimed at his chest. Leaping over the deadly appendages, Watcher landed on the creature's back. Needle came down upon the monster, smashing into its HP. Leaning left and right, the spider tried to dislodge him, but Watcher grabbed a handful of its fuzzy hair and held on as he swung his blade over and over. At the same time, Er-Lan appeared from nowhere, attacking the vicious creature with his own razor-sharp claws. The monster screamed in pain and fear, then disappeared, leaving behind three glowing balls of XP and a handful of silken thread.

Meanwhile, the cavalry stomped through the spider ranks, tearing great swaths of destruction. With the mounted warriors on one side and the infantry on the others, many of the spiders chose to flee instead of standing their ground. This emboldened the horsemen and horsewomen to charge at their foe, striking at the fuzzy bodies with their weapons and tools as the monsters tried to escape.

Someone cried out in pain to his left. Watcher spun and charged toward the sound, where Saddler was battling one of the only spiders left behind. It had the strangest claws: they were colored a dark green instead of the normal midnight black. Saddler's chainmail was shredded in places where the monster's claws had struck it, leaving her skin exposed. With her sword pointed defensively at the creature's neck, the NPC tried to back up, but she bumped into another villager, leaving her no room to escape.

The spider sprang forward, dark green claws streaking through the air.

"NOOOO!" Er-Lan shouted, sprinting toward the villager.

Watcher was a step behind the zombie, but he knew they'd be too late.

Saddler managed to block one of the claws on the right side, but she didn't see the attack from the left.

The spider hit her in the side, its pointed claw digging through the chain links and sinking into the villager's soft flesh.

Saddler screamed in pain and flashed red instantly, which was unusual. Watcher and Er-Lan reached her side moments later and attacked the spider. Needle blocked one of the spider's slashing green claws, but another scraped across Watcher's enchanted armor, tearing a deep gash in the metallic surface. Er-Lan brought his sharp claws down upon his enemy, making her flash red, but the spider ignored the pain; all eight of her eyes were focused entirely on the boy with the red hair, an insane, vicious look on the creature's face.

Watcher rolled to the left, slicing his blade across the monster's side. With a scream of agony, the spider stepped back, eyes burning with hatred, then attacked again, ignoring her peril. It swung two claws at Watcher from the left, then brought one up from the right. He blocked the first two, but never saw the third. The dark green claw tore through Watcher's armor and sunk deep into his side. Pain exploded across Watcher's stomach, and then spread throughout the rest of his body as if fire were pumping through his veins. It was unbearable, and he fell to his knees before finally collapsing to the ground.

Er-Lan leapt onto the spider's back, slicing into the creature's HP while the monster's poisonous claws poked at the zombie, but the poison had no effect; the undead were immune to the poison. In fact, it had the opposite effect: it healed the zombie. Er-Lan, consumed with rage and maxed out on HP, destroyed the monster quickly.

Watcher, laying on his side, stared helplessly as Saddler writhed in agony, her body flashing red as it took damage.

"Help," he said in a weak voice.

"Someone help!" Er-Lan's voice was frantic. "Watcher needs help!"

"Watcher . . . what's wrong?" Planter dropped her axe and ran to his side. Kneeling, she cradled his head in her hands. "Are you alright?"

He shook his head. "Something's wrong . . . poison and . . ." He was too weak to continue speaking.

"The spider must have poisoned him and Saddler." Er-Lan paced frantically back and forth, terrified for his friends.

"Mapper, Cleric, come quick!" Planter laid his head on the ground, then stood and searched for the two men.

The sounds of battle had drifted away as the spiders retreated, the NPC cavalry in hot pursuit.

"What is it?" a familiar voice said.

"It's Watcher—he thinks he's been poisoned!" Planter sounded terrified.

Watcher's vision began to waver as the poison surged through his body, the pain overwhelming his senses.

Cleric knelt at his son's side.

"Saddler . . . help Saddler," Watcher croaked, his voice barely a whisper.

Cleric pulled out a bottle of milk and gave it to Planter, then moved to Saddler's side.

Suddenly, a clicking sound filled the air; a spider had landed on the ground right behind Planter, having lowered itself noiselessly to the ground. She turned to confront the monster, but the creature was standing on her axe; Planter was defenseless.

But then Saddler, using the last of her strength, sat up and pulled out her husband's pickaxe. She threw the precious tool at the dark nightmare, the metallic instrument tumbling through the air until the sharp tip embedded itself into the spider's side. The force of the blow pushed the beast back a step. Planter sprinted toward the spider. Bending over, she scooped up her axe without even slowing, then brought the golden edge down onto the spider over and over again until its HP was destroyed.

Putting her axe away, she turned toward Saddler only to see her collapse back to the ground. Cleric tried to offer her milk, the usual antidote for spider poison, but it was too late; she was beginning to fade in and out, parts of her body becoming transparent. She turned her head toward Watcher and, with a look of confidence in her eye, she spoke.

"I know you can do it. Save my daughter, please . . ." Then she disappeared, a lone tear falling to the ground.

"No . . ." Watcher moaned. A glass bottle was put to his lips. Cool liquid came pouring down his throat. *It's milk . . . they're giving me milk,* the boy realized.

He swallowed, then let them put more into his mouth. The milk seemed to extinguish the fiery agony that pulsed through his body, bringing him back from the brink of death. Mapper stood over him, then dropped a splash potion of healing on his chest, the red liquid sinking into his flesh and replenishing his health. He coughed, then sat up as the last of the poisonous fire in his body finally died down and was extinguished.

"I'm alive . . . I'M ALIVE!" He yelled as he turned and glanced at Saddler, but only found her inventory scattered across the ground; she had disappeared. His smile quickly turned to an expression of horror as he realized what had happened.

"I didn't save her. I let Saddler die." Grief crashed down upon him like a merciless wave, driving a deep sadness into every fiber of his soul. "I promised I'd protect her . . . and now look what I've done." His guilt-ridden eyes sought out the only person he thought could help him: Planter. "Help me, Planter. I don't know who I'm supposed to be to all these people. . . . I can't protect them. I can't protect anyone."

She reached down and took his hand, then helped him to his feet. "You just need to be you." Her voice was soft and lyrical, the melodious words easing some of his grief. "It isn't possible to protect everyone. All we can do is prepare the best we can and be ready." She took his hand in hers. "Saddler knew the risks, and broke her oath to come with us. She was helping her daughter, Fencer, and would do anything for her." She moved closer and lowered her voice soothingly. "In the end, did she blame you for her death?"

Watcher thought back. The image of Saddler's face just before she died was etched into his brain; he'd never forget it. The woman's expression was not one of anger or accusation, but of hope, as if she were relying on Watcher to do what was necessary to save her daughter.

"No, she wasn't blaming me." Watcher's voice was soft and weak. He bent over and picked up Needle from where he'd dropped it, putting the weapon back into his inventory. "In fact, it seemed as if she knew I could help her daughter . . . but how could she know that?"

"Perhaps it wasn't knowledge, but faith," Er-Lan said from behind.

Watcher turned and glanced at his friend. The zombie's claws were still extended from the end of his stubby square fingers, each razor-sharp tip reflecting the light of the moon that had just emerged from behind a bank of clouds.

"It seems like all the spiders ran off," Cutter boomed. "I guess they had enough from us."

He sounded happy, as if this were some kind of game.

"We crushed those filthy monsters, and we'll do it again." Cutter held his diamond sword high over his head.

The villagers applauded, many of them banging their weapons or gardening tools against their chests. It sounded like a celebration, with NPCs smiling and cheering.

"This wasn't a victory . . . it was a defeat!" Watcher shouted, his rage barely held in check. "Many of our friends and neighbors died here. Don't just ignore their sacrifice." He glared at the villagers, then raised his hand high into the air, fingers spread wide, performing the Salute for the Dead; it was a tradition amongst villagers in Minecraft since before the Great War. Slowly, he clenched his hand into a fist, the rage and sorrow and guilt squeezed tight within his palm. His knuckles popped as his clenched fist started to turn white.

"Watcher, lower your hand," Planter whispered calmly. "Release your fist . . . it's okay."

Glanced up at his fist, he could see his arm shaking with the exertion. Slowly he lowered his arm and opened his hand. Four deep grooves were carved into his palm where his fingernails had dug into his skin.

"It's not your fault," Planter murmured softly into his ear.

He turned and stared into her deep, green eyes. Tears tried to escape from his own blues, but he refused to set the cubes of moisture free. The time for weeping was later; right now, they had to find those spiders.

Blaster handed a colorful pickaxe to Watcher, its handle decorated by a child's hand; it was Saddler's, the weapon responsible for saving their lives. Watcher stared down at it, running his hand down its handle. He knew how much Saddler loved this tool, how it had reminded her of her husband and daughter. It was a precious heirloom.

"I'm going to make sure Fencer gets this back." Watcher put away the tool, then spoke in a clear voice, his body feeling like an old kitchen towel, wrung out and devoid of emotion. "We can't stay here any longer. It's time for us to follow those spiders back to their lair, and then we'll save the witches. This isn't over . . . not by a long shot."

"But son, you should hear what the spiders did at the village," Cleric said. "They showed up looking for—"

Watcher wasn't listening. He had spotted the trail left behind by the retreating spiders and started to run, chasing his prey through the dark forest, a thirst for revenge filling his soul.

CHAPTER 13

They moved quietly through the spruce forest, Watcher following the small scratches and dents left behind in the ground by the spiders' sharp claws. The villagers walked, some leading horses by their reins, allowing the animals and the battle-weary combatants a brief respite.

"So, you're telling me the spiders attacked the village, all because they were looking for me?" Watcher still couldn't believe it. "I was hoping all this boy-wizard stuff was over. I don't want to be a wizard; I just want to be me."

"We know." Cutter's voice wasn't very convincing . . . In fact, it sounded a little sarcastic.

Watcher glanced at Cutter, annoyed, casting him a questioning gaze. The big NPC flashed him an insincere grin, then turned to Planter, who was now walking at the warrior's side. Glancing at the two of them out of the corner of his eye, Watcher noticed how close they were to each other, their steps synchronized. He felt something stir in the dark parts of his soul. With an unanswered glare, Watcher turned his attention back to the ground and continued following the monsters' trail. *Why did he say it like that? And why are they walking so close together, whispering?*

The big NPC muttered something just out of Watcher's earshot, causing Planter to laugh. The sight of Planter's smile brought joy to his heart, but when she glanced at Cutter, the joy in Watcher seemed to turn sour. She had a look of adoration and respect on her beautiful square face, as if Cutter was the greatest person in the world.

Anger and jealousy swirled around within him like a poisonous serpent, its fangs ready to strike at his soul. Everything about Cutter made him mad for reasons he didn't quite understand: his bulging muscles, his confidence, his fancy armor, his incredible diamond sword . . . he hated it all.

His father put a hand on Watcher's shoulder. "Did you hear what I said?" Cleric asked, voice soft and calming.

"Ahh . . . no, sorry."

"I said, one of the spiders that came to the village had poisonous claws." Cleric stopped walking and turned to face his son.

"You're saying the spider had poison, just like the one that got me and killed . . ." He didn't want to finish the sentence.

Cleric nodded gravely.

Watcher lowered his voice. "Did you see the poisoned spider's face?"

His father shook his head.

"The monster didn't care if would be hurt by my sword, it just wanted to attack." Watcher lowered his voice to but a whisper, making sure no one else could hear. "It looked crazed, as if its mind was completely consumed with violence and hatred. I got the impression the spider had no choice; it was compelled to attack and keep attacking, all because of the insanity that had consumed the creature's mind. These monsters are something new and dangerous to every living thing in the Far Lands. How could a creature become so twisted and evil?"

"I don't know, son." Cleric put a hand on the boy's shoulder. "But it's no way to live . . . always being consumed by hate with an unquenchable thirst for violence. You have to pity a creature like that."

"Yeah," Watcher agreed.

"The poisoned spider is why we pursued you. We think the spiders are capturing the witches, maybe to make poison for those monsters . . ."

"Or maybe something else," Mapper suggested, then shrugged.

"If the spiders are collecting the witches, then they'll have them imprisoned somewhere, right?" Watcher didn't expect an answer; he was just talking out loud. "If we can find where they're holding them, then we can. . . . Hey, where'd the trail go?"

He dropped to his hands and knees and ran his fingers across the spotted podzol, frantically searching the ground as if he'd lost something valuable.

"What's wrong?" Cleric knelt at Watcher's side.

"The trail . . . it's gone." He moved his hands across the ground again, feeling for the telltale signs of the spiders' passage, but found nothing. He glanced up at his father. "I can't see where they went. It's as if they disappeared."

"What are you saying?" Cutter asked. "The spiders just flew away?"

"I don't know what happened," Watcher snapped. "Their trail is just gone. They must have done something we didn't expect."

"This is great." Cutter's tone was sarcastic again, at least to Watcher.

"Why don't you come over here and find their trail?" Watcher's face was red with anger. The fangs of that serpent within him stabbed at his soul.

"No, I'm sure you'll find it." Cutter waved a hand, dismissing the offer.

Is he mocking me?

"We need that trail," Planter said.

"I know that!" Watcher shouted, then cringed. He didn't mean to shout, but he was so frustrated with Cutter, not to mention scared they might never find the spiders or their lair.

At that moment, the image of Saddler's face just before she died appeared in the back of his mind. *I know you can do it. Save my daughter, please . . .* Her last words echoed through his brain.

He glanced at Planter. "Sorry I yelled at you. It's just that I promised Saddler I'd . . ."

"You promised her you'd save her daughter?" Planter's green eyes were filled with compassion.

Watcher nodded. "I can't fail her. Back there in the forest, when I thought there was no hope, I thought I'd failed you as well. That was a terrible feeling I never want to experience again."

"You need to realize that failure is part of life." Planter put a reassuring hand on his shoulder. "You can only do your best."

"But what if my best isn't good enough?" He glanced at Cutter, expecting more sarcasm, but found the big warrior silently listening, face hard to read.

"Then you make the best decision you can, and I'll be there for you." She moved a little closer, then whispered. "I'll always be there for you."

She gave him a strange look he didn't quite understand, as if she were suggesting—

"So how are we gonna find the spiders now?" Blaster's voice startled Watcher, making him jump and causing Planter to step back and look away.

"I can only think of one way." Cutter stepped past Planter, then stood directly in front of Watcher and stared down at the boy. "The zombie warlord's armor . . . you need to put it on."

"But last time, it almost killed him," Planter objected.

"He can handle it, I know it. Besides, it's the only way." The towering NPC glanced down at Watcher. "You must do it."

"No . . . it's too dangerous." Planter pushed Cutter aside, then glared at Watcher. "You can't."

He sighed. "Cutter's right, I must." Watcher gave her a smile. "This is the only way." Removing his magical iron armor, he set it on the ground, then pulled out the enchanted chainmail he'd taken from the zombie warlord. "Mapper, you have more of those healing potions?"

The old man nodded. "Yep, I'm ready."

"Okay, here goes." Watcher slowly lowered the enchanted armor over his head, then settled it onto his shoulders.

Instantly, the armor reached out for his HP. Daggers of pain stabbed at him from all over as his health gave energy to the enchanted chainmail. Closing his eyes, Watcher focused his thoughts on the spiders. A group of black, fuzzy creatures appeared in his mind. They were running across the tops of the tall spruce trees. He smiled. There were far fewer there than had been when they originally attacked; Cleric's cavalry had inflicted considerable damage.

Moving his thoughts across the landscape, he focused on the monsters' final destination. A cave materialized in his mind, showing chamber after chamber crawling with spiders. A huge cavern then came into focus in his mind. It was filled with thousands of dark eggs, each covered with bright red spots. Blocks of spiderweb surrounded them, likely to hold the eggs in place and provide some protection. They were all about the same size, which meant they'd likely hatch at the same time.

"Can you see where it is?" Planter asked. She placed a hand on his and squeezed his stubby fingers. The sensation filled him with strength.

I'm not gonna let her down. The pain was intense, like fire spreading across his body and burning away at his flesh, as well as his courage, but with Mapper continually pouring healing potions over him, Watcher could stay alive, even if it was agonizing.

He pulled back his vision, moving away from the spider caves until his mind was floating somewhere outside. Before him was a huge mountain, but not like any other he'd seen before.

The armor tore into his health again . . . agony on top of agony.

The mountain was made of ore: iron, coal, lapis, emerald, gold, redstone, and diamond. A strange purple glow surrounded the cubes like a protective shield; the mountain was enchanted, likely to keep the ore from being taken.

The speckled blocks gave the peak a spotted look, as if it had some kind of multicolored disease. At the foot of the mountain was a gigantic opening leading into the dangerous caves underground.

The pain exploded in his mind again—it was getting worse. He could feel liquid running down his back, but the healing potions couldn't seem to keep up with the health cost the Mantle of Command demanded. Slowly, his HP was decreasing and decreasing; Watcher was losing the battle.

The image grew blurry. Watcher knew he had to get the enchanted armor off before it was too late. He reached up and tried to lift the sparkling chainmail off his shoulders, but it felt as if it weighed a million pounds.

The armor stabbed at him again, and he fell to his knees, crying out in pain. Focusing on the image, Watcher tried to figure out the location of the mountain, but all he could see around the spotted peak was a sea of stone . . . and then relief finally came as the armor was removed.

Watcher lay on the ground panting, his nerves still screaming at him. Another healing potion smashed against his chest, but this time, the rejuvenating liquid was able to extinguish the flames surging through his body; slowly, his HP returned.

"You came close that time," Cleric said. "I don't think using that armor again is a good idea."

"I wholeheartedly agree." Watcher took a flask of red liquid from Mapper and drained the contents. The potion flowed through his body, accelerating the healing process and making it feel as if he was among the living again.

"What did you see?" Planter asked as she took the empty bottle from his hands.

"I saw a mountain of gold."

"A mountain of gold?" Blaster asked.

"Well . . . not just gold, but every ore in Minecraft."

"A mountain of jewels . . ." Mapper was lost in thought.

"We need to find that mountain." Planter stared at Watcher, an expression of determination on her beautiful face. "That's where all the witches will be held. To save Fencer, we need to rescue them. We must do this . . . for Saddler."

"But how do we stay ahead of the spiders?" Cleric asked.

"What do you mean?" Mapper sounded confused.

"Somehow, the spiders knew Watcher had been in the savannah village." He looked at his son. "The spider warlord wants to kill the boy-wizard."

Watcher nodded, then sighed. "I don't know how the warlord is doing it, but that spider can see where I am."

"It's probably because you're a wizard," someone suggested.

"I'm not a wizard!" Watcher snapped.

Cleric put a calming hand on the boy's shoulder, then spoke in a soothing voice. "What do you mean, son?"

Watcher glanced at Planter and Blaster, then gazed at Cutter and shuddered. They'd come close to being overrun by the spiders, and if it hadn't been for Cleric and the other villagers, they'd all be dead.

"The spiders were clearly waiting for us," Watcher said. "They set up a trap, and when the time was right, they lowered themselves down from the treetops and surrounded us. It was a perfect strategy, and should have been successful, except for—"

"Except for us." Winger's voice was filled with pride.

"Exactly." Watcher nodded. "If we're gonna find the spider lair, and sneak in there without ending up in another trap, we have to move faster than the spiders expect us to."

"You're saying we need more horses." Cleric started pacing back and forth, lost in thought. "But we don't have enough for everyone. We can only move as fast as the slowest person."

"Maybe we can put three NPCs on each horse," Blaster suggested.

"We could leave some people behind," someone else said.

"Maybe if we . . ." More ideas were being shouted out by the NPCs. Arguments broke out as people debated what to do.

"The villagers need the Horse Lord." Er-Lan's voice was weak at first, but then it grew louder. "The villagers need the Horse Lord!"

No one was listening.

"THE VILLAGERS NEED THE HORSE LORD!" Er-Lan yelled, his voice like the thunderous roar of an ender dragon.

Everyone heard him now, and the villagers grew silent, many of them turning wary eyes toward the green creature.

"Er-Lan, what did you say?" Cleric asked.

"Since the Great War, zombie parents tell their children about the Horse Lord." Er-Lan turned toward Watcher. "There was a time, before the War, when zombies were friends with some wizards. The Horse Lord made zombie horses and gave them to many in the zombie nation. My mother used to love telling the tale."

"But this Horse Lord is obviously gone now." Cutter's comment sounded like an accusation.

"Cutter is correct, the Horse Lord was killed in the Great War." The villagers moaned in frustration. "But the Citadel of the Horse Lord is rumored to still exist."

"What did you say?" Mapper turned to Er-Lan. "What did you call it?"

"The Citadel of the Horse Lord. That is where they made the first zombie horses before the Great War. It was—"

"I've heard that name before." Mapper pulled out a book from his inventory.

"What's that?" Cleric asked.

"I've been copying things from old books stored in the many libraries around the Far Lands, especially the Library of Alexandria." The old man pulled a stack of books from his inventory and dropped them on the ground. He knelt and looked through the tomes until he found the one he wanted. Opening the pages, he quickly flipped through it, searching for something specific. "I wrote down a section about the Citadel, but never really understood what it meant. I thought it was a—a misspelling." He laughed, then stopped turning the pages and stared into the book. "Here . . . it says, 'The Citadel is the *mane* place, the Citadel is the *mane* place.' The book repeated that phrase over and over. I thought the word *mane* was misspelled, but now I understand what they were saying."

"Mapper, what are you talking about?" Watcher asked, confused.

The old man moved next to a large white horse and reached up to the creature's neck. "The hair along the animal's neck . . . that's called a mane." He paused for a moment, waiting for the others to get it, then sighed. "The Citadel is where you find animals with a mane . . . that's horses!"

"Great, but that doesn't help us," Cutter said. "We still don't know where this Citadel is located."

"Oh, haha, but we do." Mapper put away the book and pulled out a map. He unfolded the parchment and placed it on the ground. "We're here, in this mega taiga biome. You see this symbol here." He pointed a red dot at the center of a huge "U". "That's the Citadel. And now that I see it, the shape around it looks like a hoof print . . . I should have seen it long ago. I thought it was—"

"What's the green surrounding the Citadel?" Watcher pointed at the map.

Mapper held the map close to his eyes. "It says 'The Sea of Spines.' I don't know what that means, but it seems as if we must go through it to get to the Citadel of the Horse Lord."

"I don't like the sound of that," Blaster said. "The word *spine* reminds me of the spine of a wither. I hope it's not a sea of withers."

"That would be bad," Planter said.

"Regardless, that's where we need to go." Watcher patted Mapper on the back. "Without more horses, we'll never be able to sneak up on the spider warlord, and I won't turn back. I made a promise to Saddler, and I'm gonna keep my word."

Cleric looked at his son with a prideful expression on his face, then put an arm around him and gave him a hug. "Okay then. We're going to the Sea of Spines." He glanced at the map, then turned to Watcher. "You're our leader . . . so lead."

Watcher glanced at the map, then pulled out a compass to get his bearings. With Needle in his right hand, he took off running in the direction of the Citadel while others mounted their horses and rode double, following him.

Glancing at the forest around him, Watcher still felt as if the spider warlord were somehow still watching. "I have a bad feeling about all this." His voice was but a whisper. "But we have no choice."

Pushing aside feelings of doubt and fear, he shifted to a sprint while Saddler's last words echoed in his mind.

CHAPTER 14

The spider stumbled around spotted eggs as she scurried across the Hatching Chamber floor, heading straight toward her warlord. The weak creature's eyes were a pale, faded red as her strength waned.

"Shakaar, the sisters were . . . defeated." She flashed red as her health dropped to near death.

Shakaar quickly grabbed a clump of green moss sitting next to a spotted egg. She stuffed the fuzzy strands into the spider's mouth. The wounded creature's eyes grew brighter. Her mandibles clicked together, then skewered another clump of moss and crammed it into her slitted maw.

"Tell me, sssissster, what happened." Shakaar backed away.

"We were waiting for the wizard and hisss companionsss, jussst like you ordered." She finally was strong enough to stand again on her fuzzy legs. The sister grabbed another tuft of moss and devoured it, her eyes glowing brighter. "They were right where you sssaid they would be, in the giant foressst."

"Go on, sssissster."

The spider nodded. "We lowered down from the

branchesss and sssurrounded the wizard and hisss underlingsss."

"Yesss . . . why didn't you dessstroy him, then?" Shakaar's voice was agitated, her eyes glowing dangerously bright.

The sister tried to take a step back, but bumped into a block of spiderweb. She lowered her head to the ground in resignation. "A group of NPC warriorsss appeared out of the darkness. They were on horssseback and charged through our liness." She glanced up at her warlord. "Many sssisssstersss were killed in their firssst passs, and then they turned and attacked again and again."

"I can't imagine a mounted villager being a threat to a sssisssster." Shakaar couldn't believe what she was hearing.

"There were two on each horsssse, one guiding the mount and usssing a sssword, while the other fired a bow. No sssisssster could get near."

"But you could have—"

"They cut usss to piecesss." The spider lowered her head, expecting a fatal blow as punishment for her failure. "I'm sssorry, warlord. I wasss in command. I failed."

Shakaar sighed in frustration, then glanced around the Hatching Chamber. The smaller cave spiders were scurrying all throughout the cavern, tending to each of the eggs as if they were precious, which they were. Sisters stood outside the entrance, guarding the warlord. If she chose to punish this sister with a fatal blow, no one would see.

As a claw extended from one of Shakaar's legs, the razor-sharp tip scratched across the stone, making a high pitched *screeeeech.*

The spider before her shook in fear.

"The price for failure isss clear." The spider warlord's voice was quiet, yet menacing.

"Yesss, warlord." The doomed spider did not move, her body shuddering ever so slightly.

Raising her dark talon high in the air, Shakaar was about to bring it down on the condemned spider when she glanced again around the chamber. *I do not want this to happen amongst my unhatched children.*

She lowered her arm and instead of striking, gently patted the sister on the head. "You will not die today."

The spider breathed a sigh of relief and glanced up at her warlord, a look of adoration in her eight red eyes.

"Come with me, sssissster." Shakaar walked to the entrance of the Hatching Chamber. Her two guards instantly snapped to attention. She turned to one of them. "Take this sister to the surface so she can get some sun and recharge her health."

"Yesss, Shakaar," the monster said.

They moved off, with the reprieved sister between them, but Shakaar reached out, grabbed one of the guards, and pulled her back. She moved close and whispered in her ear. "That sssissster failed to stop the boy-wizard. Ssshe failed her warlord and ssshe failed everyone. Dessstroy her outssside of the lair. If ssshe dropsss any ssspider eyesss, take them to the witchesss ssso they can make more poissson for usss."

"Yesss, warlord." The spider nodded, understanding, then scurried away.

Shakaar moved back into the Hatching Chamber and rested a claw on one of the eggs. The sticky green ooze clinging to the shell smelled of tangy nether wart; she hated the odor, but knew it was necessary.

"I musssst know where the boy-wizard isss heading now."

The spider warlord reached into her inventory and pulled out the Eye of Searching. She strapped it to her head and positioned the glowing lens over one eye. Instantly, pain radiated throughout her body as the ancient relic drew energy from her health. The image she saw through the lens showed the wizard-boy running through the tall woods, ranks of mounted warriors galloping at his side. There were far more NPCs than before; at least a hundred, if not more.

She also saw a lone zombie running at the wizard's side. "How can that be?" she asked herself as pain splashed through her body again. A leafy mass was stuffed into her mouth—likely one of the brothers was feeding her some of the green moss.

She focused her attention on the zombie, using the Eye's powers to inspect it. And then she saw it and gasped: there was the faintest spark of purple light within the monster. It was nestled deep within the zombie's mind, far from being released, but when it did come to the surface, everything would change for that zombie and for the monsters of the Far lands.

Shakaar smiled. She pulled back her vision and watched the army of villagers from high overhead. They were moving quickly through the forest. Ahead was a huge desert, and at the center of that desert was . . .

Shakaar smiled. "I know where you are going, wizard. You cannot essscape my sssight." The warlord removed the Eye of Searching just as another clump of moss was fed to her.

She shoved the brother aside, her mandibles stuffing the rest of the rejuvenating green moss into her mouth. Slowly, her health returned, the echoes of pain caused by the magical relic slowly fading away.

Glancing at the entrance to the Hatching Chamber, she saw her guards had returned. Shakaar clicked her claw onto the stone floor, calling her attendants. The two creatures quickly scurried to her side.

"Yesss, Warlord," they said in tandem.

"Call all sssisssstersss to the Gathering Chamber. I know where the wizard isss heading. We will be waiting there with a little sssurprissse."

"Yesss, Warlord." The two spiders ran off, heading in opposite directions, announcing the commencement of a gathering.

Shakaar smiled. "I will destroy thisss wizard jussst

like the great ssspider warlock Shakahri destroyed countlesss wizardsss in the Great War. We will ssstop thisss wizard, and then my hatchlingsss can flow acrosss the Far Landsss like a dark tide of dessstruction."

She ran from the cavern and headed for the Gathering Chamber, her eyes glowing bright red with the anticipation of war.

CHAPTER 15

Watcher was mounted behind a tall, skinny villager named Farmer, both atop a sandy brown mare. The lanky NPC rode like an expert, moving with the horse as if it were an extension of his own body; clearly, Farmer had spent a lot of time in the saddle.

The army of villagers rode through the mega taiga forest in silence, each with their eyes cast upward, looking for more spiders. With only thirty horses remaining after some were killed by the spiders in the battle, more NPCs had to run and keep up as best they could. Each horse held two riders, sometimes three, causing the animals to tire quickly. At times, everyone walked, giving the horses apples or handfuls of wheat, but eventually they'd run out of food for the animals and would have to go even slower.

"That was some battle," Farmer said.

Watcher said nothing, just grunting a noncommittal response.

"If we hadn't come along when we did," Farmer continued, "I don't think you'd be talking with me right now."

The image of Saddler's face right before she died haunted Watcher's mind. Her dark brown eyes, filled with fear and sadness, seemed to be begging him to help, but he couldn't save her. Watcher had just laid next to her as the poison from the spider pulsed through his own body, as it had hers.

"You should have seen the look of surprise on those spiders' faces when we charged into them. . . . It was great."

Watcher could still feel the faintest bit of that poison in his system; his tongue had a slight metallic taste to it and his eyes stung. Watcher suspected the effects of the poison would never completely be out of his body.

"But I have to say, that was some trick by the spiders; lowering themselves down from the treetops." Farmer steered the horse around a tall spruce. "Too bad we couldn't have been up there with a set of shears. It would have been fun to cut their silk threads and watch 'em fall to the ground."

Why didn't I think of that? Watcher thought. *I should have shot their webs and let them fall to the ground. Maybe the spider that poisoned Saddler and I would have died.*

But he also knew that he hadn't been able to see their threads very well, and at that distance, it would have been impossible to shoot through them anyway.

"You know, Planter had me ride with you because she said you needed to be distracted." The tall NPC glanced over his shoulder at the boy. "She said you liked to talk." The lanky villager laughed. "Apparently she doesn't know you very well."

"It's not your fault, Farmer," Watcher said. "She's right . . . she's always right. And I do appreciate your efforts. It's just . . . that was a terrible battle, and I know we're gonna see more like that before we're able to rescue the witches."

"You think this is still about the witches?" Farmer's voice grew soft, meant only for Watcher's ears. He slowed the horse to a walk so Watcher could hear him over the hoofbeats. "The spiders in the village said something about destroying the boy-wizard. That's you, right?"

"That's what they think, but I don't feel like a wizard." Watcher scanned the forest.

They were almost to the end of the mega taiga biome and could now see the desert extending before them from between dark tree trunks.

"I wish I had magical powers, so I could blast away all these monsters and keep us safe, but that isn't happening. If I *am* a wizard, then I'm the most pathetic one in existence," Watcher said sadly.

Then he grew silent, reliving the battle in his mind. As they rode, the sun crept up from its hiding spot behind the eastern horizon, announcing its appearance with bright shades of reds and oranges. White clouds floated across the crimson sky, fleeing the sun and heading to the west; it was beautiful, and Farmer commented on it, but Watcher was lost in his own personal nightmare and couldn't appreciate the spectacle.

Soon, they passed from the forest into a pale, empty desert. The landscape was sand as far as the eye could see . . . no scrub brush, no cactus, nothing. It was as if the surface of Minecraft had been scrubbed clean of all living things; it made Watcher nervous.

The oppressive heat of the biome slammed into the villagers like a hammer. Sweat instantly beaded up on their flat foreheads, the cubes of salty moisture trickling into their unibrows. The company stayed mostly silent, with only a handful of hushed conversations here and there. Everyone felt the unusual emptiness of this desert and it made them uneasy.

The army moved across rolling dunes, the ground constantly undulating as it were an ocean frozen in time. Some of the NPCs had difficulty riding in the soft sand, but Farmer was never phased. He still moved as if he was in perfect harmony with the horse, like a seasoned cavalryman.

"How do you know how to ride so well?" Watcher asked. "I don't imagine in that savannah village, with a huge wall around community, there's much need for a cavalry. Where did you get your riding experience?"

"Well . . . it's a long story," Farmer said, his voice tentative as if the subject made him a little uncomfortable.

Watcher said nothing, just waited. The silence grew between the two villagers until Farmer spoke again.

"You see, I'm not originally from the savannah village; I was from one further south. We were on the great plains, with flat stretches of grass extending as far as the eye could see. Horses spawned all around, so each villager had a horse of their own, as long as they cared for it and kept it fed. Mine was a black stallion I named Midnight. She was the fastest horse on the plains."

"Was?" Watcher felt him tense up in the saddle.

"She was taken." Farmer grew quiet for a moment. "They attacked at dusk to take our horses. . . maybe a hundred skeletons. The filthy monsters had some kind of magical weapon that could turn our horses into skeleton horses. You see, skeletons won't ride a regular horse, something about touching their flesh; they'll only sit on bones . . . it's strange. . . . Anyway, they attacked and took what horses they could. We fought back, but there were only a couple dozen of us and a lot of them. When the battle became too fierce, we had no choice and fled, leaving the herd for the skeletons." He grew silent and his body tensed as if he were reliving the experience in his mind. "The skeletons came back again and again until—"

"Slow down . . . something's ahead!" Blaster was shouting from the back of a white mare, two other scouts riding at his side. The army slowed from a gallop to a canter, then finally stopped.

"Blaster, what is it?" Watcher dismounted and ran to the boy's horse. "What did you see?"

"I saw what looked like a green sea. I guess that's what the map meant; the Sea of Spines." He removed his pale-yellow cap and smiled at Watcher, though his black curls were covered with sweat and matted to his head. "But you aren't gonna like this sea."

"Not gonna like it? Why?" Watcher was confused.

Blaster led him to the top of a sand dune and pointed. Watcher climbed to the crest of the hill and stared down at the desert. A huge, unnaturally flat section of sand stretched out as if someone had stomped the parched landscape into a featureless, smooth plain, the edges ringed with sand dunes. The plain was hundreds of blocks across; it seemed completely out of place, as if it had been manufactured, somehow.

At the center of the plain was a bright green field of . . . something. It seemed to glitter in the morning light, as if wrapped in some kind of magical enchantment. The green field surrounded a gigantic hole at the center of the flattened desert that was easily visible from their vantage point. Watcher could just barely make out stairs leading down into the darkness of the basin, torches mounted to the sides of the pit, illuminating the steps.

And then he realized what the glittering green field really was: cacti.

"The Sea of Spines." Watcher nodded. "That's a lot of cacti out there surrounding the gigantic hole. I bet the Citadel of the Horse Lords is in that gigantic pit."

"You're probably right," Mapper said, appearing suddenly behind them. He pulled out his map and checked their location. "Sure enough, that's the place."

"I'm just glad it was cactus and not what I thought it would be," Blaster said.

"And what was that?" Mapper asked, curious.

"You know, spines . . . like bones . . . like a wither's spine." Blaster sighed. "I don't think I'd want to be near a sea of withers." He glanced at Watcher. "There are paths leading into the cactus field, but it's like a maze. Likely it's impenetrable."

"What do we do?" a soft voice asked from behind.

Watcher could feel their panting breath on the back of his neck; he knew it was Planter.

Watcher had been growing tense, the wall of cactus looked like an impassable obstacle. But with Planter nearby, a sense of calm spread through him, as if everything was somehow going to be alright.

Turning, Watcher gave her a smile. "We go down there and figure it out."

She nodded, then led the way down the slope, the rest of the army following close behind, all of them on foot, leading the horses by the reins.

As they approached, something about this place had Watcher worried. It was as if there was a distant memory in the back of his mind, struggling to surface, but it was trapped somewhere in the dark recesses of his brain. Something about that submerged memory tugged at his courage, wanting him to be wary . . . but of what?

CHAPTER 16

They walked to the edge of the cactus field and stopped. Sharp spines stuck out from the rectangular bodies of the cacti, waiting to catch the unwary if they stumbled or fell. A soft purple glow enveloped the base of the thorny plants, revealing some kind of enchantment at work, but Watcher had no idea what it did.

The morning sun shone down upon the desert, causing the temperature to climb slowly upward. Each cactus stood out in stark contrast to the surrounding desert. Nothing else had any color in the parched landscape, and the green of the plants was almost shocking to their eyes.

"The Horse Lords protected their Citadel well," Er-Lan said.

"That they certainly did," Cleric replied, patting the zombie on the back.

"Er-Lan's mother never spoke of the Sea of Spines." The zombie sounded apologetic.

"It's not your fault, Er-Lan," Cleric said. "A goal without obstacles is not a worthy goal."

The zombie nodded.

"You see the spider silk?" Blaster pointed with one of his curved knives.

Watcher turned to where his friend was pointing. Clumps of white string lay on the ground throughout the Sea of Spines, some dangling from sharp thorns.

"You think the spiders tried to get through the maze?" Planter asked.

Watcher shook his head. "No, if a spider had died, then there would be balls of XP nearby as well."

"That's weird." Planter moved to his side and stared at the string.

Watcher smiled as she brushed against his shoulder.

"How could it get there if it wasn't from a spider being destroyed by cactus spines?" Planter sounded confused.

"I don't know." Watcher, too, was perplexed.

"Who cares about a bunch of string?" Cutter barged forward and pushed his way between Watcher and Planter. "We need to get in there and get our horses." He stared down at Watcher. "How are we gonna do it?"

Watcher scowled. Cutter's voice seemed to have an accusatory tone to it. *And he pushed right between me and Planter, too. Maybe Cutter knows how I feel about her, and he's trying to get in the way. It's as if he's calling out my failings as a leader to embarrass me in front of Planter.*

Anger stirred deep in his soul, the serpent of jealousy within him growing restless. Watcher wanted to yell at him, tell him to stay out of their relationship, but the fact of it was . . . there wasn't a relationship. He hadn't said anything to Planter, not yet, and he knew why: he was afraid to confess his emotions to her. Cutter, the famous warrior, was probably afraid of nothing, including a short, blond-haired girl, but Watcher was terrified of her. *I'm pathetic.*

Watcher glanced up at the warrior's steely-gray eyes. They were filled with such confidence and strength, but not the smallest bit of anger or resentment. *Maybe Cutter isn't so bad after all.* But then the big NPC glanced at Planter and gave her a warm, lingering smile. Instantly, anger bubbled up from that serpent again, rekindling Watcher's jealousy and resentment. *He had to know I'd see that,* Watcher thought. *Did he do it on purpose?*

He didn't like Cutter like this; he missed his friend. Watcher glanced at Planter. She gazed up at Cutter, then cast him a look before moving off to help one of the elderly. Planter was always doing that, helping others. It made him smile.

"Well . . . you got any bright ideas?" Cutter asked again.

Watcher glared at him. "Well . . . we could build over the cactus."

"Nope," Blaster said. "Tried it already. You put a block on top of a cactus and the spines start tearing into the material right away. Anything you put on top of the Sea of Spines only lasts for a minute or so . . . not enough time to get everyone across."

"Hmmm . . ." Watcher paced back and forth, lost in thought, then stopped. He could feel Cutter watching, probably glaring at him . . . or was that his imagination? "If we can't go over, we'll go under." He pulled a shovel out of his inventory. "We'll tunnel."

He moved a few blocks from the edge of the Sea of Spines, then dug into the sand. After creating a set of stairs descending down three blocks, Watcher carved a horizontal tunnel through the sand. A few blocks fell as he dug, the sand unable to hold its position without support. But when he reached the edge of the Sea, he found the sand enveloped in a purple glow. His shovel banged harmlessly against the pale cubes of sand as if they were blocks of obsidian. He put away his shovel and pulled out the pickaxe that had belonged to Saddler's husband. He swung it with all his strength, but the iron tip just bounced off the blocks as if they were impenetrable.

With a sigh, Watcher climbed back up the stairs and shook his head. "They're enchanted. We can't dig under them."

Watcher paced back and forth, staring at the prickly obstacles. He reached out and touched one of the spines. "Ouch!" He pulled his hand back and put the injured finger into his mouth.

"That was smart," Cutter said with a chuckle.

Planter and some others giggled. Watcher scowled at the big warrior, but remained silent, staring at the field of cacti, trying to ignore their laughter.

"So, we can't go over them, and can't go under them," Cutter said.

Watcher nodded.

"Then I say we go *through* them." Cutter pulled out a razor-sharp iron axe and started to swing at the nearest cactus.

Slowly, jagged cracks formed on the green cube, stretching outward until the fissures had wrapped their dark fingers all the way around the cube. The top of the cactus disappeared with a pop. Cutter turned and cast Watcher a satisfied grin, but before he could turn back around, the prickly cube regenerated completely, reappearing in a cloud of sparkling purple light.

"You three," Watcher pointed to three villagers. "Use your axes on the same cactus, but focus on the bottom part."

The three NPCs pulled out iron axes and went to work on one of the cacti, digging their sharp tools into the prickly body. Cracks formed around the bottom of the cactus until it shattered, the top half disappearing with the bottom. This time, it took longer for the plant to reappear.

Pacing back and forth, Watcher thought about the problem. He could feel the solution lurking in the back of his mind, an elusive idea hidden in shadows of uncertainty and doubt. Off to the side, Cutter and Planter talked. It looked, on the surface, as if they were discussing possible ways to get through the cactus . . . but was that what they were *really* talking about?

The occasional smile spread across Planter's lips, along with a satisfied grin on the warrior's face.

What are they talking about? Jealously bloomed within Watcher, making it difficult to think. He glanced at the impassable cactus and knew he had to find a way past that obstacle, but his mind was completely distracted. Just then, the image of Saddler came to his mind, her sad eyes imploring him to help her daughter. *"I know you can do it. Save my daughter, please . . ."* The voice echoed in his mind, pushing back on the jealous monster growing in strength within him.

Slowly, Watcher was able to focus on what was important: getting past the cactus. It felt as if Saddler were watching him as he focused on the obstacle. Crazy thoughts sailed through Watcher's skull as he considered all the possibilities, with Saddler, in his mind, nodding at some and shaking her head at others. Each idea presented itself to him, but was instantly assaulted by the many ways in which it would fail. Eventually all the ideas seemed to crash together in an explosion of frustration.

And then Watcher smiled. "Explosion of frustration."

"What?" Planter asked.

"I think he's going crazy." Cutter shook his head as if Watcher were already insane.

Watcher gave Cutter an annoyed glance, then turned his gaze to Blaster. The boy put on his leather cap, the pale-yellow armor allowing him to blend in with the desert sand.

"You think you could put your special skill to work on this sea of cacti?" Watcher asked.

Blaster looked confused for a moment, then turned and stared at the pointed spines. Watcher could tell the boy was lost in thought as he calculated how many blocks he'd need . . . and then he smiled and nodded.

"Let's do it." Blaster turned back to Watcher, a huge grin on his square face. "This is gonna be fun!"

CHAPTER 17

Blaster paced back and forth, wringing his hands nervously. Watcher knew he'd done all the calculations and checked the aim of each mechanism carefully, but the boy was still worried.

"Tell me again why we can't use the horses after Blaster does his thing?" Cutter asked.

Watcher sighed. "We can't take the horses down the stairs and into the pit, and there's nowhere safe for them to stand; the cacti extend all the way to the edge of that hole." Watcher glanced up at the big NPC and rolled his eyes. "If we use the horses, they'll all be killed."

"Better them than us."

"Your concern for the animals and their well-being is inspirational." Watcher glared at Cutter, letting his sarcasm linger in the air for a moment.

"That supposed to be a joke?" the warrior asked.

"How someone treats an innocent creature, like a horse, says a lot about how they'll treat people who are important to them." Watcher's voice was loud; he hoped Planter would hear. "Animals, like people, should not be mistreated just because it's convenient."

"What are you talking about?" The growing frustration

in Cutter's voice was clear. "You think I don't care about other people?"

Watcher shrugged. "A person's actions show who they truly are. Your willingness to sacrifice the horses says a lot." He knew this wasn't about horses; this was about his own frustration over the relationship that seemed to be growing between Planter and Cutter. It was his own insecurities rising to the surface, giving voice to his jealous thoughts.

"What? You think I'm going to start sacrificing people next?" Cutter was getting angry, but he also had a confused expression on his square face.

Watcher shrugged again, his voice growing louder. "Maybe . . . who knows?"

"What are you two arguing about?" Planter said, her words soft and spoken deliberately slowly, but with the force of a giant's hammer behind them.

"I have no idea. Watcher just started screaming at me about horses."

"You're the leaders of this army and you're here, bickering like a couple of children." She glared at Cutter, then focused her gaze upon Watcher. She raised one side of her unibrow, an unasked question in her eyes. "What's this all about?"

"It's just that . . . well, the horses, Cutter wanted the horses to—"

"All you had to do is say 'no' instead of going nuts and talking about people getting sacrificed," Cutter said. "You know I wouldn't want to hurt anyone or anything if it can be avoided." He threw his hands up into the air, frustrated and confused. "I don't know what's wrong with you these days. You're so sensitive." Cutter turned and walked away.

Planter looked at Watcher, and the expression on her face changed from annoyance to concern. "What *is* going on with you?"

Her voice was soft and soothing, easing some of Watcher's fears, as it always did.

Watcher brought his eyes to the ground, ashamed.

"What's *really* going on here?" Planter asked again.

"Well, Cutter was saying we could use the horses, but after the . . . it doesn't matter." He glanced up, his gaze drawn to her beautiful, emerald-green eyes. "I reacted poorly to him. For some reason, I snapped, I don't know why." *I know exactly why.* "It won't happen again."

"It can't." She placed a hand on his arm; it felt like fireworks. "Everyone looks up to you two. Both of you must work together to keep the rest of the army functioning." She paused for a moment to let her words sink in. "You don't need to prove that you're better than everyone else." She took a step closer, her voice intimate and soft, barely a whisper. "I know you're an amazing person." She moved even closer. "I have faith in you and always will."

"But I—"

"Just be yourself. . . . That's all I ask." Her soothing voice seemed to melt away his fears.

Watcher nodded.

"Now, do you think we can make it through the Sea of Spines after Blaster does his thing?" Planter's voice now had a worried, fearful tone.

He glanced at the prickly cactus. "Based on Blaster's experiments, we'll have time."

"When do we start?" Planter asked.

Watcher glanced at Blaster. The boy was checking and double-checking each apparatus, making sure the aim and all the delays were set correctly. They both watched him as he streaked from one to the next, making sure it would all work. If it didn't, then it was likely many of the villagers would be injured . . . or worse.

Satisfied it was ready, Blaster moved everyone away from the contraptions and positioned himself next to the lever.

"Everyone needs to be fast. I don't really know how much time we'll have before the cacti appear again." Blaster grinned, clearly excited, but nervous as well.

"How will we get out after we get in there?" Planter asked.

Blaster pointed to Watcher. "I'm leaving that up to him."

Cutter scowled, then took off his armor and moved next to Planter. "Everyone, remove your armor; you'll be able to run faster."

"That's a good idea." Watcher glanced up at the big warrior and nodded, hoping to show his appreciation and make amends, but Cutter was looking away. With a sigh, Watcher scanned their surroundings, looking for monsters; none were around. Satisfied it was safe, Watcher removed his enchanted iron armor and stuffed it into his inventory. "Let's do it."

Blaster removed his own leather armor and gave him a nod, then pushed the lever. A series of plopping sounds could be heard, followed by the splashing of water and a loud hiss.

"Here it goes!" Blaster was so excited.

All around them, TNT cannons were glowing as their redstone blocks gave off a bright crimson glow. The first TNT cannon detonated, shooting a blinking cube into the air, followed by another and another and another. Watcher wasn't sure how many cannons Blaster had built, but he'd made them to shoot in a specific sequence.

The first explosive cube landed on the edge of the cactus forest, with other cubes landing nearby. While more of them were flying through the air, the first ones exploded, tearing into the prickly plants.

"Now . . . RUN!" Watcher sprinted straight for the explosion.

By the time he reached the site of the detonation, the cacti were gone, but the enchanted sand was untouched. More blocks of TNT exploded before him, just out of reach. The smell of sulfur filled the air, reminding him of creepers; all of the gunpowder had come from those deadly creatures.

He ran faster, trying to get as close to the next explosion as possible without being hurt. The bombs detonated one after another like a series of beats being played on a giant's drum. They erased the cacti from existence, carving a wide path through the Sea of Spines. But Watcher could see cactus already starting to appear again at the edges of the cleared trail.

He ran even faster, his heart pounding in his chest. *Will we make it in time?*

The last few blocks exploded at the inner edge of the cactus field, revealing a clear passage to the safe section at the middle of the sandy plain; it was only two blocks wide. Watcher bolted through the opening and stood on the sandy strip ringing the gigantic hole. Er-Lan skidded to a stop right next to him, panting heavily. The villagers streamed through the cleared trail and spread out around the edge of the bottomless pit, giving others room to exit the cactus field.

"It's closing up!" someone shouted in warning.

Watcher turned. The outer edge had healed itself, the cacti slowly reappearing in a creeping wave that closed in on those still running. His sister, Winger, was the last of the group.

"Hurry, Winger!" Watcher screamed. "It's closing up."

Winger glanced about, noticing the cactus slowly advancing on her. She reached into her inventory and pulled out a flask filled with a bright green liquid. She drank the potion, then dropped the empty flask to the ground. Instantly, bright green spirals formed around her head, then drifted up into the sky and disappeared.

Watcher was confused. "Faster, Winger, faster!"

"Er-Lan isn't sure if Winger will make it," the zombie moaned in terror.

"She'll make it," Cutter snapped.

Winger smiled at her brother, then pulled out her Elytra wings and put them on as she sprinted.

"What's she doing?" Planter asked.

Watcher shook his head. "I don't know."

The cacti were getting closer, filling in the trail behind. Cacti on either side of the wide swath of cleared desert were slowly appearing, causing the path to get narrower and narrower.

"She's not gonna make it." Planter's voice was but a whisper, her voice already filled with grief.

Watcher reached out and grabbed Planter's hand and squeezed it tight. "She's gonna make it . . . she has to."

The cactus closed in tighter and tighter until the sharp spines were nipping at her heels. She was four blocks away, but the cactus before her were already beginning to appear, their razor-sharp spines blocking the way.

"She's not gonna make it," someone said.

"Oh no." Watcher's blood went cold. He felt a hand grab his shoulder and squeeze; it was his father, Cleric, an expression of horror painted across his square face.

"No . . . you have to make it!" Cleric's voice was weak and sad.

But just then, just before the razor-sharp spines enveloped her, Winger leapt high in the air, much higher that anyone thought possible. Leaning forward, she opened her Elytra wings and glided through the air as the rest of the cacti appeared, sealing the path in. Turning in a graceful arc, Winger landed lightly on the sand beside them, a satisfied grin on her face. "Now *that's* how you make an entrance."

"You had us all scared to death," Watcher chided.

His sister shrugged. "If anyone was gonna be last, then it had to be me. I knew I could fly over a small part of the cactus. My plan worked perfectly."

"Yea, except for the fact that you had me terrified," Watcher complained. "I guess I'll just count that as a bonus," his sister replied, smiling.

Cleric wrapped his arms around his daughter and squeezed, color finally coming back to his wrinkled face.

"I like her style," Blaster added, then looked down into the huge pit. "There's something down there, but I can't tell what it is."

Watcher moved to the edge of the massive hole and peered into the darkness. There was something creepy about the hole, as if it knew they were there, and was waiting for them.

"The Citadel of the Horse Lord . . . lies down there in the darkness." The zombie was still out of breath after sprinting through the Sea of Spines. "It is there where all must go."

The zombie gave Watcher a strained smile that looked more like a grimace.

"I guess we're gonna take those stairs over there and find out if there are horses down there for us." Watcher glanced at the zombie. "Er-Lan, why don't you lead the way?"

The zombie seemed excited. He moved slowly through the crowd of NPCs, careful not to brush against the spines of the cacti or fall into the deep abyss. When he reached the stair, he glanced at Watcher, an expression of uncertainty on his scarred face, then slowly descended into the darkness. Another NPC, Farmer, quickly filed in behind the zombie, a look of excitement filling his eyes. The rest of the villagers followed, all of them looking more like the zombie than Farmer.

"Into the maw of the beast," Blaster said with a chuckle.

Planter punched him in the shoulder playfully. "We're all scared enough. We don't need your help."

He shot her a smile, then moved down the stairs.

Watcher waited until all the villagers were on the steps, then followed, his eyes peering into the hole. There was something down there in the shadows. His keen eyes could not pierce the darkness, but somehow, he could feel it, and it knew they were coming.

CHAPTER 18

The stairway spiraled downward along the wall of the huge pit, the width of the abyss making the opposite side difficult to see. Torches had been set in the walls near the surface of the desert, but as they went deeper into the gaping hole, they were replaced with blocks of netherrack, each perpetually-burning cube set behind iron bars, splashing the stairs with a flickering glow.

As they descended deeper, a structure at the bottom of the abyss came into view. It was a huge castle built from cobblestone and stone brick, with a fortified wall surrounding the main structure. Cylindrical turrets sat on each corner, the towers dotted with holes for archers to cover any approach by enemy forces.

The main structure was gigantic. Multiple buildings soared upward to impossible heights behind the fortified barricades. The structures were connected by covered walkways that stretched from one building to the other, creating a complicated series of causeways that was maze-like in its complexity. From within the castle, flickering light streamed out of barred windows, giving it the appearance of being occupied. But Watcher knew better. He could see the thick layer of dust on the ground and across the tops of the towers. This place had not been visited by the living for centuries.

The castle was built upon what seemed like a replica of a grassy plain. Thick, verdant grass grew around the walls, the blades curiously still; it was something you didn't usually see in Minecraft. But then Watcher realized there was no breeze down here. The normal east-to-west wind was blocked, leaving the blades of grass standing at attention and stationary, as if carved from green stone.

A wide set of gates sat open in the fortified wall, the iron bars rusted and crumbling apart from the ravages of time. On either side of the huge entrance, two statues loomed. They were built to resemble horses, and both black-and-white-spotted animals were sculpted to look like they were rearing up, their front hooves reaching high into the air. They were built from blocks of quartz and obsidian and were the most spectacular things Watcher had ever seen.

"I can't believe it." Farmer moved to one of the statues and ran his hand across the blocks making up a rear leg. "My brother and I heard about this place, but we always figured it was just a myth. I wish he could have lived long enough to see it."

"Your brother is gone?" Watcher asked.

Farmer glanced at Watcher and nodded. "It was during the last skeleton attack. He was killed trying to protect the herd. At the end of the attack, I saw him slumped over on the back of his horse, a dozen arrows sticking out of him. I rode as fast as I could to get to him, but Trainer fell off and died just as I approached." He paused for a moment to fight back the emotions, then his voice grew very quiet. "We never had a chance to say goodbye." A pained expression came across Farmer's face, but when he stared up at the magnificent sculpture, he smiled. "Trainer would have loved this."

Farmer raised his hand into the air, fingers spread wide in the salute to the dead, then squeezed his hand into a fist. Watcher thought the tall villager was about to weep, but when he looked up at the huge spotted horse, he just smiled.

"Look, Trainer . . . I'm here!" Farmer's voice reflected off the walls of the castle and echoed back at them. He turned and glanced at Watcher. "Now, my life is complete."

"Don't you want a peek inside?" Watcher asked.

Farmer nodded, then ran under the stone horse and through the crumbling gates.

A huge courtyard made of mossy cobblestone and stone bricks stretched from the walls to the buildings. Multiple doorways stood open, wooden doors lying on the ground in splinters; they had not aged well. One of the buildings was much larger than the rest, with what appeared to be corrals inside, though most of the wooden fences had fallen over. Farmer headed into the large building, the rest of the villagers following.

The interior was poorly lit, with only a few blocks of netherrack burning near the entrance. Farmer moved near one wall and placed a torch on the ground. It cast a weak glow throughout the building, the thick shadows pushing back with remarkable strength. Watcher figured there was some kind of enchantment working throughout the entire Citadel; the rules of Minecraft were probably altered.

Watcher moved to the torch and stared at the nearby wall. It was gray, like the stone bricks surrounding them, but this wall was different. Many of the blocks were not just brick, but decorated with pairs of dark gray spots. It made it seem as if they had eyes. Beneath the two dots, round openings filled with shadow yawned like gaping mouths. On the ground next to the strange blocks, a stone pressure plate sat on the cobblestone floor. The gray upon gray would have been easy to miss—someone not paying attention could have easily stepped on the triggers.

Planter moved to his side and stared at the strange blocks.

"Dispensers," he said, pointing to the dark opening. "Don't step on the pressure plates. Who knows what will happen."

The villagers stayed away from the walls, congregating in the center of the dark room.

With an apple in one hand and a torch in the other, Farmer went deeper into the building, hoping the fruit would attract a horse, but none came.

"I don't understand. This is the Citadel of the Horse Lord. Shouldn't there be horses here?"

"Something is wrong." Er-Lan grabbed Watcher's arm, his stubby claws digging into the enchanted iron armor and scratching the reflective surface.

"You mean the horses?" Watcher asked.

The zombie shook his head. "Er-Lan saw something in a vision . . . something that's gonna happen in the future."

"What did you see?" Watcher motioned Cutter and Planter to come near.

Er-Lan glanced around at his friends, a look of uncertainty on his scarred face. "It is not well understood. Last night, Er-Lan had a vision of this place. The two stone horses were in it, as was this building, but it was all flooded."

"Flooded?" Planter asked.

The zombie turned to her and stared into her bright green eyes. "Er-Lan saw a flood of darkness covering this castle, as if midnight had swallowed it. This zombie expected to find everything filled with dark water, yet everything is dry. But Er-Lan's visions of the future are never wrong."

"You're just talking crazy," Cutter said dismissively. "I don't see any water around us. We're still in a dry desert."

Watcher scowled at the big NPC, then put a reassuring hand on Er-Lan's shoulder.

The zombie shrugged, confused and uncertain. "The visions never lie."

"I think I found something over here," Farmer shouted.

Watcher ran to the tall villager's side. He'd moved a bale of hay from one of the corrals and found a chest hidden beneath the straw.

"Stand back; it might be a trap." Watcher pushed him back, then knelt off to the side.

Carefully, he opened the box with an outstretched arm as Farmer moved to investigate another part of the building. Inside the chest, a weapon like Watcher had never seen sparkled with magical energy. He reached in and withdrew the object. It had a wooden handle that was half the length of a sword, with one end wrapped in dark leather, the surface worn from use. The other end had a chain attached to it, with a large spiked cube connected to the links. The entire thing sparkled with magical energy.

"What's this?" Watcher asked.

"Ahh . . . I know what that is," Mapper said as he approached. "It's an ancient weapon called a flail. I've seen references to these weapons in many books." He reached out to touch one of the spikes, but then pulled back his hand cautiously. "I've never heard of one being enchanted before. I bet getting hit by this weapon is unpleasant."

Watcher nodded. "Probably true."

"Er-Lan saw that weapon in the vision," the zombie said. "The flail appeared just before the flood . . . it must be coming now."

Watcher glanced at his friend. Er-Lan was terrified, the green of his face growing pale with fear. He moved to his side and was about to say something to the zombie when a strange sound seemed to encompass the room. Tiny little scratching noises drifted to them from all sides . . . it was strangely familiar.

"Blaster—torches." Watcher pulled out a handful of torches, and his friend did the same.

They moved quickly through the building, placing torches on the ground, lighting their surroundings. The flaming sticks were able to push back some of the darkness, but even so, they still barely illuminated the walls and high ceiling.

The scratching sound grew louder as it seemed to move closer to the ground.

"What is it?" Planter asked, afraid.

Cutter moved to her side, his diamond sword drawn and ready.

"I'm not sure." Watcher glanced at the other NPCs . . . they all were terrified. He saw Cutter at Planter's side and wanted to say something, but the fact was, he was glad the warrior was at her side. Planter's safety meant everything to him, even if Cutter was responsible for it.

Winger drew an arrow back and fired it at the ceiling. The shaft instantly caught fire, the *Flame* enchantment on the bow giving the arrow fiery life. The flaming arrow streaked through the air and stuck into the stone ceiling. The flickering light from the shaft cast a yellow glow, revealing . . .

"Spiders!" Watcher quickly put the flail into his inventory and pulled out his own bow. He launched more burning arrows up towards the ceiling; his flickering shafts joining his sister's and helping to reveal the room fully.

All across the underside of the sloped roof, hundreds of black spiders clung to the surface, scurrying slowly down the walls. There were so many of them, it was as if the ceiling was covered with black fuzz. They flowed down the walls like an endless river of black hatred.

"The flood is here," Er-Lan moaned, his claws slowly extending from his stubby fingers.

The monsters streamed down every wall, forming a black barrier of anger and spite around the NPCs. They were surrounded . . . and there was no escape.

CHAPTER 19

The spiders covered the entrance to the building, then began flowing across the dusty stone floor. The villagers backed away, moving from the entrance to the back of the structure.

Strangely, the spiders remained completely quiet, their pointed mandibles held motionless before their slotted mouths; the silence was unnerving. They scuttled across the floor, moving closer to the villagers and pushing them further from the only exit in the building. And then they stopped. The monsters stood motionless, staring at their enemy with glowing red eyes filled with rage. Some swayed back and forth, clearly anxious to attack, but their rage was somehow held in check. Then, a larger spider moved forward, away from the rest, her crimson eyes glaring at Watcher.

"Wizard, your time isss up." The spider then clicked her mandibles together. This caused the rest of the spiders to follow suit, creating an almost-deafening storm of noise.

"I'm not a wizard, I'm just a villager who—" Watcher tried to explain, but was interrupted.

"Don't play gamesss with me, wizard. I am Ssshakaar, the ssspider warlord, and I will do anything to protect my people from dessstruction." She took a step closer. "Krael told me what you are planning. You want to ressstart the Great War. My sssissstersss and I are going to ssstop you."

"I don't want to start any war." Watcher put his bow back into his inventory and held his hands out, showing he was unarmed. "We don't—want any trouble with you." Watcher's voice cracked with fear. "Just give us back the witches and we can all go our own way."

"We will give you nothing," the fuzzy monster said. "But inssstead, we will take . . . your livesss."

"It's not necessary to solve our differences with violence," Watcher pleaded.

"The wither king told me you'd want to talk." The spider warlord took a step closer. "Krael told usss how cowardly you villagersss are. It isss a wonder the wizardsss won the Great War. The ancient NPCsss mussst have done sssomething dissshonorable."

"This isn't about the wizards and warlocks." Watcher took a step closer.

"Watcher . . . what are you doing?" Planter said in a low voice behind him. "Get back here."

He ignored her complaints and moved closer. *I must stop this violence before more people get hurt.* "The Great War was hundreds of years ago. It's ancient history, and doesn't involve either of us."

"Perhapsss, but the ssspidersss remember the terrible thingsss done by the villagersss. We do not forget." The spider's eyes narrowed, as if preparing for something, then she leapt into the air.

Instantly, Watcher pulled out his shield and sword. With the wooden rectangle held over his head, he braced himself for the spider landing on top of him. But before the monster touched him, Er-Lan dashed across the battlefield and jumped into the air, knocking the spider aside. The two creatures rolled across the ground, the spider trying to reach Er-Lan with her wicked, curved

claws while the zombie shoved them away with his own clawed hands.

Pushing the zombie away with her back legs, the spider warlord stood and glared at Watcher, then yelled at the top of her voice.

"Ssspidersss . . . ATTACK!" Her screechy voice caused the other monsters to spring into action.

"Archers . . . open fire!" Planter shouted.

A volley of pointed shafts streaked through the air, striking the front ranks of spiders, but the monsters didn't stop.

"Fire again!" Her voice sounded frantic.

More arrows fell upon the monsters, a few of the creatures disappearing under the onslaught. But still the attackers refused to slow. Some of the villagers were building single block towers to climb and shoot at the advancing mob, but it would not protect them from the spiders; the creatures would just climb the blocks.

Watcher grabbed Er-Lan and dragged him away from the monsters. He pulled out his bow and notched a fire arrow to the string. Drawing back, he aimed at the spider warlord and released. The arrow streaked through the air, tiny red embers falling off its shaft, leaving a glowing trail in the air. But before the projectile coul reach its target, another monster moved in front of Instantly, the spider burst into flames. The warlo realizing she was in imminent danger, retreated to rear, away from Watcher's bow.

Many of the warriors put away their bows and their swords and shields, the loot found under the now finally being put to good use. They charged attacking horde, their battle cries mixing with the ing of spiders. The two forces crashed togeth gargantuan waves, claws meeting swords in a maelstrom of violence.

Both villagers and spiders screamed in weapons found flesh, but with so many spider ing, every time one fell, two took its place. Th

slowly backed away, each NPC fighting for their life. Mapper and Cleric stood on a tall platform built from cubes of dirt, pointing out breaks in the lines, but it was Watcher who was really guiding the conflict. He ran across the battlefield, hitting spiders with Needle as he streaked past.

"Blaster, Cutter . . . the left flank!"

The two villagers gathered soldiers and stopped the spiders from sneaking around the edge of their formation to attack them from behind. But it weakened the front, causing the villagers to fall back even more. Countless NPCs fell under the barrage of razor-sharp claws, but Watcher didn't have time to think about those poor souls; he had to figure out some solution that would allow them to survive.

The spiders, sensing victory, pushed harder, driving the villagers back to the wall covered with dispensers. It wasn't clear what would happen when they were activated. . . . Would they shoot out arrows, or fireballs . . . or something worse? As they were slowly forced back, getting closer to the pressure plates, Watcher feared they would soon find out.

A spider leapt high into the air and landed right in front of him. With his wooden shield held before him, Watcher blocked a savage attack at his head, forcing him backward. The heel of his foot brushed against the pressure plate on the ground, activating the dispenser. Watcher ducked, expecting a deadly arrow to come out of the dispenser, but instead, a horse appeared suddenly with a saddle on its back. The spider, shocked by the appearance of the large animal, took a step back, then lunged and, with an outstretched claw, pulled the shield from Watcher's hand.

Spinning away, Watcher leapt into the horse's saddle, then turned the animal around and charged at the monster, swinging Needle with all his strength. The spider stepped aside, stabbing at his hand with her curved claw, and knocked Needle from his grip. Reaching into

his inventory, the boy pulled out the flail and swung it at the creature. Instantly, the enchanted weapon began to tear at his health, using his HP to charge its enchantment. But when the spiked cube hit the spider, the monster flew across the room, flashing red and disappearing in an instant. Watcher reeled in the saddle, weakened from using the incredible weapon, then urged his horse forward.

"Mapper, I need healing potions!" He guided the animal into the battle lines, swinging the flail at the spiders. With the terrifying beasts so closely packed together, the weapon struck multiple creatures, knocking their health down severely, causing the wounded spiders to scurry away.

More monsters approached, but Watcher was already swinging his new weapon. The spiked cube smashed into a large group of spiders, the chain somehow extending out to reach the creatures. It tore through their HP like a razor-sharp blade through paper. But wielding such a powerful tool was taking its toll. The weapon stabbed at his health again and again, causing pain to explode throughout his body. His vision blurred for an instant as waves of agony crashed down upon him. Then, suddenly, a splash potion shattered against his back, recharging his HP. But the healing liquid did not protect him from what came next.

An incredible wave of sorrow flowed through Watcher's mind. He thought of Saddler, and the terrible look on her face when she disappeared.

I failed to keep her safe. She died having faith that I'd help her daughter, but in the end, I couldn't even help her, he thought. An overwhelming sense of failure filled his mind along with the image of the terrified expression in Saddler's eyes.

"Watcher . . . watch out!" Planter's voice shook him from the memory.

The spiders were attacking again, all of them charging toward Watcher. Swinging the flail over his head, he drove the spiked ball into the creatures, crushing their HP. Kicking the horse forward, he charged at the monsters, striking more of them with the enchanted weapon. Splash potions fell upon him as Blaster ran behind, throwing the bottles of healing with all his strength.

Watcher swung the flail with everything he had. The spiked ball tore through the spider ranks as if they were not even there, the weapon destroying scores of the monsters in a single pass. But at the same time, emotions of grief and remorse surged through his soul. He relived every failure he'd ever caused in his life, the memories pounding him relentlessly, as if they were happening again . . . and again . . . and again. It was almost too much to bear. Watcher thought about dropping the terrible weapon, just to be rid of it forever, but he knew he had to endure this torment for the sake of his friends.

Finally, the spider warlord ordered a retreat. The spiders turned and sped from the building, leaving the battlefield covered with glowing balls of XP, spider silk, and countless piles of items from fallen villagers. The assault was over . . . at least for now.

"When we meet again, you'll feel the full force of my army, not jussst thisss sssmall group here," Shakaar shouted from the entrance. "Sssoon, when we help the wither king complete his plan, you will be begging for mercy at my feet. We will meet again, wizard. This isss not over."

Then the spider warlord turned and fled.

CHAPTER 20

"Watcher, come quick," Planter shouted.

Watcher pulled on the reins and galloped toward his friend. She was kneeling on the ground, next to someone grievously wounded, her golden blond hair spilling over her shoulders. Jumping out of the saddle, he ran to Planter's side just as the prone body flashed red.

Farmer was lying there on the ground, his chainmail armor ripped to shreds. Pale green spirals floated about the villager's head, his skin pale as a skeleton's bones.

"One of the spiders with green claws got him." Planter's voice was soft and sad.

"Does anyone have some milk!?" Watcher shouted.

"I do," someone replied, their footsteps growing louder as they approached. A bucket of milk was offered to Planter. She took the pail and moved it to Farmer's lips.

"I don't think it will help." Farmer's voice was weak and difficult to hear.

"I don't care," she said. "Drink!"

Planter poured the milk into his mouth, but Farmer was right; the milk had no effect. It must have been some new poison milk had no effect on.

"You can't die, Farmer; you didn't see what I found." Watcher stood and quickly grabbed the reins of the horse and pulled it close. "Look."

Farmer's eyes moved to the horse, and a satisfied smile spread across his face. He flashed red again.

"Can you see her, Trainer?" the villager said in a weak, cracking voice. "You were right. The horses are still here." Farmer paused as if listening to a voice in his mind. "I know, she is a beauty. I'm looking forward to riding with you again. I think I'll be there soon." He listened again, then nodded and laughed.

"You aren't going anywhere, Farmer. You have to get better so you can teach all these villagers how to ride," Watcher said.

Farmer shook his head, then coughed, flashing red. "I think my time is over in the Far Lands." He moved his gaze from the horse to Watcher. "You can do this, Watcher, just have faith in yourself and don't let the setbacks get to you." He motioned for Watcher to move closer as his voice grew weaker. "This battle cannot be viewed as a defeat."

"But lots of villagers lost their lives here," Watcher said. "How can I not see this as a defeat?"

"My father taught me something a long time ago . . ." his voice grew weaker, forcing Watcher to move his head in still closer. "Defeats are a chance to learn, not a reason to give up."

"But I don't know if I can do this." Moisture started to build up in Watcher's eyes, but he refused to let the tears loose.

Farmer motioned for Watcher to move closer, then he reached up and pulled him down, placing the dying villager's lips right next to the boy's ear. "Why do we fail?"

"What?" Watcher was confused.

"Why do we fail?" Farmer sounded frantic, as if this was some universal truth that would help Watcher in his quest.

Watcher stayed silent, still perplexed, his worry for his new friends making it difficult to think.

The dying villager let go of Watcher's head and gazed into his blue eyes. "So we can—" and then he disappeared, the last of his HP giving in to the poison.

"Farmer . . . no . . ." His sister put a hand on Watcher's shoulder, then wrapped her arms around her brother.

"You can't go . . . you need to explore the Citadel. This was your dream . . . you can't be dead," Watcher whispered.

"Watcher, he's gone." Winger's voice was filled with grief.

He pushed her arms off him and stood up, his entire body tense. But then he glanced at the ground where Farmer had lain. Three balls of XP and the villager's items floated on the ground, rising up and down silently, as if floating on some kind of magic carpet. Suddenly, he no longer had the strength to stand, and he collapsed to the ground.

"Watcher!" Planter ran to his side, catching him before he hit the ground. She cradled him in her lap, holding him tightly.

"Look around you, Planter . . . I did this." He gestured to the piles of items that still floated off the ground. "These lives were my responsibility, and I failed them all."

"No, Watcher, we're all in this together."

"But I'm the one who's supposed to be in command. It's my job to keep everyone safe. Cutter did it when he was in command, but he gave that job to me . . . I don't know why."

"Watcher, you've been a pain in the neck since we left the savanna. I don't know what's wrong, and honestly, I don't really care." Cutter glared down at the boy, but then his gaze softened and grew compassionate. "I gave you the job of commander because I believe in you." Cutter's voice was unusually gentle. "I've been a soldier all my life, and I know a commander, a *real* commander, when I see one . . . and you're that person."

"But . . . you've been so mad at me. I thought you hated me because of . . ." Watcher glanced at Planter but never finished the statement. She didn't seem to notice.

"Don't be ridiculous, I don't hate you." Cutter rolled his eyes. "I was just mad at you because you weren't being the leader I *knew* you could be. Instead, you were getting sidetracked by petty arguments and insecurities instead of doing what you do best, and that's lead."

"But look around, I got all these people killed."

"No!" Planter's voice was strong, almost angry. "You saved all these people with that horse and enchanted weapon. You destroyed half the spiders all by yourself. If you hadn't charged into battle like you did, we'd all be gone."

Watcher stood, then sighed and shook his head.

"She's right, son," Cleric said reassuringly. "You saved us all."

"But what do we do now?" Watcher's eyes were pleading for help.

"We continue." Cleric's voice was sympathetic, but strong. "That spider warlord said something about helping the wither king, and we know he's up to no good. We must find out what he wants with those witches, and don't forget that Fencer still needs us. They're probably able to keep her alive with the potions of healing, but just barely. No one knows how long she'll last."

Watcher sighed, then thought about the flail. That magical weapon had forced him to confront his failure at protecting Saddler from the spiders, and now Farmer, too. *What was it Farmer was trying to tell me at the end? Why do we fail? So we can . . . what?*

Watcher felt as if this was something he needed to understand, but he wasn't sure what Farmer had been trying to tell him.

"We need to get moving before the spiders return." Planter's voice was like a soothing balm to Watcher's emotions. He wanted to wrap his arms around her and weep, but he still wasn't sure if she knew how he felt, or what she felt about him. Confronting her about his emotions was just as scary as facing off against the spider warlord.

Defeats are a chance to learn . . . Farmer's voice echoed in his mind. *Defeats are a chance to learn, not a reason to give up.* Watcher could feel the truth in these words.

He drew the flail from his inventory and grasped the handle. The magical enchantment dug into his health, causing pain to radiate throughout his body, but he didn't care.

"Watcher, what are you doing?" Planter said.

Others called to him as well, but he shut them all out. Instead, he listened to the magical weapon. It whispered its name to him: the Flail of Regrets. And in that moment, the images of Farmer and Saddler filled his mind. The weapon drove his emotions to the forefront of his mind, making him feel responsible for all the deaths of the day.

Why do we fail, so we can . . . learn, but learn what?

The Flail of Regrets projected images of his village, burned to the ground by the skeleton warlord weeks ago. The responsibility of it wrapped around him like a leaden cloak, but he refused to give up. *Why do we fail, so we can learn to . . .* what was Farmer trying to tell him?

Images of NPCs captured by the zombie warlord months ago filled his mind. They toiled in the mines, digging up gold for the king of the withers, and many died in those dark and gloomy passages, suffering terrible beatings by their zombie guards. If Watcher had freed them sooner, then maybe some of them would have survived.

The Flail of Regrets stabbed at his HP, agony blazing through every nerve. He felt Cleric's hand on his arm. It gave little relief, but the sorrow for those poor NPCs surged through his mind. *Why do we fail, so we can learn* . . . It was on the tip of his tongue, he almost understood, but . . .

More pain blasted through his body. A liquid splashed across his back, rejuvenating some of his health, but not enough to fully counteract the effects of the flail. This was a powerful weapon, a demanding weapon, and Watcher felt he had to control it, or they would be lost.

Why do we fail, so we can learn to . . . and then he felt Planter's gentle touch on his square cheek.

I can feel the answer, just at the edges of my mind . . . but he couldn't reach it.

"I'm sorry, I don't understand," Watcher whispered, his health waning. "But I'll try to figure it out. I won't give up . . . I promise."

His words, spoken truthfully, seemed to bring some relief to his regrets. It seemed to bond him to the flail, allowing the magical enchantment from the weapon to flow into his body instead of attacking his mind. Images flashed through his brain at an unbelievably fast rate. Normally, he wouldn't have been able to understand them, but the flail was teaching him, and those lessons were now and forever part of his memory. His skin gave off an iridescent purple glow as the magic from the flail merged with his own XP, causing all the other villagers to step back . . . except for Planter.

He opened his eyes and smiled at her. "Why do we fail? Farmer was trying to tell me something."

"What are you talking about?" Planter asked, confused.

"I don't understand it yet, but I know I will . . . soon." Confidence seemed to fill the boy as the truth of the words permeated his soul. "I will understand soon, Farmer; this is my pledge."

Watcher glanced at the place where Farmer died, then raised his hand high into the air, fingers spread wide. *I won't forget you, Farmer!* He shouted his thoughts out into the fabric of Minecraft, and somehow, Watcher thought he could feel the fabric smile back.

"It's time we stopped being afraid. No, it's time *I* stopped being afraid." His gaze found Cutter, and he saw that the big NPC was as confused as the other villagers. "I'm sorry I've been a pain in the neck. I've mistreated you because of my own insecurities, and that wasn't fair. I've yelled at you and treated you like an enemy because I was afraid of losing something." He glanced at Planter, then brought his gaze back to the big warrior. "But I know now, I must let things play out the way they're meant to, and let everyone make their own choices." He wanted to look at Planter again, but didn't dare. "You're my friend and I want it to stay that way, no matter what."

"Really have no idea what you're talking about, but I never stopped being your friend," Cutter said as he slapped the boy on the back, almost knocking him down. "If you think you can get rid of me by just being a jerk, then you don't know me at all."

Watcher smiled and nodded. "Then it's time for us to do something."

"What's on your mind?" the big warrior asked.

"It's time we brought the pain to the spiders." Watcher's voice grew a little louder. "I'm tired of being ambushed by these spiders. I'm tired of being afraid they'll jump out of the shadows, and I'm *tired* of seeing our friends being injured or killed by these monsters. It's time this stopped . . . NOW!"

"Alright!" Cutter smiled. "*That's* our leader . . . Watcher the Wizard!" He raised his diamond sword high over his head, causing the other NPCs to cheer.

As the villagers shouted, Watcher thought about the images the flail had shown him, then smiled at the big warrior.

"First, we need to collect a few artifacts, and we also need what we came for." He took Planter by the hand and led her to the wall of dispensers. "These will only work for each of you once." Watcher whistled, bringing his mount to his side. "I already have my horse. Everyone else needs one."

"But how do we get out of here?" Blaster asked.

Watcher closed his eyes for a moment and played back the many images the Flail had put in his mind. "There's a portal in the building next to this one."

"How do you know that?" Blaster sounded skeptical.

"The Flail of Regret showed me." Watcher held the weapon in the air, then put it in his inventory.

Moving to where Needle lay on the ground, he bent over and retrieved the blade and his shield, then jumped on the back of his horse and moved to the building's entrance. The sky overhead was blushing a soft crimson as the stars faded from sight, the sun beginning its climb into the sky.

"It's time to ride." Watcher glanced down at the spot where Farmer had died. "Defeats are a chance to learn," he said in a soft voice, a single square tear tumbling down his cheek. "I won't forget, Farmer, I promise you that."

The sound of whinnying horses filled the air as each villager, one at a time, stepped on a pressure plate and collected their mounts. He urged his own horse forward, then headed out of the building and toward the portal that would take him from the Citadel of the Horse Lord and closer to the lair of the spider warlord.

CHAPTER 21

"How many made it out of that cactusss foressst?" Shakaar paced back and forth amidst the tall sunflowers.

"Almossst all ssspidersss were quick enough to run acrosss the blocksss of ssspiderweb we put on top of the cacti. Mossst made it across the websss before the cubesss broke, without taking too much damage." The spider general took a step back, out of reach of the warlord's claws.

"But fifty of my sssisssstersss perished. FIFTY!" Shakaar slashed angrily at a nearby flower, shredding it in seconds. "That boy-wizard cossst usss many sssisssters. He mussst be dessstroyed."

"Yesss, warlord." The general backed away more.

"Relax, general, you are sssafe." The spider warlord moved closer to her commander. "I may get angry, but I would not vent my anger on a sssisssster general like youssself. You are far too important to our planss."

"Thank you, warlord," the general said, her body finally relaxing.

"The ssspidersss have resssted enough. We mussst keep moving." Shakaar gave off a loud screech, getting her warriors' attention. "Everyone, back to the lair. We mussst move quickly."

The spiders all stopped basking in the light from the noon sun, their HP now recharged. They had walked all through the morning, trying to escape the oppressive heat of the desert. When the sun neared its zenith, they'd finally left the baked landscape and entered a narrow strip formed from a sunflower plains biome. But now their rest was over. The spider army stood and scurried through the cool landscape, the tall yellow flowers getting trampled by fuzzy black bodies as they headed for their distant spiders' lair,

"Warlord, do you have a plan for the villagersss?" the general asked.

"Yesss, general, I have been conssssidering what we will do to that wizard."

Shakaar stepped out of the sunflower plains and into the next biome. It was a mountainous landscape with steep hills jutting up from the grass-covered ground. Flowers of every color imaginable covered the ground, the perfumed air making Shakaar slightly sick.

"Sssoon, we will passs by a zombie-town and a ssskeleton-town. You will sssend my sssisssstersss to them and order them to help usss." Shakaar's eyes glowed bright.

"But what if they refussse?"

"You will have the king of the withersss, Krael, with you." Shakaar pulled out the enchanted Eye of Searching. She slowed to put the enchanted artifact over one eye, then adjusted the strap around the back of her head, and instantly, the spider warlord flashed red as the magical device drew on her HP for power. Concentrating on her target, an image of Krael burst into Shakaar's mind. Instantly, she felt the cold and dangerous presence of the wither king in the back of her head.

"Krael, we found the wizard," Shakaar said aloud, her thoughts echoing in the dark monster's three heads. "We need your help."

I will be there soon. The wither's thoughts echoed through the spider, causing a strange chill to settle across her body.

Reaching up, she removed the ancient relic before it took more of her health and put it back into her inventory.

"The wither king will be with you to encourage the zombiesss and ssskeletonsss to help." Shakaar smiled. "If they disssobey, then you'll get to sssee Krael's flaming ssskullsss in action."

The spider general nodded, her eight eyes burning bright red with excitement.

"We will sssend groupsss of ssspidersss and zombiessss and ssskeletonsss from all across the Far Landsss in sssearch of thisss wizard." Shakaar smiled and clicked her mandibles together. "They will harasss them by attacking at every opportunity, slowly decreasssing their numbers. When we finally meet the villagersss in battle, their forcesss will be pathetic compared to our ssspider army." She laughed. "Sssoon, we will sssee thisss boy-wizard begging for mercy, then we will dessstroy him."

Her eyes gave off a brilliant red glow as she clicked her mandibles together and the rest of the spiders joined in, filling the air with their excitement and thirst for destruction.

CHAPTER 22

Watcher stood next to his horse, waiting impatiently for the other villagers to get their own mounts, as well as repair cracked and dented armor and eat so their HP would be replenished. The horse nuzzled his neck with a cold and wet nose. Reaching up, he scratched the animal's ear, the mare leaning into the caress.

He turned and gazed at the portal. When Watcher had first come into this second building, the blocks making up the portal had been dark, as if asleep. But when he drew closer, the strange cubes began to glow from within, giving off a pale bluish-white hue. The edges of each bright cube were trimmed with a thin border of sea-foam green. It reminded him, for some reason, of the ocean . . . strange.

Within the ring of glowing blocks, a sparkling silver translucent field now undulated and pulsed with magical power. It seemed to sense Watcher's approach, for it had grown brighter the closer he'd gotten, until he could no longer see through it. In fact, Watcher could now see his reflection as if he were staring into a mirror. It was then that he noticed his hands were sparkling with a subtly iridescent purple glow.

Before he had a chance to investigate further, the other villagers began filing into the portal room behind him, each on their new mounts, the horses filling them with a new sense of courage.

"These horses will, for the first time, let us move faster than the spiders." Watcher's voice filled the stone-lined structure, reflecting off the mossy brick and echoing back from all sides. The portal reacted to his voice, bulging outward as if were trying to reach out and grab him.

"Any idea where this portal leads?" Planter asked.

Watcher shook his head. "The Flail of Regret showed me this portal, as well as some other things I don't fully understand. All I know is that our path leads through this portal."

He turned in the saddle and smiled. Planter's blond hair glowed in the harsh light of the portal, appearing as if it were somehow electrified and giving off its own light. Overcome by her beauty, all he could do was gaze at her, transfixed. He felt like he needed to say something to her. He'd mistreated Planter as well when his jealousy over Cutter had flared, but Watcher didn't know what to say to apologize. He didn't even know how she felt. *Maybe I should tell her that I—*

"Watcher . . . you're glowing." Planter pointed to his arms.

His thoughts interrupted, Watcher glanced down at his hands and remembered the faint purple light wrapping around them like velvet gloves.

"Yeah, I know."

"What does it mean?" she asked.

"I don't know." Watcher shrugged, trying to look nonchalant, but actually, he was a little afraid. *Have I been infected, somehow, by that flail? What's happening to me?* The urge to pull out the flail was great, but Watcher resisted and kept his hands on the reins.

Staring out at the sea of mounted villagers, he could tell they were nervous, but willing to follow him. Many glanced at Watcher's glowing hands, but instead of being afraid of him, they seemed proud of his affliction, as if the magic that had leaked into his body might somehow save them, so they could save Fencer. Watcher wasn't convinced.

This unexpected gift could be a curse, he thought, but he knew it was too late. The die had been cast, and now all they could do was wait to see where they landed.

"Let's get this party started!" Blaster shouted from the back. "I need some spider's silk and maybe a few spider eyes, and I only know one way of getting them: by destroying spiders!"

Many of the villagers chuckled, their laughter breaking the tension.

"Here we go." Watcher urged his horse forward.

He rode through the portal, the silvery membrane bulging outward to envelop him in its magical grasp. A tingling sensation spread across his skin as he passed through the field, and then suddenly, he was out of the Citadel of the Horse Lords and in the middle of a birch forest.

Glancing over his shoulder, he saw Planter appear out of thin air, followed by Winger, then Cleric, then the rest of the army. Each time another NPC passed through the portal and emerged, the horse and rider were surrounded by a dusting of silver sparkles that clung to their skin for just a moment as they fully materialized.

"Well, that's not something I do every day," Cutter said, brushing at his arms as if trying to get rid of the shimmering particles, which were already disappearing on their own.

"Everyone make it through? Okay then, come on . . . this way." Watcher pulled on the reins and urged his horse into a gallop, heading through the birch forest toward something dark in the distance.

"You have any idea where we're going?" Cutter asked.

Watcher shrugged. "Not exactly, but I have this

strange feeling telling me where our next destination is located, and it's this way."

"Maybe we should be figuring out where the spiders' lair is hidden and head for that," Cutter suggested.

Turning in his saddle, Watcher stared at the big warrior and shook his head again, his arms glowing brighter. "This is the right way."

"I think we should listen to him," Blaster said. "Being a wizard and all, he seems to know what's going on."

"He isn't a wizard . . . he's just Watcher." Cutter gave Blaster a scowl. "Enchanted items don't make someone a wizard. If they did, then my armor would make me some kind of legendary sorcerer."

"Cutter's right . . . I'm not a wizard. At least, that's not how I think of myself," Watcher said as he stared at the other villagers. "I'm just me . . . just Watcher. But for some reason, I can feel our next location, and we *must* go there, or all will be lost."

Someone said something, but Watcher didn't hear what was said. A gentle tug pulling at the back of his mind urged the boy forward. He ignored the discussion and turned toward the path laid out before him. Giving his horse a gentle kick in the ribs, he trotted through the forest. Watcher ignored the questions being levied toward him; he was completely focused on where they were heading. The path ahead now looked like a line of sparkling particles to him, similar to those around the portal; the silvery sparks hovered just off the ground in a neat line.

Watcher turned to Planter as his side. "Can you see them?"

"See what?" She sounded confused.

"The shining particles on the ground . . . you can't see them?"

She shook her head. "Sorry, no. But if you can see them, that's good enough for me, as long as you're okay." Planter reached out and put her hand on Watcher's, a concerned expression on her square face.

His heart soared.

"I'm okay," Watcher said. Glancing down at her hand, he smiled.

"I know you are," she replied. "I'm just worried about you. . . . Many of us are."

"Well, you don't need to be. I know where we're going and I know what I'm doing, for a change." Watcher could feel the certainty in his words, but still saw the worry in his friend's eyes.

They rode in silence, weaving around the white-barked trees with ease. Gradually, Er-Lan caught up with Watcher and rode at his side.

"You're doing well on the horse," Planter said to the zombie.

"Er-Lan understands animals and they understand Er-Lan." The zombie smiled an eerie, toothy smile. "That makes it easier."

"Did you have horses when you were a child?" Planter asked.

But suddenly, her faced changed to one of fear. Pulling her horse to a sudden stop, she reached into her inventory, pulled out her enchanted golden axe, and pointed with the glowing weapon.

Watcher also brought his horse to a halt. The birch forest had ended, and before them stood a roofed forest, the wide, interlocking leafy canopy blocking most of the sunlight from reaching the forest floor.

"We're going in there?" she asked, frightened.

Watcher nodded. "Our path leads through this forest."

"But monsters are always in dark forests. They like the shadows and being out of the sun for some reason."

"*Zombies* like the dark forests," Er-Lan moaned.

"I know," Watcher said. He raised his voice so all could hear. "Our path leads us through this forest. We'll stay in a close formation and ride fast. Speed will be our ally, and no monster will dare confront us."

Many of the villagers seemed worried and doubtful.

They all knew roofed forests were dangerous places in the Far Lands. Uncertainty and fear were visible on their faces, their courage close to shattering.

Just then, an old man from the savannah village kicked his horse forward to the head of the column.

"What are we waiting for?" he said with a scratchy voice, his frail body barely able to stay in the saddle. "Fencer needs a golden Notch apple, and the spiders have all the witches." He turned and glared at all the NPCs, his wrinkled face a visage of courage. "If going through this forest will help us save those witches, which will in turn help us save Fencer, then what are we waiting for?"

Still, no one moved.

"Oh, I get it," the ancient villager continued. "You're afraid of a little darkness. Well, don't worry. I'm Carver, knight of the wooden sword."

He pulled a wooden sword from his inventory and held it high over his head. The weapon was almost useless. Many of the villagers laughed. Even Watcher had no choice but to shake his head at how ridiculous it was.

"If you are afraid, I'll protect you." Swinging the pathetic weapon over his head, the old man kicked his horse forward and headed into the roofed forest, stopping at the first tree. "Take that, tree monster!" he cried fiercely, swinging his wooden blade without effect at a dark oak standing on the border of the biome. As he slashed at the woody adversary, his weapon bouncing harmlessly off the tree's thick trunk, more villagers laughed, then urged their horses forward.

"Come on, Watcher, let's get this done," Cutter said. "I don't know about you, but if Carver's able to summon the courage to push forward, I think I can as well. So lead the way."

Watcher smiled, then snapped the reins and galloped into the dark forest, unaware of the lifeless eyes watching from behind them.

CHAPTER 23

They rode through the roofed forest, moving as fast as possible. Watcher followed the sparkling particles that only he could see, weaving around trees and splashing through narrow streams. At times, they had to pass between two trees at a time, their trunks growing close together.

Every now and then, Watcher caught a glimpse of the sky overhead through the smallest of gaps. It was growing dark, and fast. He wasn't excited about being in this terrifying forest at night, even though the lack of sunlight would likely do little to make it darker; the leafy canopy blocked most of the sunlight, even during the day.

The branches from the dark oaks stretched out far, interlocking with the neighboring trees and creating a green roof of leaves overhead that was, in some places, completely solid. Even the rays from the afternoon sun were unable to penetrate the leafy covering at these places, leaving the ground cloaked in shadows. But in other places, where the trees were further apart, the leafy canopy left openings for the light of the sun to leak through and cast its rays on the forest floor.

"Watcher, where is it we're heading?" Planter asked.

"What?" Watcher put a hand to his ear. It was difficult to hear over all the hoofbeats.

"I said," she shouted, "where are we heading?"

He slowed to let his horse rest. The animal panted,
taking in huge gulps of air. Watcher moved his spotted
horse right next to Planter's chocolate brown animal.
His leg brushed against hers; it felt electric. *Should I say
something now . . . let her know how I feel?* Fear exploded
within him at the thought of confessing his emotions.
She could reject him, or laugh, or . . . it was a terrifying
prospect. Just then, a group of villagers rode near, slowing their horses to let them rest. *No, this isn't the time,
but will there be time later?* Uncertainty filled his soul.

"All I saw was a vision of the destination. It looked
unlike anything I'd ever seen in Minecraft." He glanced
around, then lowered his voice so only she could hear.
"It's a building constructed during the Great War."

"You mean some kind of castle?"

He shook his head. "No, not a castle, but a mansion.
In my vision, it looked like the biggest house you've ever
seen, with countless rooms. The vision said I had to go
to the second floor and look at the walls. I didn't understand, but I know it's important. When we get there, I'm
gonna—"

"Something's up ahead," a voice shouted from the
darkness in front of them.

Blaster emerged from the shadows wearing his favorite black leather armor and riding a bright white horse.

"What is it?" Cleric asked.

"I'm not sure," the boy replied. "I've never seen anything like it before. It looks sorta like a . . . "

"A mansion?" Planter said.

"Exactly." Blaster nodded, an expression of surprise
on his face. "How did you know that?"

Planter just glanced at Watcher and smiled. His
heart skipped a beat.

He heard Cutter giving commands at the back of the
formation, deploying archers and swordsmen along the

edge of the group. Watcher glanced over his shoulder and saw the big NPC on his horse, brimming with confidence and strength. Then he glanced at Planter. She too was looking at the back of the group, and toward Cutter.

The vicious fangs of jealously again stabbed at his heart. He hated it when Planter looked at Cutter and smiled; it made him feel on fire inside, with a jealous rage bubbling deep within his soul. But he couldn't worry about that now. This path, laid out by the Flail of Regret, was fraught with countless perils; if he were to become distracted, it could cost someone their life.

"I must focus," Watcher whispered to himself. "I can't let myself get distracted by thoughts of jealousy and self-doubt. The spider warlord must be stopped . . . for Fencer and for the Far Lands."

He turned and found Planter staring at him, confused.

"What?"

"Ahh . . . nothing." Sitting up high in the saddle, Watcher spoke to the villagers. "That's our destination up ahead." He cast his gaze across their faces. Many were scared, as was he, but Watcher knew they *had* to push ahead, or they'd ultimately fail in their quest. "There's something we need in there, on the second floor. I'm not sure what it is, or whether there's something standing in the way of us getting it."

"Or maybe some*things*," Cutter said.

Watcher nodded. "Cutter's right . . . maybe some*things*, so we need to stay together. Search every chest you find; we could always use more enchanted weapons. Be on the lookout for pressure plates and tripwires— there might be traps in there waiting for us, just like in many of the other ancient structures in the Far Lands."

He nudged his horse forward, moving at a slow walk, the rest of the army following.

Blaster moved to his side. "Just so you know, I heard monsters in the forest and inside that mansion. Zombies and skeletons, I think. "

"I'm not surprised; they like the darkness," Watcher said.

"But it's different." Blaster lowered his voice. "We'd expect a skeleton or two, but by the sounds I heard, there are a *lot* of them moving about in the forest. I also heard lots of monsters inside the mansion." His voice became a nervous whisper. "But there was something else . . . a growling, wailing sort of sound I've never heard before. I'm kinda worried about that. I don't think getting trapped in this building with lots of monsters inside and out is a very good idea."

"We have no choice." Watcher stared at Blaster, then smiled. "Besides, if we get trapped in there, I bet you can figure out a way to create a new exit."

Blaster grinned, then scowled again. "That's only if these walls can be damaged. If it's like the sand in that cactus forest, then we might be in trouble."

"Let's not worry about problems that aren't here yet." Watcher put a hand on the boy's arm. "Don't worry, it will be alright."

"If you say so, but I'm still gonna worry," Blaster said.

"Me too," Watcher said, and for the first time, he saw something in his friend's dark brown eyes he hadn't ever seen before: fear.

CHAPTER 24

As they neared the mansion, the sounds of monsters greeted their ears. The creatures weren't very loud—the thick wooden walls muffled their voices—but they could still hear the moans and clattering of bones. The sounds caused little square goosebumps to form on Watcher's arms. When they moved through the last of the trees and saw their first glimpse of the mansion, Watcher pulled his horse to a halt.

"It just looks like a big house," Mapper said skeptically.

"But not just big . . . *really* big." Blaster dismounted and tied the reins to a tree branch, then helped the old man dismount from his horse. "It must be at least sixty blocks wide."

Watcher nodded as slid off his horse and tied it up, then turned and faced the woodland mansion.

The outside walls were constructed from dark oak planks, an ornate line of stone separating the bottom floor from the one above. Huge windows adorned the walls of the second floor, the gigantic openings spilling light out onto the forest roof. The third floor was smaller than the second, but the windows there were also filled with a flickering glow.

"It's from before the Great War." Watcher pointed at the roof. "There's something on the second floor that we need . . . that's our goal. The only problem is, I don't know which room."

"Any idea what the thing we need is?" Mapper asked.

Watcher shook his head. "The enchanted weapon we found in the Citadel of the Horse Lord, the Flail of Regret, showed me a vision of this place." He pointed at the second floor. "There are monsters all throughout the building . . . I saw some of them with those windows in the background, but I also saw some creatures I didn't recognize at all."

"There is great danger here," Er-Lan said in a low voice. "Something from the distant past. It is wise to avoid this place."

"I can't do that, Er-Lan. I must go in." He put a hand on the zombie's shoulder. "You can stay out here if you wish, though I suspect there are threats out here as well."

"Er-Lan stays at Watcher's side." The zombie's voice was loud and filled with confidence.

"Okay then. I'm always glad to have you next to me." Watcher patted him on the back. "Let's go knock and see if anyone is home."

The rest of the villagers tied their horses to trees standing next to the structure, then moved to the front entrance.

The doors of the mansion stood open, inviting anyone to enter . . . or daring them. Bright crimson carpet covered the floor, a white border around the edges. The carpet stretched off to the left and right, with a cobblestone stairway directly in front of them, leading to a carpeted landing. The steps then split to the left and right, disappearing into shadows.

Watcher stepped inside the structure and glanced down the long passages. The sky could be seen through the huge windows at the end of the hallways. The one pointing to the west showed the sun settling down upon the horizon, while the one to the east revealed the silvery face of the moon peeking over the mountains.

Suddenly, the sounds of zombies, along with the rattling of skeleton bones, filled the air, the eerie noises bouncing off the wooden walls. It was a creepy sound, loud, as if they were right nearby, but none could be seen.

"There must be rooms on the other sides of these walls." Cleric moved to one wall and patted it with his hand. The moans grew louder.

"I don't like hearing monsters I can't see." Blaster scowled in the direction of the moans.

"Me neither." Planter pulled out her golden axe and drew her red shield with the three dark skulls adorned across the center.

But then came another sound mixed in with the clattering bones and sorrowful moans, something Watcher had never heard before, and that worried him.

"I'm thinking there are some monsters here." Blaster smiled, removing his leather armor and donning a set of iron.

Watcher glanced at him, perplexed.

"I don't have any leather armor that'll match the color of this carpeted hallway." Blaster gave him a mischievous smile. "Might as well wear something durable and strong."

Watcher nodded, grinning. "Okay, here's what I want to do. I need to go upstairs and find something, but I'm not really sure what. I need everyone to search the rooms and take any enchanted artifacts that may be hidden here."

He turned and scanned the faces of the villagers congregated around him. When his eyes fell upon Er-Lan, Watcher instantly recognized something was wrong. The zombie seemed unusually terrified, his normally dark-green skin pale with fear. He shook almost uncontrollably.

"Er-Lan, you okay?" Watcher asked.

The zombie shook his head. "Evoker . . . evoker."

The monster wasn't making any sense.

"What do you mean, Er-Lan?" Planter asked. She put an arm around her friend and tried to calm him, but it had little effect. "Just take a deep breath and tell us what's wrong."

Cleric took a bottle of water from his inventory and handed it to the zombie. "Here, drink."

Er-Lan took the flask and drained its contents, then finally calmed down. His eyes darted to the left and right as if he was searching for something sneaking up on them.

"An evoker is speaking into Er-Lan's mind," the zombie said. "It was thought they were gone, all destroyed in the Great War, but one still lives."

"Er-Lan, you aren't making any sense." Watcher moved to his side and grabbed his face. He turned the monster's head so they were looking eye-to-eye. "Tell me what an evoker is."

The zombie was still shaking. "Zombie history, passed down from parent to child, teaches about what happened during the Great War." He glanced to the left and right again, searching for threats, then continued. "Near the end of the war, when the warlocks could tell their enchanted weapons were not able to compete with those of the wizards, a new strategy was formed. Instead of making swords and shields, living weapons were made."

"And an evoker was one of them?" Mapper asked.

Er-Lan nodded. "Evokers have some of the magical powers of the warlocks, but only very specific powers used for very specific attacks. These are very dangerous creatures and should be avoided. All must leave this mansion while it is still possible."

Watcher sighed. "I know you're concerned, but there's something here I must see."

As he thought about the image the flail had shown him, his hands began to glow a soft purple. He had seen a room with books covering one wall, a wide table in the middle with a map of the Overworld covering its surface. Many of the villagers stepped back, afraid. Watcher glanced down at his arms, then looked at the NPCs. He could see the fear in their eyes; they were afraid of him.

"All must be wary of the evokers . . . they are very deadly." Er-Lan's voice cracked with fear.

"I think we should listen to our friend here," Cleric said. "Maybe instead of everyone just spreading out, we break up into two large groups."

"I think you're right." Watcher nodded. "Cleric, you and Cutter take half the army and search this floor. Planter and I will lead the rest of the army to the second floor and search there." He turned to face the zombie. "Er-Lan, I want you right next to me the whole time. I'm gonna keep you safe from this evoker thing."

The zombie mumbled something low and unintelligible, then nodded.

"Okay, everyone . . . eyes sharp. Let's find us some loot, then get out of here." Watcher reached into his inventory for a weapon. His fingers brushed the handle of the flail and instantly, thoughts of his many failures burst into his head. Pushing the weapon inside, he found Needle's hilt, drew the sword with his right hand, and held it high over his head. With his left, he pulled out a wooden shield and held it close to his body.

"Everyone . . . go!"

Half the army moved off to the right while Watcher ascended the stairs, the sound of monsters growing louder and louder.

CHAPTER 25

At the top of the stairs, Watcher placed a torch on the ground, then turned just as an arrow streaked past his head.

"Skeleton!" he called out in warning, and held his shield up just in time to catch the next pointed shaft. It thumped into the wooden square, the sharp tip sticking through the back. Arrows streaked past Watcher's shoulders as the other villagers fired on the creature. The monster fired again, but was quickly silenced.

Watcher checked the hallway and found it clear of threats, but he could still hear moaning and growling; the monsters were close. A torch flickered at the end of the passage, but the side rooms were all cloaked in darkness, and with monsters nearby, darkness was the enemy. Putting away Needle, Watcher pulled out a stack of torches, then handed them to Er-Lan. "Come on, you're gonna give us some light. Stay right next to me."

He moved along the red carpet, Er-Lan right at his side. Every dozen blocks, the zombie placed a torch on a wall, splashing a flickering glow on the corridor. The moans of zombies were growing louder and angrier. Moving to a doorway on the left side of the passage,

Watcher stood next to the entrance and drew his sword and shield, his hands both glowing with a purple luster that matched his enchanted blade.

"As soon as we go in, put torches on the ground," he told the zombie.

Er-Lan nodded.

Just then, they heard fighting on the floor below, iron clashing into iron. The sound caused the hairs on the back of Watcher's neck to stand up, his whole body quivering just a bit.

I hope they're okay, he thought.

An angry growl came from the room he was about to enter. It was a zombie-like groan, but it sounded more vicious somehow than any zombie he'd heard before.

"Here we go," he whispered to Er-Lan, then ran into the room.

A loud growl floated out of the darkness. Er-Lan placed a torch on the ground, revealing a dining area with table and chairs, as well as a gray carpet trimmed in white covering the floor. At one end stood a villager zombie with gray skin. His bulbous nose, hanging down across his mouth, was a charcoal color, as were his eyes. The monster wore what looked like a military uniform of some sort, his jacket dark with gray buttons running down either side. A pair of dark bluish-green pants covered the monster's legs.

"I've never seen zombies looking like them before," Watcher whispered to Er-Lan. "What are they?"

The zombie-villager's hands were linked across his chest, but as soon as it heard Watcher's voice, the monster pulled out an axe and charged. A bloodcurdling scream filled the room as the zombie attacked. Watcher brought up his shield just in time to deflect the axe's blow, the impact almost tearing the wooden rectangle from his grip. The stench from the creature was terrible, its rotting flesh smelling just like decaying meat.

Swinging Needle, he pushed the monster back, the zombie's axe blocking his attacks. Two more of the creatures emerged from the shadows, their angry, insane howls filling the room and their axes shining in the flickering light from the torch as they spotted Planter by the entrance.

"Vindicators . . . they're vindicators!" Er-Lan shouted in warning.

"Not for long," Blaster said.

He charged at the two monsters, his iron armor shining bright. He slashed at them as he ran by, his curved knives slipping past their vicious axes. Planter fired at the creatures with her enchanted bow, striking one but missing the other. It didn't even slow their advance. Putting away her bow, Planter drew her golden axe and ran toward the zombies. More villagers charged in, but it was difficult for them to help in the confines of the small room.

The vindicators attacked with such vicious anger and rage, as if they'd been programmed to hate NPCs. They moved completely differently from regular zombies or zombie villagers, sprinting across the floor instead of moving at a slow shuffle. They charged at their enemies without concern for injury; they were consumed with a thirst for violence. But the worst parts about the creatures were their eyes and their screams; both were filled with terrible, unquenchable hatred.

An axe thudded against Watcher's shield, causing a crack to form down the center. He pushed the monster backward, then allowed his awareness to flow through Needle. Somehow, he seemed to merge with the weapon, the enchanted blade becoming part of his body. Needle moved on its own, but this time, it was smarter and faster.

The shimmering weapon slashed at the vindicator, hitting it in the shoulder, then the knee, then across the ribs. The monster groaned in pain, but never stopped attacking. It was as if it had no choice but to attack; these vindicators, or whatever they were, indeed seemed to be like living weapons, made by the warlocks during the Great War.

The vindicator charged at Watcher again, but Blaster slashed at it from behind. The vicious zombie screamed, then turned toward its attacker. Instantly, Watcher charged, Needle tearing into the monster's HP.

Planter backed away from her attackers, letting the villagers from behind open fire with their bows. A dozen arrows fell on the other two monsters, their cries of pain as they were defeated mixed, not with fear, but rage. These were creatures bred for only one purpose: destruction.

The closest vindicator charged at Watcher, its axe held high over its head. Watcher rolled to the left and hacked at the zombie's legs. Flashing red with damage, the monster wailed, then attacked again without even slowing, but Blaster emerged from the shadows, his dual, curved knives slashing through the air with steely purpose.

With one last crazed scream of fury, the vindicator disappeared, leaving an emerald and three glowing balls of XP on the carpeted floor.

"Is everyone okay?" Watcher asked.

His companions nodded.

"Search the room—they must be protecting something in this mansion."

The villagers spread out, knocking over chairs and tables, even tearing up the carpeting. They found nothing.

"Let's go to the next room." Blaster put away his knives, then wiped his brow. "There's nothing here."

The next room was just like the last; a dining room with tables and chairs, but this one had no monsters. It, too, was empty.

Suddenly, the floor beneath them shook and footsteps reverberated down the hallway. Watcher quickly had all the villagers file into the room, then move against the walls. He stood on one side of the doorway, Blaster on the other, while Er-Lan extinguished all of the torches. Then, somehow, Watcher was able to still the magical enchantment in Needle. The iridescent glow normally wrapped around the blade grew dim, as did the glow from his hands. The darkness grew deep, hiding the villagers from whatever approached.

The footsteps grew closer, the floor shaking with the pounding of boots.

"Get ready," Watcher whispered. He couldn't see the other villagers, but he knew there must be expressions of fear painted across their square faces.

The footsteps were right outside the room, but suddenly they stopped. Slowly, a hulking, shadowy shape entered the room, holding something that resembled a shaft of ice.

"Any monster in here better get out of the way," a deep voice boomed.

It was Cutter.

The villagers in the darkness laughed as Er-Lan pulled out a torch and placed it on the ground.

"Oh, there you are," the big NPC said. "What are you all doing in the dark?"

"Apparently, hiding from you," Watcher said, grinning.

"That doesn't seem very smart." Cutter laughed. "Did you find what you were looking for yet?"

Watcher shook his head. "There's one more room at the end of this hallway. That must be the room we need."

"I saw it; follow me." Planter held her axe high in the air, then ran into the corridor, heading for the last room.

Watcher followed her along the red carpet running down the center of the passage. The last room had an entrance larger than any of the others, with a complicated pattern of blocks and slabs around the doorway making it look like a wide arch. The room smelled stale and rotten, as if something ancient were decaying on the dust-covered floor.

"Don't go in," Er-Lan whispered, the zombie's face pale almost devoid of color. The creature was so scared, he almost couldn't stand.

"Is the evoker in there?" Watcher asked in a hushed voice.

The zombie nodded. "Walk away."

"I can't. There's something in there I must see." He put a hand on his friend's shoulder. "I need your help. Can you help me?"

Er-Lan moved his head up and down almost imperceptibly, then sighed, an expression of resignation on his scarred face.

"Everyone ready?" Watcher cast his gaze across the faces of the villagers huddled together in the hallway.

Just then, a terrible, low-pitched sound came from the dark room. It was something between a moan and a growl; it sounded angry beyond reason, as if the beast within had lost every bit of its sanity, and only evil and rage remained. A shiver of fear slithered down Watcher's spine. His heart pumped faster, his breaths shallow and raspy. That monster's growl nearly drove the last bit of courage from him, making him want to run and hide. But a distant voice in the back of his mind whispered something faint and ancient: *Someone must stand against the storm.* Watcher knew that person had to be him. The iridescent glow from his hands grew brighter, then slowly crept up to his elbows and pulsed with life, the power filling his mind from some other place . . . or maybe it was some other *time?*

Gripping Needle firmly, Watcher forced the magic deep into his soul, causing his sword and arms to grow dark, until only the faintest wisp of lavender hugged his skin. Stepping toward the entrance, Watcher turned and glanced at his companions.

"Here we go."

Then he ran into the dark room to face the ancient terror waiting for its next victim.

CHAPTER 26

"Er-Lan, place a torch on the ground," Watcher said. The zombie shuffled into the darkness, unable to function due to fear. Blaster took the torches from the monster's shaking hands and started putting them on the ground. The light revealed a large room with a huge square table at the center and chairs lining its edges. Across the table was a gigantic, pixelated map of the Far Lands. One wall was completely covered with book cases, their shelves filled with ancient books.

The growling moan sounded again, this time from the back of the chamber.

Watcher glanced urgently at Blaster. "More torches."

The boy nodded, then ran through the room, placing torches on the floor. Leaping across the wide table, he placed some high up on the opposite walls, then sprinted back for the entrance.

On the far end of the room, standing in a corner, was another of the gray-skinned villager-zombies. This one wore a long brown smock with a wide gold stripe running down the center. He had his arms tucked into his sleeves, as if hiding something. This creature wasn't like the vindicators they'd just faced. There was a sense of power about it, power that was old and mysterious.

Watcher put away his weapon and lowered his shield. He slowly raised his hands to announce that he was unarmed. At that moment, his arms started glowing again, giving off the iridescent purple glow as magical power seeped from his soul.

The evoker's eyes shifted to Watcher's arms, then grew wide with surprise.

"WIZARD!" the monster shrieked.

Raising his arms over his head, the zombie-villager growled some kind of incantation, the words unintelligible. Gray spirals of mystical power poured out of the monster's brown sleeves. Watcher could feel the buildup of magic in the room, the energy from the evoker stabbing at his mind.

"Evoker . . . evoker," Er-Lan moaned in terror.

Suddenly, tiny demons appeared in the air, each colored the same as the zombie-villager: a colorless gray, but with stains of crimson across their bodies, as if they were splashed with . . . Watcher didn't want to think about it.

The small demons floated up into the air on pointed wings, each with a sword in their miniature hands. They laughed evil, maniacal laughs as they streaked toward Watcher. His blood froze as the wicked creatures descended upon the villagers, screeching in terrifying glee.

"Vexes," Er-Lan moaned. "The evoker summoned vexes." The zombie sounded terrified.

"Everyone, scatter!" Watcher called as he drew his blade and shield, then charged at the nearest monster.

The dreadful shrieks from the vexes chilled Watcher's blood, echoing off the bare wooden walls and reflecting back to him from all sides—it was the worst thing he'd ever heard.

Swinging with all his strength, Watcher attacked the vex, but it was so small and fast that it easily evaded Needle's path. Then, a blade sliced into Watcher's shoulder. He grunted in pain, and spun around to attack the monster, but the vex who had cut him laughed, then flew away higher into the air, out of reach.

The flying demons swooped down upon the NPCs, slashing at them with their tiny swords, stabbing at exposed backs. Villages shouted out in pain and fear, their voices barely audible over the frightening shrieks of the winged monsters. He could hear bodies hitting the ground as the HP of his friends and comrades was consumed, and Watcher had had just about enough of that.

Rage exploded within him. "No more . . . NO MORE!"

Putting away his sword and shield, Watcher pulled out his enchanted bow and fired at the creature. His arrow struck it, causing the monster to flash red. It screeched in pain, then swooped down, causing the boy to dive to the ground. As it passed by, Watcher stood and fired at its back, his pointed shafts striking the creature's wings. Others were already following Watcher's lead and using their bows on the vexes, but the evoker was summoning more and more of the creatures into existence. They flitted about the map room, dive-bombing the villagers and driving them back into the hallway.

With a hideous laugh, the evoker strutted toward Watcher as the rest of the NPCs retreated.

I must destroy that monster before he summons more of the vexes, Watcher thought.

Just as he was about to charge toward it, the zombie-villager raised his hand over his head again, but this time, instead of summoning more of the flying demons, a deep, horn-like sound resonated off the walls. A line of metallic jaws, like the snouts of carnivorous animals, burst upward out of the floor and tried to devour Watcher. One of them caught his leg and bit down, causing pain to envelop his senses. He struggled for freedom, but the iron teeth held him firmly for just an instant, then released and descended back into the floor.

Watcher quickly dashed out of the room, the evoker in pursuit. When he reached the hallway, Watcher had an idea. Pulling out blocks of stone, he put two of the cubes under his feet so he stood high in the air.

"Everyone, get on top of two blocks of stone or wood!" he shouted to the others.

With his bow, he fired at the vexes as they dive bombed him, but stayed on his tower of stone; he hoped the metallic jaws couldn't reach him at this height. When the evoker stepped out of the map room, Watcher turned his bow toward the zombie-villager. Notching three arrows, one of them a fire arrow, he pulled back the bowstring, then released. The shafts hit the monster, setting him ablaze. Shouting in rage, the magical creature raised his hands, summoning the fanged attack again, but this time, the shining teeth snapped at stone; they could not reach high enough. The metallic teeth harmlessly brushed the soles of Watcher's boots, but that was all.

"Everyone, shoot the evoker!" Watcher shouted.

A dozen arrows fell upon the evoker, stabbing at the monster's HP. The creature screamed in pain, summoning the fanged attack again, but those closest stood on blocks of stone, too high for the metallic jaws to reach. Watcher drew and fired faster than he thought possible, his body moving without thought, instinct ruling his arms. Finally, his arrows took the last of the evoker's HP from his magical body. Giving off one last shout of animalistic rage, the magical creature fell to the side and disappeared, dropping something that looked like a small doll.

Watcher jumped down and grabbed the idol, then turned his bow upon the flying demons. Their shrieks of anger and pain filled the passage as arrows flew through the air, tearing into the tiny monsters' health. But without the evoker adding to their numbers, the little vexes quickly fell to the villagers' pointed shafts.

A cheer rang out within the halls of the mansion. The NPCs celebrated their victory, but Watcher remained quiet. He saw the piles of items left behind by the fallen; the battle had cost many lives.

"I hope this was worth the sacrifice," Cutter said sadly as he scooped up some of the items on the ground.

Planter put a hand on Watcher's shoulder, reassuring him after Cutter's harsh words, but he knew the big NPC was right. Watcher had no idea why this was so important; it was just something the Flail of Regret had projected into his mind, and he could feel the importance . . . but what if he was wrong?

Reaching into his inventory, he pulled out the doll dropped by the evoker. It was a small figurine made of woven gold cloth, the inside stuffed with something soft, probably wool. It had piercing green eyes that seemed alive somehow; Watcher could almost feel them staring at him. He stuffed the little totem back into his inventory, grateful to be away from its lifelike stare. He didn't know what it was or what it was for, but if the evoker had the tiny object in its inventory, it must have been important.

With a sigh, he looked out around the map room, hoping to find whatever it was the flail had sent him here to find.

I hope something's here, or I've caused all these deaths for nothing. A feeling of dread filled his mind as he walked back into the room and searched.

CHAPTER 27

"**O**kay, what are we searching for?" Cutter asked, looking around the room.

Watcher shrugged. "I'm not sure."

"You're not sure?" Cutter stomped across the room and stood right in front of the boy. "We just fought a battle against a warlock and—"

"Not a warlock, just one of their weapons," Er-Lan said.

"Whatever!" The big warrior glared at the zombie, then brought his gaze back to Watcher. "Well? Show us what was so important."

Moving about the room, Watcher ran his fingers over the backs of chairs that sat around the large table dominating the room. The villagers spread out, searching the room, looking for hidden doors and chests under carpets, but they found nothing.

With the monsters destroyed, the NPCs spread out through the entire structure, doing a more complete search of the mansion. They worked all through the night, looking for some undefined hidden treasure, but found nothing. Finally, in frustration, they all congregated back in the map room.

Mapper peered over the table with Cleric at his side,

the gigantic map on its surface showing the Far Lands in spectacular detail. There was a faint shimmer to the map, as if it were enchanted.

The two old men debated where they were on the map, pointing out known landmarks.

Mapper moved his face closer to the map, then shouted. "I found it!" He stood up straight and smiled. "The Jeweled Mountain! I found it on this map. We can head straight for it—if that's still the plan."

"It is," Watcher said before anyone could speak. "We still need to get a golden apple for Fencer. Without it, she'll likely perish. And we must stop Krael's plan, whatever that is."

"Then let's get going." Blaster removed his iron armor and put on his favorite black leather, allowing him to merge with the dark forest hugging the mansion outside. "There's nothing here."

Through the huge windows, the rising sun was painting the horizon with rich colors, brightening the room and bathing the dark wooden walls with a warm crimson hue.

"No, we can't leave yet." Watcher shook his head. "There's something else here, something the magical enchantment in the Flail wanted me to see."

"You talk as if it's alive," Planter said.

"That's exactly how it felt: as if there were a living presence within that weapon." Watcher walked along the outer edge of the room, running his fingers across the walls, wiping centuries of dust from the surfaces and leaving behind clear streaks.

"Why do you think the windows on the wall are not centered?" Winger asked.

"What?" Watcher was lost in thought.

"I said, why do you think they put the windows into the wall without centering them?" She pointed to the two huge windows that stared out upon the forest. "They could have moved the window on the right over two spaces . . . then it would have been centered with the other one. But it looks shifted to the side."

"Or maybe the wall was shifted," Blaster said with a mischievous smile.

"What are you talking about?" Watcher asked.

But Blaster was already moving toward the bookcase, an iron axe in his hands.

"No . . . not the books!" Mapper shouted in horror, but it was too late.

Blaster tore into the bookcase, carving through the books and shelves in seconds. "Well, well, look what we have here."

The boy put away his axe and gave Watcher a smile. "Seems the bookshelves were a false wall. There's more space behind it, and something else."

"What?"

Blaster smiled, then pulled out a torch and disappeared behind the wooden shelves.

Watcher followed him, holding a torch as well. Behind the bookcases was a narrow room only three blocks deep. A gigantic painting covered the wall, with meticulous figures drawn here and there.

"We need to see the whole thing." Watcher placed his torch on the ground, then pulled out his own axe. "Sorry, Mapper!" he shouted, then glanced at Blaster.

The dark-haired boy smiled again, then pulled out his axe as well. The two friends went to work on the bookcase, tearing down the structure quickly.

"Look at this." Blaster finished taking out a section of the bookcase, revealing a chest hidden underneath. He flipped the lid open, the hinges screeching from centuries of neglect. "My, oh my." The boy glanced at Watcher and smiled.

"What is it?" he asked.

"Something I think you need." Blaster reached into the chest and pulled out a set of diamond armor. He tossed the pieces to Watcher. "Put them on. A commander should be properly clothed."

Staring at the armor in his hands, Watcher smiled. He removed his enchanted iron armor and donned the diamond plating. Instantly, the crystalline items hugged his skin as if bonding with him. Watcher ran his hand across the surface of the armor and found spots where it was cracked and gouged. This armor was battle-seasoned . . . all the better.

"Now that's more like it." Blaster gave his friend a grin, then finished removing the bookcases.

When they'd brought the rest of the shelves down, Watcher stepped out of the cloud of dust and torn pages, then placed another torch on the ground. The diamond armor reflected the torchlight, making the Watcher that emerged glow as if ablaze himself.

"Look! It was my birthday, and Watcher gets a set of diamond armor." Winger laughed.

"It could be worse," Cleric said. "We could still be captives of the zombie warlord, like we were a couple of months ago."

"I suppose that's true." Winger smiled at her father.

Many of the villagers stared in awe at Watcher and his new armor, but the young boy ignored their stares. Instead, he scanned the crowd of faces until he found Planter. Her eyes were wide with surprise, a beautiful smile on her square face. It made Watcher's heart race.

Pulling his attention away from her, he placed more torches on the ground, then backed away from the wall.

"This is a fantastic painting," Cleric said. "Look at the detail. How could someone ever come up with this? The artist had quite an imagination."

"This is what we fought for . . . a painting?" Cutter said, his voice sounding irritated.

"No, it's not a painting; it's more." Watcher stared at the pictures with amazement.

"What do you mean, son?" his father asked.

"This is not just a painting, it's a mural showing the history of the Great War. Look, over here is the start of the war. You can see villagers and monsters battling. But then over here you can see the wither army entering the battle."

"It seems like the wizards did something to get the withers into a huge cave," Planter said, pointing.

"The Cave of Slumber," Mapper said. "I read about that in an ancient book."

"That's what the wither king was trying to do with the zombie warlord," Watcher said. "He was trying to awaken the withers in the Cave of Slumber by getting a huge pile of gold together."

"But I don't understand the next part of the painting." Planter moved to the right side of the mural and pointed to a group of villagers. "These characters, they look like . . ."

"Us," Watcher said, amazed.

He stepped forward and placed his rectangular hand on the tiny image of himself painted on the wall. A purple spark leapt from his hand to the map, a loud snapping sound filling the air.

At that moment, the mural sparkled with an iridescent lavender glow, then slowly changed, revealing a new image. Krael, the King of the Withers, wearing his Crown of Skulls, was shown amongst spiders and witches. The wither moved across the painting as if it were animated, vials of some kind of potion floating next to him as the black, three-headed creature entered the Cave of Slumber and splashed the potions across the imprisoned monsters. The withers then poured out of the cave and covered the map with their dark bodies until the entire mural was as black as midnight, the dark eyes of the wither king still staring out at them from the center. Watcher backed away from the painting as if afraid the wither might reach out for him.

Why do we fail? Farmer's voice said in his mind.

Watcher thought about the riddle. He knew it was important, somehow, but the answer still eluded him.

"I think we found what we came for," Cleric said.

"You think?" Cutter added, uncertain.

Their voices brought Watcher out of his deep thoughts and back to the moment.

"This is the wither's plan." Watcher turned and faced the other villagers. "The king of the withers is using the witches to brew potions that will awaken the other monsters in the wither army. If they are successful, they'll blanket the Far Lands with death and destruction."

"That doesn't sound very pleasant," Blaster said. "And remember the poisonous spiders. The witches are probably also being forced to make poison for the giant spiders, making them even deadlier."

Saddler, Watcher thought, closing his eyes. The image of the old woman's face in that moment when the spider's poison took the last of her HP still haunted him. *Help my daughter . . . you must help her,* the image spoke again to him in his mind. *I will. I promise, Saddler, I'll help your daughter.*

He couldn't bear the thought of more villagers suffering the same fate as Saddler, but what choice did they have? Watcher had to stand against the storm, or they'd all be swept away. If they didn't stop these monsters now, then everything would be lost.

He opened his eyes. "This is why we're here, to stop the spiders and the withers."

"You want to take on an entire army of withers?" Cutter asked.

"If not us, then who?" Watcher replied, looking the big warrior in the eye.

"But if the witches have given their poison to the new spider hatchlings, there might be *hundreds* of poisonous monsters waiting for us," Cleric said. "We don't have enough forces to defeat them."

"If not us, then who?" Watcher said again, turning to face his father.

"And if that wither king is there with the spiders, then we'll have enemies on the ground and in the air," Blaster said. "How are we gonna defend against that?"

"If not us, then who?" Watcher cast his gaze across the faces of the villagers.

"Me," an uncertain voice said from the doorway.

Everyone turned to find Er-Lan standing there, a sword in his green hand. He pulled out an iron chest plate and lowered it over his head, then banged on the armor with the hilt of the sword.

Crash!

"Er-Lan will do this, that's who," the zombie growled. "The Great War cannot happen again. The horrors of that conflict are well-known to the zombies. Er-Lan will not allow those atrocities to be relived. The withers and spiders must be stopped. As always, Er-Lan stands with Watcher."

He banged his sword against the metallic skin again, the sound echoing off the walls of the forest mansion.

Crash! . . . Crash!

"I stand with Watcher," Planter said as she pounded the hilt of her axe against her chainmail, the armor jingling like a set of wind chimes.

Crash!

"And I," his sister said, pounding her bow against her chest.

Crash!

"And I . . ."

CRASH!

"I stand with Watcher . . ."

CRASH!

"I'm there with you . . ."

CRASH! . . . CRASH! . . . CRASH!

The shouts of support filled the chamber as villager after villager slammed their weapons to their chests. With each voice and each *crash* of weapon against armor, Watcher's fears of failing receded into the recesses of his mind. A purple glow seemed to spread around him. Looking down, Watcher realized he'd pulled the Flail of Regret from his inventory without realizing it.

Was this what you wanted me to see . . . this mural of the past, and the future? The weapon was silent, but somehow, Watcher could sense that the presence that lived within the weapon was smiling.

He brought his eyes to Planter, then smiled. "Let's go bust up some spiders."

She nodded. "Absolutely."

CHAPTER 28

Shakkar stepped into the huge cavern that served as her personal chamber under the Jeweled Mountain. This was the ancient home of the spider warlock Shakahri the Deadly, and the spider warlord could somehow feel the great spider's presence in this hallowed hall. Late at night, when the lair was quiet, she'd close her eyes and imagine what it had been like when the powerful spider warlock had walked these ancient passages.

A spider suddenly ran into her chamber, the creature's mandibles clicking together nervously and a concerned expression on her dark face.

"What isss it?" Shakaar snapped.

"We received word from the ssspidersss in the roofed foressst." The creature lowered her eight eyes to the stone floor and waited for her spider warlord to approach.

Shakaar moved silently across the ancient cavern, then reached out and lifted the monster's chin so they were looking eye to eye.

"Ssspeak."

The spider took a breath, then reported her news. "The villagersss went into the ancient woodland mansssion in the middle of the foressst. There was great fighting. The zombiesss and ssskeletonsss that had been sssta-tioned there fought valiantly, but were defeated."

"If they fought valiantly, then they would have won." Shakaar was angry.

The smaller sister took a step back, afraid of being punished for bringing the spider warlord bad news.

"Be calm, sssissster." The warlord put a reassuring claw on her head and stroked her short, stubbly hair. "Tell me the ressst."

"There were also ancient warlock weaponsss in the mansssion. The villagersss defeated them."

"They defeated them?" The spider nodded. "The boy-wizard must have usssed sssome kind of powerful enchantment on them." Shakaar paced back and forth across the chamber floor, lost in thought. "Thisss wizard isss becoming a problem and mussst be dessstroyed. Follow me."

Shakaar moved out of her chamber and through the maze of tunnels that wove their way through the huge mountain. At some places, piles of gravel and sand spilled into the passage where the occasional cave-in had caused the spiders to divert the passage by digging around the obstruction. The smaller spider glanced at the gravel, then eyed the ceiling of the passage with suspicion.

"Do not fear, sssissster, the tunnel isss sssafe," Shakaar said.

"The cave-insss make me nervousss." The sister clicked her mandibles together nervously as they scur-ried past the obstruction. "Why would the great sssspi-der warlock build her lair here, under thisss mountain of gravel and sssand?"

"I'm sssure Ssshakahri had her reasssonsss," Shakaar said. "When they cassst the enchantment to change the mountain to ore, I believe sssomething hap-pened, causssing the magic to only change a portion of the mountain, leaving much of it in itsss original form . . . sssand and gravel."

"If our great warlock'sss enchantment had worked, and thisss mountain wasss made of ore, it would have made for an excellent ssstronghold."

"I agree, sssissster." Shakaar nodded. "But we cannot know what happened back in the Great War that causssed thisss failure."

They continued through the passages in silence. When the two monsters reached the hatchery, Shakaar glanced into the chamber. The smaller cave spiders moved quickly, checking each egg with care. She stopped at the entrance for just a moment.

"Grow ssstrong, my little hatchlingsss." Shakaar clicked her mandibles together once, as if adding an exclamation point to her comment. "You will be needed in the war that approachesss, and the new poissson the witchesss are brewing will make you unbeatable."

"Warlord, I do not mean to bother, but I have a quessstion," the smaller spider said.

"Ssspeak."

"Why do only half the witchesss make potionsss for usss? The othersss are making sssome other kind of potion."

"That isss true." The spider warlord nodded. "The other witchesss make potionsss for the wither king . . . it isss related to the wither army that sssleepsss in the Cave of Ssslumber."

"Krael wantsss the potionsss to awaken the other withersss?"

Shakaar nodded again. "I believe that isss true."

"But doesss the wither even *know* where the Cave of Ssslumber isss located?"

The spider warlord shrugged. "I don't know and don't care. If the witchesss deliver our poissson, then they can do whatever they want for the withersss—it isss of no concern to me."

"But if the wither army isss awakened, will they not eventually attack usss?"

"They wouldn't dare. Krael and I have an agreement, and he will keep hisss end of the agreement or he will be dessstroyed."

Shakaar turned from the Hatching Chamber and continued on through the tunnel. Finally, they reached a huge chamber, the largest in the lair: the Gathering Chamber.

"Bring all the sssisssters here; we have a trap to lay for the boy-wizard and hisss friendsss." The warlord grinned. "When thossse pathetic NPCsss come into my lair, they will have a sssuprissse waiting for them . . . and it will be the lassst sssuprissse they ever sssee."

CHAPTER 29

They rode in silence with expressions of grim determination on their square faces. Watcher rode at the front of the army, his mount from the Horse Lord's castle galloping with seemingly unlimited strength and endurance.

They left the roofed forest in the early morning after searching the third floor of the mansion; a secret room had been found, but no artifacts were discovered. They passed into a frozen river biome when the sun was at its peak, the bright rays heating the dark forest but doing little to warm this frozen terrain.

The chilly biome was a big change compared to the dark forest with its green roof. They were surrounded by white and blue, the snow-covered land stretching out in all directions as a frozen river wove a meandering path through the landscape.

Watcher was shocked by the drop in temperature. His breath now billowed out in clouds of white, as did that of the horses. His diamond armor had been too warm in the forest, but was now not warm enough.

"Are you sure you know where we're going?" Watcher shouted to Mapper.

The old man smiled, then veered to the left so he was right next to the boy, their horses galloping in lockstep.

"That map in the forest mansion showed the entire area." Mapper glanced down at Watcher's forearms; they still gave off the iridescent purple glow of magical power. He looked up into the boy's blue eyes. "The strange thing was, when we entered the room, I thought the map showed a different part of the Far Lands, but when you laid your hand on it, the map seemed to change, giving a view of the Far Lands that you needed."

"You think the map was enchanted?"

The old man glanced at Watcher's hands, then shrugged. "Maybe it wasn't the map, maybe it was . . ." He didn't finish the sentence.

"Maybe it was me. . . . That's what you mean?"

Mapper just shrugged again. "There is much in the Far Lands that I do not understand."

Suddenly, the moans of zombies filled the air. Watcher slowed his horse and drew his sword and shield. A company of the green monsters flowed out of a dark hole nearby, some with weapons and armor, some armed with just their razor-sharp claws.

"Attack them as we pass," Watcher shouted. "We don't slow down!"

Kicking his horse into a gallop again, he charged at the monsters, his shield knocking aside zombies on the left while Needle cleaved a path of destruction on the right. The other NPCs, following his example, slashed at the creatures as they passed, slaying some, but just wounding many.

The zombies growled in confusion as the villagers left them behind, refusing to engage them in battle for long. Many of the NPCs wanted to slow down and fire at them with their bows, but Watcher urged them forward.

"Our enemies lie ahead in their underground caves. Those zombies are but a distraction."

Some of the villagers complained.

"You heard Watcher," Winger snapped. "Ignore the zombies and ride."

The warriors sighed with disappointment, but still turned their mounts and followed Watcher. Planter moved forward and rode at Watcher's side. Her long blond hair bounced across her back like a golden waterfall; it was mesmerizing. She said something, but he didn't hear.

Watcher snapped out of it and glanced at her. "What?"

She laughed. "I said, why do you think the zombies were out here? It was as if they were waiting for us."

"Zombies must have leaders." Er-Lan rode next to Planter. "Without leaders, zombies will take orders from any monster strong enough to give them."

"I suspect the spider warlord is doing exactly that . . . giving them orders. As Er-Lan said, without the zombie warlord, the zombies are leaderless and likely easily manipulated." He scanned the terrain, looking for more threats. "Next will be the skeletons."

"You think?"

He nodded, then turned in his saddle and glanced behind him. The warriors rode in no formation to speak of; he needed to remedy that. "Swordsmen to the outside of the formation with shields drawn, and archers right behind them! Be ready for a skeleton attack."

"Why do you think it will be skeletons next?" Planter asked.

"Those bony creatures are also leaderless. The spider warlord will pressure the other monsters to assist her." Watcher paused to scan their icy surroundings. "She's likely sending these monsters out after us, trying to reduce our numbers and slow us down. We aren't gonna accommodate her. Speed is our weapon now." He held his own shield high over his head. "Faster . . . we must ride faster!"

Just then, an arrow whizzed by his shoulder. Lowering the shield for protection, he scanned the terrain again. Something was in the snow up ahead, but it was difficult to see . . . and then he realized what it was. Skeletons—a lot of them—stood in ranks, barring their path.

"I have an idea," Blaster said. "Stop here; you're far from the monsters, and it'll be difficult for them to hit anything at this range." The boy smiled. "Wait for my signal."

"What'll your signal be?"

Blaster just grinned. "You'll know it when you hear it."

Watcher nodded. "Everyone stop and dismount. Keep your shields up."

An arrow streaked overhead, landing in the snow far behind the group.

Blaster grabbed another soldier and both jumped onto the back of his white horse. As they galloped away, Blaster changed into white leather armor, then handed a similar set to the soldier with him.

"What's he doing now?" Cutter asked, annoyed, staring at them ride off.

"I don't know." Watcher moved to the left, then extended his shield, stopping an arrow that might have hit the big NPC in his inattention. "He said wait for his signal and—"

"Look!" someone shouted.

The white horse galloped toward the side of the skeleton formation, going just behind the monsters' ranks.

"Everyone, make some noise so the skeletons look toward us," Watcher said.

The villagers shouted and banged their weapons against their shields and armor, making as much noise as possible. The skeletons stared at their enemy, unsure what was happening.

Blaster and his cohort dashed behind the bony creatures. The young boy pulled out a block of TNT, then his companion lit it with flint and steel. As soon as it started to blink, they dropped it, then pulled out another explosive cube. Dashing right behind the skeletons, they dropped block after block, not slowing to see what would happen.

The first one exploded right behind the monsters, tearing a huge hole in the terrain. The skeletons, confused as to what was happening, stared at the fireball that enveloped their fellow monsters, still unaware of the rest of the explosives blinking right behind them. One block after the next came to life, bursting into existence and crushing the skeletons in their explosive grasp. The monsters yelled and screamed in surprise and terror. Those that survived the blasts scrambled away from the newly hewn craters, and those that did not were just piles of bones.

The villagers cheered as Blaster steered their alabaster-hued mare back toward the army.

"That was fun," Blaster said when he drew near.

"You could have told us what you were doing," Watcher complained.

"And ruin the surprise? I don't think so."

Watcher smiled, then turned to the rest of the army. "Everyone mount up." He glanced up at the sun. "We'll be at the lair of the spider warlord by dusk, so let's get moving."

The NPCs cheered, then mounted and followed their leader toward the Jeweled Mountain and a battle that would likely claim many lives on both sides.

CHAPTER 30

The Jeweled Mountain rose high into the air, dominating the skyline even before they were even out of the frozen river biome. Watcher knew the mountain was made up of blocks of diamond ore, emerald, redstone, coal, iron, and more, but he hadn't expected what he saw before him now. The mountain glittered as sunlight reflected off the ore, making it appear to sparkle, reflecting icy blues, greens, reds and silvers in all directions. It gave the huge peak a colorful look, as if some titanic god had sprinkled pieces of a rainbow onto its rocky slopes. It was breathtaking.

"That's about the most beautiful thing I've ever seen." Planter's voice was filled with awe.

Watcher glanced at her; the smile on her face was wonderful. "It's a spectacular sight." He wasn't really sure what he was referring to.

"You know, Watcher, that mountain sort of reminds me of you." Planter gave him a soft, peaceful sort of look, her voice only meant for his ears.

"What do you mean?" Watcher was confused. *Why is she looking at me like that?*

"Well, from a distance, that mountain is just there, but when you get up close, you see all the incredible details, like I see in you."

Now Watcher was really confused. *Is she saying she's interested in—*

"How big is that thing?" Blaster's voice cut through his thoughts. "It must be three hundred blocks high, if not more."

"Actually, there's a limit to how high things can be in Minecraft," Mapper chimed in. "Some say when you reach the top, it's like there's an invisible ceiling that stops you from placing any more blocks. Books I've read call it the maximum build height."

"That's ridiculous." Planter laughed. "How can there be an invisible ceiling?"

"I don't think the build height is our problem right now," Cutter said, annoyed. "We need to figure out how to get in there." He pointed at the huge mountain.

"I know how to get in." Watcher slowed his mount, then stopped and pulled out an apple. He tossed it to Planter, then grabbed a loaf of bread and ate it. "Everyone eat something. I doubt we'll have the opportunity once we go inside the mountain."

The other villagers took out pieces of beef and cooked chicken, sharing with those that had nothing.

"There's an entrance on the southern face. A large cluster of bushes hides the entrance, but we can climb over the top of the shrubs and get into the spiders' lair." He glanced at the faces of the villagers and could see the fear in their eyes.

"You have any plan on what we do when we get in there?" Cutter asked. "Or are we just going in blind? After all," the big NPC said as he glanced at Planter, "we have people to protect."

"I know . . . I'm working on it." Watcher gave the big NPC a scowl.

That didn't lessen anyone's fears. He saw Cutter's look toward Planter, and that didn't ease any of his other worries . . . but he had to put that aside. Glancing up at the sun, Watcher checked the time of day. It was just passing its apex, the bright, glowing square now heading down toward the western horizon.

"We need to find the entrance before it gets dark. Once the sun sets, we'll never find it." Watcher urged his horse into a gallop and charged toward the mountain, the rest of the villagers following close behind.

They raced the sun as they rode to the edge of the frozen landscape, finally entering an extreme hills biome, the Jeweled Mountain looming bigger and bigger before them all the while.

A wide stone plain stretched between them and the sparkling mound, the gray of the landscape making it appear as if all color had been sucked out of the land. The only thing lending any color to the pale landscape was the sparkling mountain. As they drew closer, the glittering mountain of light seemed to change. The individual blocks of ore making up the peak became visible, giving the landmark a speckled look, as if the Jeweled Mountain were covered with a million colored dots; black-spotted coal ore, red-spotted redstone, blue-spotted diamond ore, and many others covered the mountain top. A faint shimmer of magical energy wrapped around every cube of ore; the enchantments likely protecting the blocks from being mined.

Moving around the flat stone base, Watcher headed for the southern side of the mountain. Waterfalls careened down the slopes at places, at times merging with flows of lava, the hot and cold liquids forming layers of obsidian and cobblestone. Ash from the lava mixed with steam from the cooling stone, creating a grayish haze in the air. It made distant things more difficult to see, but that also meant the villagers would be harder to spot by nearby monsters as well.

Finally, they reached the southernmost side just as the sun started kissing the western horizon. A deep crimson glow spread across the landscape as the sun put on a show of spectacular colors and hues.

"I see some bushes over there." Planter pointed with her sparkling axe.

Watcher rode toward the foliage, then dismounted. He patted his horse on the neck, then scratched one ear. The animal nuzzled against him, then turned away and scanned the terrain for some grass to munch on; there was little to be found in this rocky landscape.

"Planter, cut through some of the leaves with your axe." Watcher pointed to one of the green, leafy blocks.

Her golden axe cleaved through the blocks with ease, quickly shredding them into pieces. When the blocks disappeared, a dark tunnel, like something from a nightmare, was revealed, descending into the bowels of the mountain.

Watcher climbed over the blocks and stepped into the tunnel. There was nearly total darkness inside, almost as if something were covering his eyes. But slowly his vision adjusted, and features started to emerge. The passage was lined with more ore blocks, but these ones were not shielded by magic; apparently, only the exterior was covered by the protective enchantment.

He glanced over his shoulder. Others were following him, but slowly, and apprehensively, each with an expression of fear on their square face.

"It'll be alright," Watcher whispered. "I know what I'm doing."

Blaster moved to his side and whispered softly. "Do you *really* know what you're doing?"

Watcher shrugged. "I'll let you know when I get it figured out."

Just then, a scratchy, croaking voice emerged from the darkness. "Villagers . . . help me."

Watcher ran deeper into the tunnel toward the sound, ignoring the terrifying places where the darkness was impenetrable. He homed in on the coughs and ragged breaths until he found a witch collapsed over a block of stone, her health dangerously low.

"Are you okay?" Watcher asked as he handed her a slice of melon.

The witch took the food and gobbled it down quickly. He handed her a pumpkin pie which she devoured as well. Planter appeared at his side, a torch in her hand. The flickering light filled the tunnel, allowing Watcher to see the witch more clearly. She wore a purple smock with a dark green stripe down the middle. The strip matched the band wrapping around her black, pointed hat, a green gem mounted at the front.

"What's your name?"

"I am called Cassandra. Before I was a witch, my name was Harvester, but after the lightning strike, Harvester was no more, and Cassandra came to life."

Watcher glanced at Planter, confused.

"Witches are created when a villager is hit by lightning," the girl explained.

Watcher mouthed, "Oh" and nodded. "How did you get here?"

"Why, the spiders brought me here, of course." Cassandra stood on shaky legs and gladly accepted a loaf of bread from Planter. "They must be stopped. If my sisters' potions work, the new generation of spiders will be deadlier than any that walk the surface of Minecraft."

"What do you mean?" a worried voice said from the darkness. Cleric stepped into the torchlight.

"The spiders are forcing the witches to make a poison that can be put on the spider eggs. When the hatchlings emerge, the poison is infused into their claws."

"We've already seen some of those monsters." Saddler's face, right before her death, popped into Watcher's mind.

"Yes, those were experiments. By now the potion has been perfected and has likely been applied to all the eggs." She leaned close to Watcher and Planter. "The improved potion poisons the target, and only death can stop its effects. Milk will not stop this poison, and no antidote exists. And that's not the worse part."

"You mean there's more? . . . wonderful." Blaster's sarcastic voice drew no laughter.

"Yes, there's more." Cassandra turned and stared into Watcher's bright blue eyes. "The potion not only makes their claws deadly, but it also poisons the spiders' minds."

"What do you mean?" Watcher asked.

"The poison makes the spiders more violent than any other creature in the Far Lands. They are born with a hatred for all living things other than their own kind. The spider warlord thinks she can control them, but I don't know." A terrified expression formed on the witch's face. "There are thousands of eggs in the Hatching Chamber. If those spiders emerge from their eggs, they will cover the Far Lands with death and destruction, and I don't even think the wizards from before the Great War could stop them."

Watcher glanced at Planter, then to Cleric. Both had worried looks on their faces.

"What about the wither king?" Cleric asked.

"Ahh . . . you speak of Krael." The witch nodded. "Yes, that evil creature took many of my sisters away. He's having them make something special for him. I think he wants to stay awake, for he's asking for a potion that will keep him from falling asleep."

"It's not to keep him awake," Watcher said. "It's to awaken the others."

He thought about the mural in the map room, and how it showed the wither king throwing some kind of liquid on the other sleeping withers, allowing them to escape the Cave of Slumber.

"I have a plan," Watcher said, trying to keep his voice low, yet still be audible to all his troops. Everyone moved a step closer. "The spider warlord has done terrible things to those unhatched spiders, distorting them from innocent spider hatchlings and engineering them into vicious, heartless killers. If we allow them to hatch, who knows how much senseless destruction they'll do to the Far Lands. We can't let that happen. We're going to destroy all the eggs in that Hatching Chamber, and make sure those poisonous spiders never see the surface of the Far Lands. That will throw all the spiders into chaos. During the confusion, we'll free the other witches and destroy every potion they've made."

"This plan will likely get the spider warlord's attention," Planter said.

Watcher nodded. "On our way out, we focus our attention on the spider warlord. We'll destroy her, leaving the spiders leaderless . . . then we escape."

"Sounds easy," Blaster said with a grin.

Cutter glanced at Planter, then to Watcher. "You have it all figured out, huh?" He moved closer and whispered in Watcher's ear. "No plan survives first contact with the enemy. . . . You better be ready. Everyone will be relying on you."

Watcher glanced up into his stone-gray eyes and nodded, trying to appear confident, but he knew it wasn't working. The big warrior cast another glance at Planter, then stepped away.

A shudder of fear slithered down his spine. *I remember how many spiders I saw in this nest when I used that enchanted chainmail,* he thought. *I'm not sure if any of us are going to emerge from these caves alive. . . . But we have to try. The spiders and the wither king must be stopped.*

He glanced at Planter and feelings of grief began to bubble up from within his soul, as if she were already gone. And then a deep voice, different from his own internal thoughts, echoed from within his mind.

Don't be afraid to . . .

"What?" he said in a soft voice.

The other villagers looked at him, confused.

Don't be afraid to be . . .

"Do any of you hear that voice?" Watcher glanced hopefully at Planter, then Blaster. They both had confused expressions on their square faces.

What are you saying? Watcher sent his thoughts out into the shapeless darkness of his mind. And then the voice, deep and ancient, returned again.

Don't be afraid to be you!

And in that moment, he knew the voice was coming from the Flail of Regret; it was alive and speaking to him, as if there were a living presence trapped within that spiked ball and chain. He hoped that the voice would bring him courage, but all it did was make him more afraid of what was to come.

CHAPTER 31

The NPCs moved silently through the dark passages, hoping to avoid being noticed by the spiders. The glow from Watcher's arms cast enough purple light for him to see, but those at the back of the formation carried redstone torches, the crimson glow lighting the area around the villagers, yet dim enough that it might go undetected if spotted by the enemy.

The strange thing was, they didn't see any of the fuzzy monsters in any of the passages. The sound of clicking mandibles and curved claws scratching against the stone floor was completely absent; it was as if the spiders' lair was deserted.

Watcher held an arm across his chest, trying to keep the plates of diamond armor from banging against each other. Cutter and the others in iron armor did the same. The only sound in the stone passage was the sound of their boots scuffing the floor and the *scratch-scratch* of Er-Lan's clawed feet.

The witch, Cassandra, led them directly through the maze of dark passages as if she had the place memorized.

"How is it you know where to go?" Planter asked her in a hushed voice.

"I've been a prisoner for a long time, and tried

to escape many times." Cassandra's voice was still scratchy, but stronger with her renewed health. "My last escape attempt was just for the purpose of mapping out all the tunnels." She turned down a passage to the left, the stony corridor plunging deeper into the depths of the Jeweled Mountain. "I'd just finished memorizing the last of the tunnels when a squad of spiders saw me. I had to hide for days as they searched for me, and I didn't have enough food. I became too weak and couldn't walk; that was when you found me."

"It was a good thing we did." Planter smiled. "I don't think you would have lasted much longer."

"You're probably right. . . . Wait, look at the ground." Watcher stared down at the stone, confused. "You see all the scratches?"

The witch knelt and ran her old, wrinkled fingers across the rock. "A lot of spiders have been through this tunnel recently."

"Where does this passage lead to?" Cleric asked.

"The Gathering Chamber and the Hatching Chamber," Cassandra replied.

"So the spiders could be in one or the other," Blaster said.

"Or both." Cutter stared down at the witch, then brought his gaze to Watcher. "The longer we wait, the stronger the spiders' defenses become. We need to move . . . now."

"You're right." Watcher helped the witch back to her feet, then spoke to the rest of the NPCs. "We stick to the original plan. The Hatching Chamber is our first target, then we'll see what's in this Gathering Chamber." He glanced at Cassandra. "Which way?"

"We follow this passage, then take the tunnel that splits off to the left."

"Let's go." Watcher's voice was just a whisper. "Everyone . . . quick and quiet."

They moved through the passage like shadows in the darkness. The few redstone torches cast a faint crimson glow on portions of the army, giving them just enough light to avoid falling into any holes or stumbling into blocks of spiderweb.

"Here it is," Cassandra whispered.

She put away the redstone torch in her hand, then pointed at the other torches. They were all extinguished, plunging them into darkness. Only the faint iridescent glows of Watcher's arms, Cutter's armor, and Planter's axe offered any light.

"Here, drink this." The witch handed Watcher a bottle with some potion in it.

He couldn't tell what it was in the darkness, but he trusted her. Pulling out the cork, he drank the liquid. Instantly, purple spirals appeared before his eyes, signifying the potion was active, and his surroundings came clearly into view, the darkness of the passage now gone; it was a potion of night vision.

Watcher moved to the entrance and peered around the stone blocks.

Inside the Hatching Chamber were thousands of dark, spotted eggs, each smeared with green goo. Blue cave spiders moved about the chamber tending to the eggs, with only a handful of the larger spiders on guard. Watcher glanced up at the ceiling and walls of the chamber. Many of the blocks of ore were missing, replaced by sand and gravel.

"Do you have any more night vision potions?" Watcher asked the witch in a hushed voice.

She pulled out a single bottle from her inventory. "This is the last one."

Watcher glanced at Blaster and smiled. "Okay . . . here's my idea. You remember the skeletons in the snow?"

"Of course."

"Then here's what I want to do." Watcher explained his plan, the smile on Blaster's face growing bigger and bigger as he spoke.

CHAPTER 32

"You ready?" Watcher glanced at Blaster. They were both clearly nervous.

Blaster nodded.

Watcher turned to Winger and Planter. They, too, had anxious expressions on their square faces. "You two have enough arrows?"

"I'd like to have more," Planter said.

"We have as many as we have," Winger said. She turned to her brother. "Don't worry . . . we'll keep them busy."

"Ready?" Watcher whispered. "Now."

Blaster led the way, sprinting along the edge of the chamber, Watcher following close on his heels. The scratching of the cave spiders' claws on the stone floor filled the air, making Watcher want to turn and flee. But he knew they had to see this through.

The spiders didn't notice them, the darkness in the chamber cloaking the two boys' presence. But before they reached the back wall, the deadly monsters began to click their mandibles together in excitement. That was the signal for the girls.

Planter and Winger shot their arrows into the cave, the pointed shafts bursting into fiery life as soon as they left their bows. The fire arrows hit the ground, illuminating the chamber near the center. The flickering light let the two archers target the blocks of spiderweb wrapped around the eggs. Shooting again and again, they lit the white fibrous cubes aflame, driving the cave spiders into a panic. The spiders in the cavern turned their attention to the flames and the villagers at the cave entrance, ignoring Watcher and Blaster.

When the two boys reached the back of the Hatching Chamber, Blaster started placing blocks of TNT on the ground, Watcher then lighting them with flint and steel. They sped through the chamber, trying to get as many explosives lit as they could before they started to detonate. They had covered most of one wall and were heading to the opposite side of the cave when the first cubes exploded.

Smoke filled the air as the TNT came to life, tearing into the stone walls with their destructive energy, ripping into the ore blocks, revealing sand and gravel. The unstable cubes fell into the chamber, the avalanche crushing many of the eggs.

Not looking back, Blaster ran to the other side of the cavern, placing additional red and white cubes, Watcher lighting each one. The cavern filled with thunder as more of the explosives came to life, causing the avalanches to spread. Blaster carefully picked the right spots along the walls, hoping to do as much damage to the structure of the cavern as possible.

"We need to get out of here now," Watcher said.

"We aren't done yet."

Blaster ran straight for the cavern entrance. By now, the spiders were advancing on the villagers there. Arrows streaked through the air, striking the fuzzy creatures, but they continued their charge.

"Watcher . . . scream," Blaster called out.

"What?"

And then, instead, Blaster let out a blood curdling scream, causing the spiders to turn around. In the moment of uncertainty, Blaster put a line of TNT around the monsters, with Watcher lighting their fuses.

"Everyone, RUN!" Blaster shouted.

The villagers retreated from the Hatching Chamber and ran up the tunnel, back toward the main corridor. Watcher jumped over the spiders, following the rest of the NPCs. He glanced back into the chamber just as the rest of the explosives detonated. A huge rumble shook the very roots of the mountain as the stone blocks crumbled under the burning fist of TNT, releasing what a torrent of sand and gravel throughout the dark cavern. The spiders screeched in fear as thousands of blocks fell upon them. Billows of smoke and dust choked the tunnel, making it difficult to see the true extent of the damage.

Skidding to a stop, Watcher turned and looked back down the tunnel. He drew Needle and prepared for an attack, but none of the spiders charged. He coughed as smoke and dust filled his lungs.

"Archers . . . get ready!" Watcher commanded.

A group of villagers knelt with bows drawn and ready, another row of archers standing behind them. Still, no attack came. When the dust from the rubble finally cleared, a huge pile of gravel covered the entrance to the Hatching Chamber.

"We did it!" Watcher exclaimed.

"What?" Planter asked.

"Most of this mountain is sand and gravel. Blaster's explosives were placed perfectly. The chamber is sealed off forever."

"You think any of the spider eggs survived?" Winger asked.

Watcher shook his head. "Let's hope not."

Suddenly, a high-pitched shriek, filled with rage and fury, cut through the passage like a knife through flesh. Many of the villagers put their hands to their ears, trying to block out the hideous sound.

"I'm thinking that was the spider warlord." Blaster smiled sarcastically.

"I suspect she isn't very happy with us," Watcher said.

"Well, we're not happy with her either." Mapper scowled toward the sound as if trying to intimidate the monster.

The other villagers laughed.

"It's time we doled out some punishment," the old man added.

"Absolutely." Watcher slapped Mapper on the back, then ran through the passage toward the Gathering Chamber and their foe.

CHAPTER 33

Watcher followed Cassandra through the dark passage, the purple glow from his arms intensifying, growing brighter . . . but his fear was building as well. The witch slowed as the passage curved to the right and descended sharply.

"The entrance is just around this curve," she said. "It's on the left side of the passage. The Gathering Chamber will be well lit, with many pools of lava along the edges of the chamber." Cassandra moved closer to him and whispered in his ear. "There will be no place to hide with hundreds of spiders all around you; this is suicide."

"You don't need to go in with us, but we must do this. If the king of the withers gets a potion that can awaken his army, then the Far Lands as we know it will be destroyed."

A gentle hand settled onto his shoulder. Turning, he found Planter's beautiful green eyes peering into his, an expression of fear on her face. "We must save the witches and stop Krael . . . it's up to us."

Planter nodded, then gave Watcher a nervous grin.

"You have a plan?" Cutter pushed the witch out of the way and stared down at Watcher. "We can't just walk in there and ask them to stop."

"I've been thinking about that." Watcher stared into the big warrior's steely gray eyes. They were filled with such courage . . . if only he could have the smallest bit of Cutter's bravery. "You remember what happened in the mega taiga forest?"

Cutter nodded his head, but looked like he still didn't understand what Watcher was getting at.

"Everyone gather around." Watcher stood on a block of stone and peered down at the terrified NPCs. "Here's my plan. If anyone has a better idea, I'd love to hear it." In a hushed voice, Watcher explained his plan, pointing out key features necessary for the plan to be successful. He assigned tasks to group of villagers, making sure everyone understood their role.

"Are you with me?" the boy asked. "I'd do this on my own, but I don't know if I can defeat a couple hundred spiders all by myself. . . . I think my arm might get tired."

The villagers laughed, then nodded their heads.

"Then let's do it." Watcher adjusted his diamond armor, then drew Needle and his wooden shield.

Stepping into the center of the passage, he walked through the tunnel, dragging Needle along the ground. It made a scratchy, screechy sort of sound that was unnerving.

"Shhh . . . they'll hear you," Cutter said in a low voice.

"They already know we're here!" Watcher shouted. "Might as well let the cowardly spiders know we're coming!"

The villagers cheered, and then all of them dragged their weapons on the ground as well, filling the passage with the sound of steel on stone. Watcher glanced at Cutter, and the big NPC nodded, then smiled and dragged his diamond blade against the wall.

They followed the curving passage, then came to the entrance of the Gathering Chamber. It was a huge opening that led to a chamber bigger than any Watcher had ever seen. The walls were roughly shaped, as if explosives had been used to carve out the space, but the floor was perfectly flat. It seemed completely unnatural, the uniform stone stretching from wall to wall. Streams of lava either splashed out of the wall or sat in small pools, filling the chamber with an orange glow, though the impossibly high ceiling was still cloaked in darkness.

At the center of the chamber stood a solitary spider, Shakaar. The prickly fuzz that covered her body was inky black, as was her skin; she was like a shadowy hole in the universe. The monster clicked her mandibles together once, the sound echoing off the walls. Then it was completely silent in the chamber. Her eight bright red eyes glared at the villagers as they entered the colossal cave, each of the glowing orbs filled with venomous hatred.

"Boy-wizard, you dessstroyed my hatchlingsss."

Watcher remained silent. He took a step toward her, gripping Needle's hilt firmly, the glow from his arms and weapon growing brighter.

"My ssspidersss will cover the Far Landsss with grief and dessspair, and you will be the caussse."

He moved closer, keeping his blue eyes glued to her red ones.

"Do you have anything to sssay for yoursssself, boy-wizard?"

"Yeah, your spiders killed innocent villagers. You kidnapped witches and have been terrifying the Far Lands." Watcher took another step closer and slowly raised his weapon. The keen edge gave off a harsh white radiance, pushing back the shadows in the massive hall. It was as if Watcher's rage was powering the weapon from within. "Actions have consequences. That's something you need to learn . . . and I'm the one who's gonna teach you." He gave the warlord an angry glare. "Spider, school is now in session."

As if on cue, the villagers clustered at the entrance all charged into the chamber, yelling at the top of their voices, each with their swords held up high. They spread out in a long line, as if getting ready to charge, then suddenly stopped and held their position.

Watcher sprinted toward Shakaar, but as he drew near, the spider took out a bottle filled with a dark green potion. She splashed it on her body, the liquid instantly coating her claws, turning them a dark green.

"Here isss a little of our new poissson for you to tassste."

Poisonous claws . . . must be careful, Watcher thought. *The slightest scratch would be fatal.* Then he kept sprinting at his enemy, swinging Needle with all his strength.

Shakaar attacked, her claw sinking into his shield, then going all the way through. Watcher could see a dark green stain across the claw where the razor-sharp tip poked through the back of the wooden rectangle; they were completely coated with poison, which meant he had to be extra careful.

The villagers moved further into the chamber while Watcher and the spider warlord battled. Needle flashed through the air, striking at the monster's side. Shakaar brought a poisonous claw up to block. The blade clanked as it struck the monster's defense, but Watcher was ready. Rolling to the side, he slashed at the creature's legs, hitting two and causing her to flash red. She screeched in pain and stepped back, glaring at her opponent.

"You know, I only need to hit you once, and our new poissson will do the ressst. You may have dessstroyed my hatchlingsss, but we will make more poissson. Sssoon, all of my sssisssterss will be as venomousss as their warlord." She held her dark green claw in the air and pointed it at Watcher. Shakaar glanced up at the dark ceiling, then clicked her mandibles together and yelled. "NOW!"

Suddenly, the sound of a million crickets seemed to fill the cavern as hundreds of spiders clicked their pointed mandibles together.

"You villagersss think you are ssso clever. Now, witnesss your doom."

Watcher stepped away from the spider warlord and glanced up at the ceiling. Hundreds of spiders were slowly lowering themselves from the roof overhead. Their eyes blazed red with hatred as the monsters glared down at the intruders. Many of the villagers shouted in surprise and fear, some wanting to flee.

"Hold your ground," Cutter boomed. "We haven't finished what we came here to do."

Courage and strength boomed from the NPC's voice, keeping the other villagers from running away.

Shakaar laughed as she watched her sisters descend from the ceiling.

"There must be a hundred of them . . . maybe two hundred," one of the villagers said. "How do we fight that many?"

Shakaar smiled.

"What do we do?" another asked.

The spider warlord clicked her mandibles together excitedly, anticipating her victory.

Watcher just stepped back away from Shakaar and stared up at the descending monsters. He didn't see any with the dark green poisoned claws, but even still, their normal claws would be dangerous enough.

"I hope I didn't doom all of my friends," he said in a low voice, then brought his gaze up to the spider warlord again.

"You look ssscared, boy-wizard."

Watcher dropped Needle, the enchanted blade clattering to the ground, then reached into his inventory and found what he was searching for.

"I'm not a boy-wizard!" Watcher shouted. He grabbed the leather-wrapped handle firmly and pulled out the Flair of Regret, the huge enchanted weapon flooding the cavern with purple light. "I'm a wizard!"

The iridescent light from Watcher's arm blazed bright purple, causing the spider warlord to shield her eyes. Now it was Watcher who was smiling. He glanced over his shoulder, then shouted as loud as he could.

"NOW!"

And the battle for the Jeweled Mountain began.

CHAPTER 34

The villagers put away their swords and drew bows. They notched arrows, then fired up into the air, but they weren't aiming at the spiders; instead, they shot at the strands of silk from which the spiders dangled as the descended. One of the arrows sliced through a gossamer strand, and the spider attached to it screeched as she plummeted to the ground, the impact fatal.

"Keep firing!" Cutter shouted.

Arrows streaked through the air, severing more strands of spider silk. The black, fuzzy monsters fell like a dark hail, their bodies flashing red, then disappearing on impact.

"NOOOOO!" Shakaar screeched as she watched her sisters perish.

Watcher moved closer to the villagers' position and glanced at Er-Lan. "You ready?"

The zombie pulled out a splash potion and held it far from his body; it was poison to him. Regardless of the danger, Er-Lan nodded to his friend.

"Let's do this," Watcher said, an expression of grim determination on his face.

He knew what was in store for him, but it was

necessary, and might mean the difference between victory or defeat.

Sprinting through the chamber, Watcher swung the flail over his head. Pain stabbed into his body as the magical weapon used his HP to recharge. He moaned, but continued to run as, swinging the weapon high over his head, he aimed at the spiders that were still descending to the ground. The chain connected to the handle extended—a lot—allowing the spiked ball at the end to slice through the strands of web hanging from the ceiling.

A dozen spiders fell to their deaths.

The weapon tore into his HP again, but then a glass bottle broke across his back, spilling a healing potion across him, rejuvenating his health a little. Watcher could hear Er-Lan's footsteps behind him, the monster staying far enough away to avoid getting splashed.

Watcher swung the flail again, the chain stretching out so the spiked ball could reach his targets. More spiders fell to their deaths.

"My sssisssstersss . . . nooooooo!" Shakaar was in a rage. "You will pay for thisss, wizard!"

Watcher kept running with Er-Lan following three steps behind. He swung the Flail of Regret again and again, the spikes cleaving silken threads, causing more spiders to crash to the ground.

Then, images of Saddler and Farmer suddenly appeared in his mind, their terrified faces staring at him, accusing him of their deaths.

I did what I could, Watcher explained to the images. *I did my best. I can't do more.*

More images of his many catastrophes surged through his mind. He thought about his village; it had been burned to the ground by the skeleton warlord. Watcher had failed to stop those skeletons from that atrocity. *It was your fault,* the image of a fallen NPC told him. *My son died in the wither king's mines,* another face accused. He hadn't freed them from the wither king's captivity at the Capitol soon enough. The images of his countless failures hammered at him from within his mind, the Flail of Regret demanding payment, not just in HP, but also in remorse.

Pain tore through his body as he swung the flail at another group of descending spiders. Some were hitting the ground and flashing red, but not disappearing; they were surviving the fall, which was bad. Another bottle of healing splashed across his back, Er-Lan keeping him alive. Watcher swung the weapon at the spiders, the spiked ball stretching out and cleaving through what was left of the monsters' HP.

He saw the faces of Planter's parents in the deep recesses of his mind. They were fighting hand-to-hand with zombies invading their home, giving their daughter time to escape through an attic window, but suddenly, they stopped their struggle and stared straight at Watcher, their eyes pleading for his help. At the time, when the zombies had invaded his village, Watcher had been unconscious, or he'd been pretending to be, at least.

I can't help you, he pleaded with the two villagers in his imagination. *But I'm helping your daughter now . . . I won't let anything happen to her.* Which was true. He'd protected Planter and many others from the violence of the zombie warlord and the skeleton warlord. Watcher had struggled, but he'd learned from his mistakes and helped those he could.

Why do we fail? . . . Why do we fail? . . . Why do we fail? . . . The deep, mysterious voice from the Flail of Regret echoed in his brain. The fog of failures grew thicker in his mind as the images of more deceased villagers stared at him, their eyes pleading for help.

I can't help everyone, but those that I could, I did, Watcher thought.

Why do we fail? . . . Why do we fail? . . . Why do we fail? . . . The magical voice grew louder, hammering away at Watcher's sanity.

And then, somehow, he suddenly knew the answer. It emerged from the deepest recesses of his soul like some kind of universal truth. "We fail so that we can learn to overcome," Watcher shouted. "Farmer . . . I understand!" Strength seemed to surge through him as the realization of this truth filled him with courage. "I did what I could and helped as many people as possible. I could have helped more if I'd embraced who I really was, but now I know the truth." He glanced down at his glowing arms and nodded. "I understand who I am now . . . I'm a wizard!" he shouted with pride, unafraid of being different from everyone else.

Watcher skidded to a stop just as a splash potion of healing shattered against his diamond armor. He turned and faced the spider warlord, who was directing her troops in the battle unfolding in the Gathering Chamber.

"I've learned from my failures and I know who I am," he said.

"What is Watcher saying?" Er-Lan asked. "Who is being spoken to?"

"I'm a wizard, Er-Lan, and I'm not afraid anymore!" He pointed the Flail of Regret at Shakaar. It no longer tore into his HP; the magical enchantment pulsing through his body was now powering the ancient relic. It was a part of him now and could never harm him; it could never harm a wizard. "I've learned from my failures, and now it's time to overcome . . . and destroy my enemy."

He walked toward the spider warlord. "SHAKAAR . . . IT'S GO TIME!"

And then Watcher charged into a battle that would only end one way: death.

CHAPTER 35

Shakaar screeched with delight, her sharp mandibles clicking together, as her foe charged.

Swinging the flail with all his strength, Watcher struck out at his enemy. Shakaar jumped into the air just as the spiked ball streaked by, passing underneath the monster. Watcher readied for another attack, but he knew a moving target would be hard to hit. Swinging the magical weapon over his head, he stepped to the side, hoping to surprise the warlord by doing the unexpected.

It worked.

A razor-sharp claw sliced through the air where he had been standing, an acidic aroma coming from the poisonous tip. The smell made his eyes sting a little. Watcher wiped at them with his left hand, then pulled out his shield again just as the spider warlord attacked again. The claw punched through the shield, stopping just inches from Watcher's face. Shakaar tried to yank it out for another attack, but it was stuck.

Pushing forward to knock the spider off balance, Watcher swung the flail at the warlord, the spiked ball smashing into her body. She shrieked in pain, then yanked her claw out of the shield and moved back. An image of Saddler appeared in his mind, reviving all of Watcher's feeling of guilt and sorrow over her death.

While the two leaders battled, the group of villagers continued to fire at the few spiders still lowering themselves from the ceiling, while rest of the NPCs built fortifications to slow the oncoming wave of fangs and claws from the spiders who had made it safely to the floor.

Winger directed the placement of blocks, allowing gaps for the archers while placing inverted stairs on the edge of the wall to keep the spiders from climbing over the tops of their defenses. Er-Lan moved across the barricade being constructed with a group of NPCs behind him, placing blocks of cobblestone as fast as their hands would work. Other groups of villages added to the barricade on the left and right, making their fortified wall wider and wider. Swordsmen stood atop the battlements, slashing at the spiders, allowing the zombie and NPCs finish the construction.

The villagers placed blocks as fast as they could, extending the wall to form a wide arc. The spider mob crashed upon the barrier like a tidal wave meeting a rocky cliff. The spiders tried to climb up the wall, but were stopped by the cubes of dirt sticking out over the edge of the barrier. Meanwhile, archers fired through the gaps and warriors stabbed at the monsters from above. But the spiders had the numerical advantage; it wasn't clear if the NPCs could prevail.

A group of spiders attacked the left flank, trying to get behind the intruders. Cutter charged at the creatures, with Planter and Winger at his side. They tore into the spiders' ranks, each watching the others' backs. Planter's enchanted axe tore through the monsters like golden fire, tearing at their HP with its keen edge. At the same time, Wingers fire-bow launched pointed shafts at the spiders, lighting them ablaze before they could ever get near.

Watcher tore his gaze from his friends and focused his attention on the spider warlord again.

"Your friendsss will sssoon be dead," Shakaar said. "My ssspidersss will dessstroy them."

"We'll see," Watcher said. He had no intention of letting that happen.

Charging forward, Watcher swung the Flail of Regret at the warlord. The spider leapt to the side, narrowly avoiding the sharp spikes. She paused to catch her breath; it was clear she was tired as she panted heavily. Watcher was thankful for the respite as well.

Farmer's lanky image appeared in his mind. The villager seemed so happy as he rode on a horse, but suddenly, his prone body began flashing red, with a terrified expression on the dying villager's square face. Watcher couldn't do anything to help him . . . he'd failed Farmer just like he failed Saddler.

No . . . my guilt lies in not learning from those failures, Watcher said, his thoughts shouting at the images. *I won't fail my friends and I won't fail Fencer. I made a promise to Saddler and I'm going to keep it. I am Watcher, and I keep my word!*

"You won't stop us." Watcher scowled at her. "We're gonna free the witches and take the potions before the wither king can get them. But first, we're gonna destroy all your followers. History will know it was Shakaar, the worst warlord of all time, who led her spiders to destruction."

The monster shrieked in rage and charged, her eyes glowing a hateful red. Watcher brought his shield up at the same time as he swung his flail. The spiked ball hit the spider, knocking her to the side. She rolled across the ground, flashing red with damage, then screeched to a halt and leapt toward Watcher again. She crashed into the young boy, her deadly legs flailing wildly.

Suddenly, a pain like liquid fire tore into his neck. Watcher kicked the spider away, then dropped his shield and felt his neck. A long, jagged scratch extended down his neck, the wound already swelling as the poison seeped into his blood.

Shakaar laughed and moved back. "It will take more than an NPC-boy to sssurvive my venom."

"NO!" a voice shouted. Planter pushed through the spiders and ran for Watcher, but Cutter caught the back of her armor and held her back. The rest of the villagers saw Watcher stumble and screamed in rage, then climbed over their own fortifications and fell upon the spider horde, fighting with a ferocity Watcher had never before seen. The spiders tried to move back, but Winger's fire arrows were taking down those that fled.

Watcher saw all this, but knew his fight wasn't over. *OK, I'm poisoned,* he thought, *but I'm not dead . . . not yet.*

Why do we fail? . . . So we can learn and overcome. The thought resonated within his mind.

"Just because I'm poisoned . . . doesn't mean I'd already dead," Watcher whispered to himself. "If I go, then I'm taking the spider warlord with me."

He charged on unsteady legs, swinging his flail with all his strength. The spider, not expecting his attack, was caught off guard. The spiked flail slammed down, slicing through more of her HP, almost taking the last of it . . . but she still lived.

Shakaar's legs started to buckle under her, as did Watcher's. They both fell to the ground. Watcher tried to swing the flail for one more hit . . . he wanted to be the one to take the last of her HP, but his strength was waning. He collapsed to the ground, almost dead. The spider, with the slightest bit of additional health, dragged herself toward Watcher. He could see it in her eyes; Shakaar wanted to be the one to end his life.

She crawled closer, but then her strength finally failed and she just lay on the ground too.

"At leassst I get to watch you die." The spider warlord smiled bitterly.

A fiery agony blasted through his body as the venom spread through him, the poison eating away at his HP.

Watcher felt his health falter as it dropped lower and lower, until . . .

A voice suddenly filled his mind. It was a deep voice, and sounded as if it was coming from a hundred blocks away . . . or maybe from a hundred years ago. *Grab the totem . . . grab the Totem of Undying.*

Watcher was confused.

Grab the totem and use your powers.

In that last moment before his death, he remembered the tiny doll the evoker had dropped in that forest mansion. He dropped his flail and reached into his inventory. There were just a few seconds left—he had to find it before then—and then his fingers brushed against the soft item. He clasped his hands around the Totem of Undying and glanced toward Planter. Driving every drop of magical power he had into the totem, Watcher tried to smile at Planter, but he lacked the strength.

Planter and Er-Lan were pushing through the remaining spiders, trying to reach him, but Watcher knew they wouldn't make it in time.

He didn't want to die, not like this. A tear trickled down his cheek, not because of his imminent death, but because he never had the chance to tell Planter how he felt.

"If I survive somehow, I'll tell her and . . ." he started to say, but then the last of his health was devoured by the poison, and Watcher perished.

CHAPTER 36

Darkness enveloped Watcher for the briefest of instants, and then his mind was filled with the most beautiful yellow sparks he'd ever seen. They reminded him of Planter's glorious blond hair and . . . *Wait . . . I'm alive . . . I'm alive.*

The Totem of Undying was gone, but he could now feel his body. He was weak . . . unbelievably weak, but the poison was gone and he was alive.

"I'M ALIVE!"

Slowly, Watcher stood and glared down at the spider warlord.

"Imposssible!" Shakaar glared up at Watcher, a confused expression on her dark face. "The poisssson continuessss until death. How are you sssstill alive?"

"You have harmed too many people, spider. It is time for you to be punished." Watcher raised the flail and spun it over his head, ready to bring the spiked ball down upon her . . . but she was helpless. The spider's health was so low, she couldn't even stand. The monster was finished.

"No . . . I'm not gonna kill you," Watcher said. "I'll figure out an even more fitting punishment."

"Watcher . . . you're alive!" Planter rushed toward him, then wrapped her arms around his weakened body, nearly knocking him over as she enveloped him in a giant hug.

"I'm okay, just a little weak," he said.

The other villagers approached as the last of the spiders were destroyed. When they saw Watcher standing near the decrepit monster, they raised their weapons high over their heads and cheered.

"Ssso, the wizard hasss a girl," the spider hissed from the ground below.

"What?" Watcher said.

And then, with the last bit of her strength, Shakaar attacked Planter, swinging her poisoned claw at the girl's exposed leg.

Watcher moved without thought, bringing the flail's spiked ball down upon the spider with lightning speed. The monster screamed in pain and fear, then disappeared before she could harm another, her poisonous claw inches from Planter's leg. All that remained of Shakaar, the spider warlord, was a clump of spider's silk, three glowing balls of XP, and something that looked like a glass lens attached to a black strap, the object glowing with magical power.

He turned to Planter. She wrapped her arms around him, squeezing his enchanted armor in a huge hug, causing some of the diamond plates to creak and bend.

"Planter, are you okay?" Watcher checked her for scratches. "Did she touch you?"

"No . . . I'm alright." She released the hug and wiped back a tear. "I thought that spider was going to poison me . . . I was so scared."

"Don't worry, she didn't get you." He breathed a sigh of relief, then picked up the magical artifact and stuffed it into his inventory. He'd look at it more closely later.

"This is the second time this happened," Blaster said as he approached, a huge grin on his square face. "Planter, you didn't give *me* a hug when you saw *I* was okay."

"Blasterrrr." Winger hit him with her bow, silencing him with a sarcastic glare.

"Well . . . it's just that . . ."

Suddenly, a cold chill spread through the chamber. It made Watcher's flesh crawl, as if death itself had just brushed against him.

"He's here," Watcher said. "Everyone look for the wither. He's probably hiding in the darkness overhead." He glanced at Winger. "How about you bring some light to the darkness up there?" Watcher pointed to the ceiling.

Winger shot a stream of arrows from her bow, the *Flame* enchantment giving every pointed shaft a wreath of fire. They flew up to the ceiling of the Gathering Chamber and stuck into the stone roof, each casting a circle of flickering light. And then one of the fire-arrows revealed a wither hiding in the darkness.

The monster was as black as coal, his three heads glaring down at Watcher. Ribs stuck out from his stubby spine, all the bones blackened, as if he'd just emerged from a furnace.

"Krael," Watcher said.

"Wizard . . . you destroyed my spiders," the center head growled.

"That displeases us," the right wither skull said.

"It makes us mad," hissed the left.

Watcher stepped away from the other villagers as he ate a piece of beef. He could feel his health returning. But just then, he noticed there was something different about the monster. Instead of just the center head wearing the Crown of Skulls, now the left head wore one as well.

"Ahh . . . I see you've noticed my newest relic from days long past." Center laughed. "While you've been playing with my spiders, we've been searching the ancient sites for relics. And look what we found: the second Crown of Skulls. When we find the third crown, we will destroy all the Far Lands, and remake the surface as we choose."

"We'll never let you do that," Watcher shouted defiantly.

"Hahaha . . . what a fool." Left glared at him, the Crown of Skulls glowing with a subtle purple hue.

"Left, be quiet," Center commanded. The center head turned back to Watcher and scowled. "I've come for the rest of the potions the witches were brewing for me. I think I'll just fly over and get them."

All three heads smiled at Watcher as the wither floated across the high ceiling. The wither king moved to the far end of the Gathering Chamber, then descended to the ground. A chest sat on the ground, its lid tilted open. Watcher hadn't noticed it before, but that was likely where the spiders had kept all their potions.

Blaster giggled.

The wither stared down into the chest, an expression of disbelief covering his three ashen faces. Krael turned and glared at Watcher.

Now Blaster laughed. "It isn't there, is it?"

"What's happening?" Watcher whispered.

"I found the chest of potions and took them all." Blaster smiled. "They've all been dumped into the lava." He glared at the king of the withers, then shouted, "No potions for you!"

Krael howled in rage, firing a flaming skull at the villagers. Watcher brought up his shield just before the projectile hit. The explosion knocked him and many others to the ground, but the shield took the brunt of the damage, splintering into a hundred pieces.

The wither floated toward the villagers as they all pulled out their bows and readied themselves for battle. Then, suddenly, a sparkling field appeared around the shadowy monster, protecting him from their arrows as he drew closer and closer. Watcher stepped away from the other villagers, advancing on the monster. He held the Flail of Regret in his hand, his fingers gripping the handle tight.

Just then, the wither fired a barrage of flaming skulls directly at Watcher. The dark projectiles, with their wreaths of blue flames, drove a spike of fear through his soul. He was petrified, with terror taking over his mind. A shout came at him from behind, but Watcher couldn't look back; he was transfixed on the burning skulls of death descending upon him.

Suddenly, a dark rectangle appeared in front of him; Planter stood in front of the flaming skulls, her red shield with the three dark heads held out to protect them both.

"Planter, those skulls will destroy that shield. You need to . . ."

Before Watcher could finish the sentence, the wither's attack smashed into the shield. The three flaming skulls crashed into the rectangle and exploded, but at the same time, an iridescent glow spread across the barrier, deflecting the blast and saving them both.

"I'm alive . . . again!" Watcher was stunned.

"Come on, it's time to attack." Planter moved forward with the magical shield held out in front of them.

Watcher drew his bow and fired arrows at the wither, but they just bounced off its sparkling shield. Watcher smiled; he knew that would happen. At the same time, the creature slowly descended to the ground. It was something they'd learned in the battle with the last wither king, Kaza. Whenever that regeneration shield appeared, the wither was unable to fly and always descended to the ground.

Continuing his assault, Watcher fired as fast as he could, trying to get the monster close to the ground so they could use blades on him. But Krael knew this as well. He kept firing his flaming skulls at the two friends, the blast of each explosion causing waves of heat to wash over them. Planter held her shield up high, deflecting the projectiles, the magical enchantment in the wooden rectangle keeping it from taking any damage.

They drew closer and closer to the wither king. With the shield in her left hand, Planter pulled out her golden axe, the enchantment wrapped around the weapon glowing bright with anticipation. Krael saw the axe and an expression of recognition seemed to flash across the center head's face. With a growl, the monster turned off his sparkling regeneration field and floated upward, allowing Watcher's arrows to strike his body. The monster flashed red with damage, but the arrows weren't powerful enough to stop the wither king. Watcher thought about shooting Needle at the creature, as he had with its predecessor, but instead, he had a different, even better, idea.

The king of the withers now hovered near the ceiling of the Gathering Chamber, nearly out of reach from Watcher's bow.

"I am not as easy to kill as that fool, Kaza," Center said. "He was a poor wither king, and I was glad to see him go. You'll find Krael to be a stronger and smarter opponent." He glanced at the other villagers.

"I bet they only have one of the Wither Shields," Right said.

"Hmmm . . . yes." Center glanced down at Planter, then back toward the other villagers.

"Maybe we should shoot our flaming skulls at the other pathetic NPCs." Left chuckled with cruel glee.

"Maybe you should just go away!" Watcher shouted.

"And are *you* going to make us leave?" Krael replied. "How are you gonna do that?"

"Like *this*." Watcher dropped his bow and reached into his inventory. His fingers found the smooth weapon and pulled it out. It was a white bow made of fossilized bone: the Fossil Bow of Destruction, the magical relic they'd taken from the skeleton king before his destruction.

"Say hello to my little friend."

Pain stabbed at Watcher as the magical bow drew its power from his HP, but he didn't care. It was time to destroy this monster.

He pulled back on the string. Instantly, a magical arrow appeared in his grip, the sparkling shaft ready to seek its target. Focusing on Krael with his mind, he drew the string back a little further, but before he could release, the king of the withers saw the magical bow and, for the first time, expressions of fear covered the three wither skulls. The monster growled at Watcher, then disappeared in a cloud of gray mist.

Watcher released the arrow. The sparkling shaft leapt off the bow and streaked up to the ceiling. It smashed through the stone covering and drilled a hole through the side of the Jeweled Mountain, the projectile seeking its target.

Another blast of pain reminded Watcher to put the bow back into his inventory. He stuffed the weapon away just as he fell to one knee.

"Here . . . eat." Planter handed him a piece of melon.

The footsteps of villagers filled the air as the rest of their army sprinted across the chamber to see if he was alright.

He ate the melon quickly, but it was not enough to completely regenerate his HP.

"I don't have any more food." Planter looked at the approaching villagers. "Does anyone have food? Watcher needs it."

"Here . . . try this." Blaster pulled something bright from his inventory and tossed it to Planter.

She caught it in the air and handed it to Watcher without even looking at it. Watcher took the food and was about to bite into it when he saw what it was.

"A golden apple?" Watcher was stunned.

"There was a whole chest of them, plus a few of these as well." Blaster held up another golden apple, one that had an iridescent glow to it, as if it were enchanted with magical power. "It's a Notch apple. I'm saving this one for Fencer back at the village."

Watcher smiled and nodded to his friend, then devoured the golden apple. Instantly, he felt his hunger disappear and his health begin to rejuvenate.

"Better?" Planter asked.

Watcher nodded.

"Was that the Fossil Bow of Destruction we took from the skeleton warlord?" Cleric asked.

Watcher smiled. "Yep. I wonder if that arrow will continue to chase the wither king."

"I remember the arrows from that bow turn and track their target," Blaster said. "It would be fun if it tracked the wither king for a while."

The others nodded.

"I think it's time we left these terrible caves and got back to Fencer." Planter put away her shield, but kept her axe out, just to be safe. "After all, we didn't come here to save the world . . . just her."

Watcher smiled, then thought about that moment just before his death. He'd made a promise to himself, and now it was time to follow through. He was about to say something when she turned and headed toward the exit of the cavern.

"Hey Planter, I wanted to tell you—" But she was already gone.

He glanced around and found his sister staring at him, a smile on her face.

"Why do we fail?" she asked.

He nodded to his sister. "I've learned from my mistakes, and now it's time for me to overcome, regardless of the outcome." Waves of panic spread through him as Watcher imagined every terrible response he might receive when he told Planter how he felt, but he refused to be afraid of that anymore. *It's time to tell her the truth,* he thought. *I just have to catch her first.*

With a sigh, he ran, chasing Planter and the rest of the villagers as they fled the spiders' lair.

CHAPTER 37

Watcher sprinted through the tunnels, trying to reach Planter, but a mass of villagers clogged the tunnel leading to the surface, making it impossible for him to pass anyone. Resigned to the fact that he wasn't going to catch up to her now, Watcher was at least happy he was leaving the terrible spiders' lair.

Er-Lan moved next to him and gave Watcher a toothy smile. "Er-Lan is proud of Watcher."

"And why's that?"

"Watcher did what many try, but few succeed."

"And what's that?" Watcher asked. "Destroy the spider warlord?"

The zombie shook his head. "Not just that. Destroying Shakaar was great, but Watcher did something more significant."

The boy looked at the zombie, a confused expression on his face.

"Watcher found the true self hiding within." The zombie put a clawed hand on Watcher's arm and pulled him to a halt. "Few ever know their true selves, but Watcher has realized his true nature."

"You mean being a wizard?"

Er-Lan nodded. "Now, Watcher must be true to another."

"You mean Planter?" he asked in a whisper.

Er-Lan nodded again. "A wizard should know the value of truth."

Watcher considered his friend's words, then steeled himself for the most terrifying thing he'd ever done: confessing his feelings to Planter.

"I'm gonna do it," Watcher whispered.

"Then don't stand here with Er-Lan . . . run!"

Courage blossomed within the boy's chest. He clasped the zombie's hand, then turned and ran through the passage. He reached the villagers filing up the passage and found Blaster in his black armor walking alone. In his hands was the Notch apple, the iridescent glow coming from the magical fruit working like a lavender torch and lighting the passage.

"So, you wanna share with me how you didn't die?" Blaster asked. "Don't get me wrong, I'm pretty happy you're alive, but that poison was deadly . . . and yet here you are."

Watcher wanted to push his way ahead through the throng of villagers, but they were too tightly packed. Frustrated, he glanced at Blaster.

"I'm not really sure, but I think it had to do with the little doll the evoker dropped in the forest mansion." Watcher lowered his voice so that Blaster was the only one who could hear. "A voice in my head told me to use the Totem of Undying . . . that was the little doll. Anyway, I sent all my power into it, and here I am. I think it was just lucky."

"You said you sent *all your power*. It seems like maybe you are a wizard." Blaster patted him on the back. "Don't worry; I still like you, even if you are magical."

Watcher smiled. "I wish I understood more, but that's all I've got."

"Seems like you need to figure this out."

"I agree." Watcher grew silent as he contemplated the terrifying upcoming event again.

"I can't believe the witches had these already made." Blaster held the Notch apple up to his face. The enchantment surrounding the fruit lit the dark passage. "There were a dozen of them, as well as many golden apples just like the one I gave you."

"I never said thank you for that. I was pretty close to dying again." Watcher smiled. "That's a funny thing to say . . . dying *again*."

"Yep, pretty strange," the boy said as he extended the Notch apple to Watcher. "You should be the one to give it to her."

Watcher's eyes grew wide with surprise. He accepted the glowing fruit and put it in his inventory. "Thanks."

"You were there with Saddler when she died," Blaster said. "I heard you promise to help her daughter . . . now you can."

Blaster slowed, then raised his hand high in the air, fingers spread wide. Watcher joined him, raising his glowing arm into the air, his extended fingertips brushing the ceiling. They clenched their fists. "For Saddler," Watcher said in a solemn voice.

"For Saddler." Blaster clenched his hand into a fist, then lowered it to his side. He reached out and slapped Watcher on the back. "Come on, let's get out of these stinking tunnels."

They sprinted through the tunnels, chasing the rest of the NPCs. In a few minutes, they'd reached the entrance to the underground passages, the blocks of leaves hiding the entrance now removed by villager axes.

"Look, our horses are still here." Blaster whistled, and his alabaster mare came running to his side. He leapt up into the saddle and smiled down at his friend. "Where's yours?"

"I'm sure it's around here somewhere."

Watcher scanned the area, but he wasn't searching for his horse. And then he found who he was looking for: Planter was talking with Cutter, the two in a hushed discussion. The dark serpent of jealousy began stirring deep within his soul. He could feel it slithering past memories of Planter and Cutter laughing together or walking near each other or . . . anger bubbled up within him, making him want to scream. But coupled with these feeling was also a wave of fear. *Am I going to lose her? Should I go up to her now? Cutter's right there. What if he's saying what I should be saying?* Voices of doubt echoed through his mind as he stood there, paralyzed with fear.

And then someone pushed him forward. Watcher glanced over his shoulder and found his sister smiling at him, her blue eyes filled with hope.

Why do we fail? he thought. And then, a strange thing happened: Watcher refused to be afraid anymore. Fear was so familiar to him: fear of bullies, fear of not being accepted, fear of failure . . . all of it weighed down on his soul.

"No more!" he whispered. *I must confront both Planter* and *Cutter. I have to know what's going on, for real.* He felt a strange, tingling warmth spread up his arms, making them feel lighter, somehow; it didn't make any sense, but he couldn't focus on that right now. He could focus on only one thing: Planter and Cutter.

Walking across the uneven stone ground, he headed straight for Planter just as Cutter turned and headed straight for him. He stopped and waited for the big NPC to reach him.

"Cutter, I know you care about Planter. I can see it in the way you look at her and talk to her, so don't deny it," he said.

"Of course I care about her." The big warrior seemed confused. "Why would I deny it?"

The serpent of jealousy coiled around Watcher's soul, ready to strike. "So you admit it?!"

"Absolutely." Cutter smiled, as if it were obvious. "She's like a sister to me."

"A—what?"

"Yeah, ever since we first met when we were chasing

the zombie warlord, Planter seemed like my kid sister. That's why I look after her and make sure she's always safe."

"You mean . . . you don't *like* her?" The slithering beast within him started to fade away.

"Of course I like her." Cutter sounded confused. "I just told you she's like a sister to me." He paused and stared down at Watcher, then nodded slowly and smiled. "Ahh . . . I get it now. You thought I felt the same way *you* do about her."

"What? I don't know what you're talking about." Watcher's cheeks grew warm as all feelings of jealousy and anger evaporated; the serpent was finally gone.

Cutter reached out and placed a hand on his shoulder. "Now it all makes sense, all the crazy way you've been acting and weird things you've been doing." He smiled, his steely-gray eyes piercing Watcher's soul, then glanced over his shoulder at Planter. When he brought his gaze back to Watcher, he continued. "You need to take care of this . . . now. And if you don't, then I will for you."

"I don't know what you mean." Watcher's cheeks grew hotter.

Cutter moved behind him and whispered in his ear. "I have been and always will be your friend. Now go take care of business before I knock that block-head off your shoulders." He shoved Watcher toward Planter, then laughed as he moved off to find his horse.

Terror enveloped Watcher's soul as he walked toward Planter, but he knew he could not retreat.

"Watcher, hi, I was looking for—look at your arms." Planter pointed.

Glancing down, Watcher found the iridescent glow that had been enveloping his hands and forearms had now spread all the way up to his shoulders. They glowed as if electrified from within, the magical enchantments— or whatever they were—pulsing with life.

"Wow . . . I didn't notice that before," Watcher said.

"Well, it wasn't there before." Planter's voice was soft, only meant for his ears. "I watched you as you came out of the tunnel. The glow was only up to your elbows."

"You watched me?" Watcher asked.

"What?" She seemed nervous, or confused by his question.

"I have to tell you something, but I'm a little afraid." Watcher stepped away from the other NPCs, many of them glancing in his direction. Planter walked with him until they could speak in private.

"What is it?" Planter asked. "You can tell me anything."

"Well, it's just that . . . you see, we've known each other a long time, and . . . well . . . your friendship is the most important thing to me in the whole world." Sweat trickled down his forehead, the square beads getting stuck in his unibrow. One of them tumbled down his face and found the corner of his mouth. It tasted salty.

A llama bayed in the distance, followed by the bleating of a sheep.

"You see . . . for a while now . . ." Watcher thought this stress was worse than battling the most ferocious of monsters. "I've been feeling . . . well . . . you know . . ."

"I *do* know," Planter said. She reached out and grasped his hand, then intertwined her fingers between his. "I've been feeling the same about you, too."

"You *have*?" Watcher was stunned.

She nodded and smiled. "I see the way you take care of everyone around you . . . especially me. I love that about you."

His cheeks felt hot as he turned away, embarrassed. Planter reached out and brought his face back toward hers. "I like you Watcher, and I believe you like me."

He nodded, his cheeks getting hotter. "I want us to be closer, you know?"

"I know." She smiled, then grabbed his other hand too. "Our friendship will always be here, no matter what, but we can be more. . . agreed?"

"Agreed." A smile burst across Watcher's face as his stress evaporated. He felt closer to her than ever before, as if the missing piece to his soul had somehow been found, and now he was complete. He felt as if he were soaring through the air, his soul bursting with joy.

"Hey! Let's get moving, you two!" Blaster shouted. "Fencer needs that Notch apple."

"Come on, let's find our horses," Planter said.

They walked back to the other villagers, hand in hand. The other NPCs were frantically searching among the horses; the animals called into existence at the Citadel of the Horse Lord would only allow the specific villagers who summoned them to ride them again now. It was chaos, with villagers whistling and calling out to their mounts. People and animals moved in all directions, but at the center of the confusion was Winger and Cleric. They stood, arm in arm, staring at Planter and Watcher, smiling with tears in their eyes.

Watcher walked toward them, uncertain what was going on.

"You know, Dad, I think I was wrong before," Winger said in a clear voice.

"What are you talking about, dear?" her father replied, confused.

"It was about what I said earlier." Winger let go of her father and wrapped her arms around Watcher and Planter, then glanced back at her father. "This is *exactly* what I wanted for my birthday."

Watcher and Planter were both confused as Winger and Cleric laughed loud belly-laughs that filled the landscape with joy, then kissed them both on the forehead.

"Let's go home," Watcher said, his cheeks turning red. "I have an important delivery to make to a little girl."

"Absolutely!" Cleric replied. "Lead on, wizard."

Then Watcher and Planter found their horses, as did the rest of the NPCs. As Watcher kicked his spotted horse into a trot, putting the Jeweled Mountain behind him, he thought about that name, *wizard*, and for the first time, instead of being afraid of the title, he wore it with pride, for it did not separate him from others or make him different. It didn't define who he was . . . his actions did that.

Watcher was still just Watcher, but now, he was also Watcher the Wizard.

AVAILABLE NOW FROM MARK CHEVERTON
AND SKY PONY PRESS

THE GAMEKNIGHT999 SERIES
The world of Minecraft comes to life in this thrilling adventure!

Gameknight999 loved Minecraft, and above all else, he loved to grief—to intentionally ruin the gaming experience for other users.

But when one of his father's inventions teleports him into the game, Gameknight is forced to live out a real-life adventure inside a digital world. What will happen if he's killed? Will he respawn? Die in real life? Stuck in the game, Gameknight discovers Minecraft's best-kept secret, something not even the game's programmers realize: the creatures within the game are alive! He will have to stay one step ahead of the sharp claws of zombies and pointed fangs of spiders, but he'll also have to learn to make friends and work as a team if he has any chance of surviving the Minecraft war his arrival has started.

With deadly Endermen, ghasts, and dragons, this action-packed trilogy introduces the heroic Gameknight999 and has proven to be a runaway publishing smash, showing that the Gameknight999 series is the perfect companion for Minecraft fans of all ages.

Invasion of the Overworld (Book One):
$9.99 paperback • 978-1-63220-711-1

Battle for the Nether (Book Two):
$9.99 paperback • 978-1-63220-712-8

Confronting the Dragon (Book Three):
$9.99 paperback • 978-1-63450-046-3

AVAILABLE NOW FROM MARK CHEVERTON AND SKY PONY PRESS

HEROBRINE REBORN SERIES
Gameknight999 and his friends and family face Herobrine in the biggest showdown the Overworld has ever seen!

Gameknight999, a former Minecraft griefer, got a big dose of virtual reality when his father's invention teleported him into the game. Living out a dangerous adventure inside a digital world, he discovered that the Minecraft villagers were alive and needed his help to defeat the infamous virus, Herobrine, a diabolical enemy determined to escape into the real world.

Gameknight thought Herobrine had finally been stopped once and for all. But the virus proves to be even craftier than anyone could imagine, and his XP begins inhabiting new bodies in an effort to escape. The User-that-is-not-a-user will need the help of not only his Minecraft friends, but his own father, Monkeypants271, as well, if he has any hope of destroying the evil Herobrine once and for all.

Saving Crafter (Book One):
$9.99 paperback • 978-1-5107-0014-7

Destruction of the Overworld (Book Two):
$9.99 paperback • 978-1-5107-0015-4

Gameknight999 vs. Herobrine (Book Three):
$9.99 paperback • 978-1-5107-0010-9

AVAILABLE NOW FROM MARK CHEVERTON AND SKY PONY PRESS

THE MYSTERY OF ENTITY303 SERIES
Minecraft mods are covering the tracks of a mysterious new villain!

Gameknight999 reenters Minecraft to find it completely changed, and his old friends acting differently. The changes are not for the better.

Outside of Crafter's village, a strange user named Entity303 is spotted with Weaver, a young NPC Gameknight knows from Minecraft's past. He realizes that Weaver has somehow been kidnapped, and returning him to the correct time is the only way to fix things.

What's worse: Entity303 has created a strange and bizarre modded version of Minecraft, full of unusual creatures and biomes. Racing through the Twilight Forest and MystCraft, and finally into the far reaches of outer space, Gameknight will face his toughest challenge yet in a Minecraft both alien and dangerous.

Terrors of the Forest (Book One):
$9.99 paperback • 978-1-5107-1886-9

Monsters in the Mist (Book Two):
$9.99 paperback • 978-1-5107-1887-6

Mission to the Moon (Book Three):
$9.99 paperback • 978-1-5107-1888-3

EXCERPT FROM
THE WITHER KING
A BRAND NEW FAR LANDS ADVENTURE

Watcher ached of a deep weariness, not just of body, but of spirit as well. Fencer and Planter had been glaring at each other all through the night, and his girlfriend's glances toward him clearly suggested he had to do something . . . but what?

I can't send Fencer back to their village without sending a couple of soldiers with her, he thought. *But keeping her here doesn't seem like a good idea, either.*

The whole situation had him completely confused.

He looked around wearily and took in his surroundings. They'd ridden hard all night and everyone was exhausted. The villagers had made it through the forest until they came across their enemy's tracks. Now, they'd followed them into the desert, the sun already past its zenith.

"Watcher . . . look out!"

He stopped daydreaming and looked ahead: his horse was heading straight for a cactus. Watcher pulled on the reins at the last second, causing the animal to veer to the left, narrowly avoiding the prickly plant.

"Maybe you should pay attention," Cutter chided.

Watcher could feel his cheeks turn red.

"It's not like we need Watcher's expert tracking skills to follow our friends' trail." Blaster pointed at the sandy ground. Footprints were burned into the surface of Minecraft as if something so incredibly evil had walked by and had damaged the landscape.

"That does make it easier," Cutter added. "What do you think is making those tracks?"

"The Eight." Er-Lan's voice was almost like a moan, drawn out and sad. "It is the mark of the Broken Eight. All zombies have heard the stories about the terrible enchantments used to create these warriors. The evil magic used to bring these creatures into existence cannot be contained within their golden armor. It leaks out and scars the land."

"Great . . . you're making me really excited to meet these creatures."

"The forest is ending up ahead." Planter pointed with her axe, then gave Watcher a glance. She neither smiled nor frowned.

What was that supposed to mean? Watcher was even more confused.

"Look, It seems as if they stopped her behind this sand dune." Mapper leaned so far out of the saddle to stare at the footprints that he almost fell off his horse. Many of the soldiers laughed.

"Maybe you should try to stay *on* your horse," Blaster suggested with a grin.

The old man nodded, embarrassed.

Watcher glanced up at the sun; its heat pounded down on the NPCs like a blacksmith's flaming hammer. Their armor was hot to the touch, and the air burned his throat a little as he breathed. It was a harsh environment, but they had to follow the trail, no matter where it led. On the ground were the remains of the cactus, the green, spiny body shattered by the charred footprints.

One of the Broken Eight must have crushed it, Watcher thought. *But why would it want to do that? Maybe they—*

"There's a village on the other side of this dune," the forward scout shouted from atop a sandy mound. The NPC sat on a light brown horse, his leather armor a dirty white, courtesy of Blaster. The villager and his mount blended in with the pale surroundings, making him hard to see when he stood still. "Hurry . . . something's happened to them."

"What do you think he means by that?" Watcher asked.

"I don't know," Planter said from behind them.

He turned and gave her a smile.

"I'm sure you'll figure it out. You always do." Fencer rode up next to him and matched his pace, guiding her horse so close that their legs were brushing against each other. She gave him an adoring grin.

"Grrr . . ." Planter growled like a zombie, then snapped her reins and galloped up the hill, her face a visage of anger as she passed.

"She seems so angry all the time," Fencer said softly, only for Watcher's ears. "Planter should be more respectful . . . in fact they all should be more respectful to you. You're a wizard after all." She leaned toward him, bringing her horse even closer. "I know how important you are. I'll never mistreat you . . . like the others do."

"Look, Fencer, you need to understand something." She had such an innocent expression on her face. Watcher felt like he was about to do something mean and hurt her. He glanced ahead at Planter. Her blond hair shone bright against the afternoon sun; it was beautiful. He turned back to Fencer. "You see, I'm with—"

"Oh no, Watcher, come quick!" Planter didn't even turn to look at him, she just shouted and then rode down the other side of the sand dune.

A jolt of fear surged through his veins. Watcher instantly nudged his horse into a gallop, then into a sprint as he charged up the sandy mound. When he reached the top, his heart sank.

Strewn across the sands were the remains of the village. Charred footsteps could be seen all throughout the area, as well as paw prints from the vicious dire wolves embedded in the sand.

Riding down the dune, he caught up with Planter, then shot past her.

"We need to search for survivors," Watcher shouted.

Someone else yelled commands to the other NPCs, but Watcher wasn't listening; he was scanning the flat, sandy plane, looking for anyone moving or crying out for help. But the village seemed completely still . . . like a graveyard.

Leaping off his horse, Watcher dashed through the smoky ruins of what looked like the blacksmith's house. Only a couple of furnaces had survived the destruction; the rest of the houses were burned to the ground. Running up to what resembling a baker's house, he kicked through the brittle remains, hoping to uncover someone hiding in the rubble. But there was no one. With panic rising in his soul, Watcher ran from house to house, digging through the wreckage, looking for any living thing.

It was hopeless.

This entire village has been erased from the surface of Minecraft, just like the one he'd seen when he used the Eye of Searching.

"Why would they do this?" Planter asked. "I don't understand."

"It is the Eight." Er-Lan moved toward Watcher, careful to step over the charred footprints left behind by the ancient warriors. "Their hatred for everything drove the Broken Eight to do this thing. There is no plan here, no strategy or goal . . . just destruction. That is why these ancient warriors were put in the Eternal Jail. It was the only way to stop their destruction."

"But these people did nothing." A terrible sadness rose up from within Watcher, but mixed in with it was also guilt. He should have been here to stop them.

Even though he knew that to be impossible, he still felt responsible for this destruction.

These creatures may have been made by the monster warlocks hundreds of years ago, but this *wizard is going to destroy them.* Watcher's thoughts raged with fury within his mind. He wanted to shout and scream, but it would not change what had happened.

There may be a way, the ancient voice from the Flail of Regrets whispered.

"What?" Watcher said.

"I didn't say anything," Blaster replied.

Watcher shook his head. *What did you say?*

There may be a way to stop the Broken Eight, the Flail said. *But it will take some thought. Likely we'll need some friends from the old days.*

What are you talking about? Watcher asked, but the voice was gone.

"You okay?" Blaster put a hand on Watcher's shoulder, startling him and making him jump. "Sorry, didn't mean to scare you. Don't blast me with any of your magical powers." He gave Watcher a smile.

"Sorry, I was talking to . . ." he lowered his voice and glanced around, "the Flail."

"Of course, you were talking to that inanimate object in your inventory."

"It's true, there's something inside it. I just don't fully understand, yet." Watcher pulled out the weapon and stared down at it. The leather-wrapped handle was worn, as if it had seen many battles, but the chain running from the handle to the spiked cube looked brand new, with each spike still razor sharp. The enchanted weapon seemed as if it had just been made, even though it had actually been constructed hundreds of years ago, during the Great War.

"Everyone, come over here." Cutter's booming voice carried across the desert with ease.

Watcher and Blaster ran toward what would have been the center of the village. Where the community's well once had stood was now just a huge, blackened crater. Watcher stood next to Cutter and stared down at the destruction.

"Why would they have destroyed the well like this?" Mapper started to move down into the crater, but Planter stopped the old man. "Did any of you notice what's at the bottom of the crater?"

Watcher held a hand over his eyes to shield them from the afternoon sun. They slowly adjusted to the dark, charred blocks of sandstone, sand and gravel . . . and then he saw it. There were steps leading down into the darkness. Everyone was pointing at them and talking all at once, but Watcher was instead looking at the landscape around them. On one side of the village was the large sand dune they had just crossed, but on the opposite side of the village was another one, identical in size and shape.

"The Dual Dunes." Watcher moved to Planter's side, then pointed. "Look . . . the Dual Dunes."

She followed his finger and stared at the two huge sandy mounds, then realization dawned on her. "It's the entrance to the Hall of Planes."

Watcher nodded.

She pulled out the Amulet of Planes and found the red gemstone in the middle, blinking as if it had a heartbeat. Stepping into the crater, Planter moved closer to the dark stairway, Watcher at her side. The ancient relic pulsed faster and faster as they moved near the shadowy passage.

Watcher glanced over his shoulder and nodded to the rest of the NPCs. "Everyone gather your things. Our path now leads downward."

The villagers moved down into the crater in complete silence. Watcher knew they were scared; he could somehow feel their tension through the magic pulsing through his body. When they reached the bottom, the company stood around the staircase, staring down at the steps disappearing into the darkness.

"This is the entrance to the Hall of Planes." Watcher turned and look at each member of their party. "We have no idea what dangers we're heading toward, but as you saw from the village around us, these creatures must be stopped, and we're the only ones here. If we don't stop these zombie warriors *and* stop the king of the withers from releasing his army, then the Far Lands will likely be in the greatest danger it's faced since the Great War." He paused to let his words sink in. "We *can* do this if we work together. Now follow me."

"I'll be right behind you," Fencer shouted.

Watcher rolled his eyes as the rest of the warriors laughed.

Drawing his enchanted blade, Needle, he headed down into the darkness.

COMING SOON:
THE WITHER KING: WITHER WAR BOOK ONE